THE
PORNO
GIRL

THE
PORNO
GIRL

and other stories

MERIN WEXLER

ST. MARTIN'S PRESS ✖ NEW YORK

The following stories appeared, in slightly different form, previously and are reprinted by permission of the author: "Waiting to Discover Electricity" in the *Sonora Review*; "Helen of Alexandria" in *Puerto del Sol*; "Pink Is for Punks" in *Phoebe*; "Solomon and His Wives" in *The Florida Review*.

www.stmartins.com

Library of Congress Cataloging-in-Publication Data

Wexler, Merin.
    The porno girl, and other stories / Merin Wexler.—1st ed.
        p.   cm.
    Contents: The porno girl—The nanny trap—Don Giovanni in the tub—What Marcia wanted—Waiting to discover electricity—Save yourself—The closet—Helen of Alexandria—The Marginot Line—Pink is for punks—Solomon and his wives.
    ISBN 0-312-31057-9
    1. Mothers and daughters—Fiction.   2. Women—Fiction.
I. Title.

PS3623.E95P67   2003
813'.6—dc21

                                                                            2003041587

First Edition: June 2003

10   9   8   7   6   5   4   3   2   1

For PJS

and

for NSW, in memory

CONTENTS

ACKNOWLEDGMENTS

I am profoundly and immutably grateful to my agent, Henry Dunow, and to Jennifer Carlson.

For her abiding faith, her extraordinary diligence, and her ever-ready wisdom, I owe an enormous thank-you to my editor, Alicia Brooks.

In addition, thank you to Chris McIlroy, Antonya Nelson, Susan Neville, Darcey Steinke, and Pete Turchi. Not to forget: David Huddle and Margot Livesey.

Also: Kaye Gibbons, Carol Hill, Paul Kafka, Charlotte Sheedy, Marisa Silver, the Heekin Foundation, the Millay Colony, the Virginia Center for the Arts, and the Writers Room.

And thank you, Peter, Liana, and Julian.

THE
PORNO
GIRL

MOTHERS

THE PORNO GIRL

This place was five blocks from my apartment but I swear I'd never noticed. I'd never seen it. I'd never wanted to. In fact, until then I'd have found it disgusting, the sick destination of desperate misogynist loners, perverts, and creeps. But everything, everything, had changed since the baby in ways beyond measure, and one of those ways was that for the first time in my life I was drawn to peep shows.

Not exactly peep shows, as nothing live was happening there. I'd heard they had live acts at the place across Eighth Avenue, but that I did not have the stomach for. What I craved were the video halls where twenty-five cents bought one minute's huffing and thrusting, lifting me from my life in a way nothing else could, at least not any way described in the postpartum handbooks. I had a new baby, a perfect baby girl whom I cradled and cherished, yet I was grieving. And my only relief was to take the quarters I should have saved for the laundry and drop them instead down the dented metal slot above the chain padlock, choose my sixty seconds of sweat from the titles rolling up the screen, and watch, tiny infant Cleo strapped to my chest.

It was unmotherly, I know, not just stepping foot into these rank infested booths with their battered saloon double-swing doors, but worse bringing my baby, however lovingly concealed in Richard's giant down parka. But I was afraid to look for motives, knowing if I got to the root of my compulsion, I would end up one of those mothers who mistakes her head for a casserole and shoves it in the oven.

It wasn't sex I was after (this I know you won't believe), the floodlit vulgarity of naked wet flesh, the prodigious moans, the expulsion of fluid. It was the shock, the sheer carnality. I wasn't aroused; I was becalmed, as if the actions onscreen confirmed my new understanding of the body, its limitations and abundance, its wrenching amalgam of pain and joy. And in that faint tranquility I could begin to feel briefly myself, meaning my prebaby self, which, since the birth, seemed to have died.

I tried telling my husband. We were eating dinner, Szechuan, delivery. Cleo was lurching back and forth in her swing. Things were relatively quiet.

"I've been doing some exploring," I said. We lived in the low West Fifties on a residential, tree-lined street almost like a stage set. The buildings had a shabby elegance that, back in the days when my life was different, had comforted me.

"Where?"

"In the neighborhood." He looked up. A lock of hair fell across his brow. It killed me, how placid he was in the thick of this.

"With Cleo?" He helped himself to a box of noodles.

"It seems dirty now, with the baby."

"Oh, honey." He looked at me tenderly.

"Oh, honey, *what*?"

"I told you last summer we should move. Remember? Before we got pregnant."

I hated that idea, as if *his* belly had been stretched and distended, his boobs like water balloons. But the one time I told him as much, he said I hurt his feelings, and he spent four hours playing Internet bridge before even looking at me again. He could take even the weather report personally. The truth was that I never knew how he would react to anything, favorably or not, and so I had learned to keep certain things secret.

Besides, I still couldn't believe that he was pleased we'd had a girl.

"You know that place on Forty-eighth Street?" I tried again.

He squinted, cocked his head slightly to one side, then nodded. He's a know-it-all. He'll say "I know" before I'm halfway through a sentence. Truth is, he's often right.

"I mean the video store," I added.

"Blockbuster?"

"No. The Pussy Cat Palace."

He looked at me quizzically.

"What video store are you talking about?"

"You know, the one with the flaming neon triple X?"

He put down his chopsticks, dabbed his mouth with a paper towel. He looked at me intently, shaking his head. Then he cleared his throat.

"If it's sex you're worried about, I told you. Whatever Dr. Massey says. I can wait." He took my hand holding the chopstick and squeezed.

If only he weren't so evolved. I would have preferred him ripping open my nursing blouse, throwing the soggy pads into the sesame noodles, and taking me here on the table now in the wallpapered dining el. What would Cleo know? She was in her own orgasmic state of swing. But Richard was too sensitive. And wasn't that why I had married him? He wasn't like those linebacker types I always used to end up with.

Be careful what you wish for.

But the truth was that I had lied. We could have hit the sheets three weeks ago, the doctor said.

I speared a dumpling with my chopstick. For a dairy queen, I had a mousy appetite.

The next day I swore not to go back to the Pussy Cat and to that end decided to spend the day inside. But by midafternoon, Cleo was shrieking nonstop and the only possible solution was a neighborhood stroll. I packed her into the carrier. By the time I got to the corner she was knocked out asleep, so I did a loop around the block. Then another loop, and another. I'd been walking at least an hour when I saw those words circling over my head like vultures searching for carrion.

Where's the harm if she's asleep?

Next thing I know, my two hands are pressed flat against that opaque glass door, pushing it open, only my hands don't have any feeling. From my head down to my toes, my body has been relieved of all sensation, as if every neuron had been snipped and excised, my legs and feet on autopilot. Then, almost like a camera, I can see how fast I'm sprinting into the booth. Only when I get inside do I find out—I haven't a single quarter. My change purse is empty.

I had to ask the clerk. I'd never laid eyes on him—always before I'd come prepared. He sat perched behind a counter on a raised platform, a large man behind round wire-rims, his skin as dark as chestnuts roasted on the street. On the shallow tabletop in front of him was a small black-and-white television, the screen no bigger than a slice of bread, and his eyes were fixed. He was watching *Leeza*. Rising on the wall behind him from floor to ceiling like a stained-glass window were dildos and vibrators in a variety of sizes, shapes, and colors. Not only dildos and vibrators, but rubber buttocks, plump oversized vulvas, phony breasts plus enough chains and leather for an entire S&M Olympics. This was his fiefdom and he was lord, the cash register his treasury. It was hard not to stare. There was stuff I had never imagined, and I would have stared at it some more but for the awareness that doing so would make me seem even more out of place than I already was. Gingerly, I set my dollar bill on the counter.

"Quarters. Please."

He stacked four on the counter, then pushed the dollar bill back in my direction.

"It's on me."

His voice was grainy and deep with an indefinable foreign accent. He had a scar across his left cheek and he was missing a front tooth. He glanced at the lump high under my coat. My face was prickly with heat. I took the stack of quarters in hand, but I didn't touch that dollar bill. I skulked to my usual cubicle and pitched a coin down the slot. The screen twitched alive, and I felt alive, too, my body limber and warm. It was like focusing a camera, when the split image in the view-finder merges into one. For this brief delirious interval, my mind and my body, which since the birth of my daughter had been violently torn asunder, were reunited.

I chose a feature. From the title it promised a group of high school seniors who turn an ordinary after-school detention class into a steaming orgy. But just as I put my finger on the selection button, Cleo awoke. I lost my concentration and regressed to channel surfing, turning the stiff metal knob, catching glimpses of body parts in motion, oversized and glistening—in no way satisfying. It was the best I could do. Cleo hung lopsided in the carrier, jabbing me in the ribs. I straightened her but the kicks kept coming, like she was sending a message. Before I knew it, the minute was up. I shoved the remaining quarters into my overalls and made my way to the door. It was papered on this side with a film poster: a full-color close-up of a giant erect penis rising against a fleet of Air Force fighter planes in V-formation in the sky. Cleo was whimpering.

The clerk called out. "You dropped something."

I pretended not to hear. My face was burning. But I heard him climb down from his stool so I turned. He was walking toward me.

"In there," he said, pointing to the booth. "Wait." He got on his knees and reached under the doors.

In the corner of my eye I saw a man with a shopping bag from Barneys browsing the homoerotica, a dead ringer for Richard's cousin Tate. Cleo began to wail.

The clerk reappeared with something dangling from his fingers. Something diminutive and pink.

"This is yours, I believe."

In his hand was Cleo's pacifier.

My heart beat so hard and so fast I could feel it in my throat.

I needed that pacifier—Cleo would not shut up without it.

The Tate look-alike was staring.

I felt rank with shame.

"Don't you want it?" asked the clerk. He turned the pacifier in his hand as if examining it. "This is a good one. NUK. Orthodontic."

"How do you know?"

"I have one."

"You use a pacifier?" I was shocked, but considering the rest of the merchandise here, *why not?*

He shook his head. "I have a baby." He handed me the plug. "Olivia. Six months."

I popped the plug in my mouth for a wash, then stuck it in Cleo's. By now I could hardly pretend to be hygienic.

"Boy or girl?" he asked.

I didn't answer. Part of me believed that if I ignored the question I could pretend I wasn't actually there, loitering in a sex shop, rocking my baby while conferring with the clerk.

"Let me guess," he said. "Girl."

I nodded.

"Have a look?" He inched closer, smelling of some too-sweet after-shave.

I opened the parka and turned down the top of the carrier to find Cleo's squishy pink face, sucking furiously.

"Beautiful. Your first?"

Again I nodded.

"Me, too." He smiled, and as he did the gap from the missing tooth seemed to widen, opening up like a black hole. I imagined a vortex hidden inside, something furious and wet, something that could suck me in. "Are you breast-feeding?"

My tongue felt like lead, immovable. I was shocked. I thought maybe this was a come-on but it wasn't. He was serious. Or maybe this was some genre I hadn't yet encountered—*lactation erotica.* Either way, what had I done in my life that brought me to this moment, here, parsing the benefits of breast-feeding with a porn salesman? Where had I gone wrong? Then it occurred to me: Maybe this was a kind of sex karma, the consequences of my actions in a previous life, like I'd been the den mother of a bordello with unfair labor practices. Or I had seduced my twelve-year-old nephew. A man stumbled from a booth, a pint of Night Train swinging from one hand, croaking for change.

"Excuse me," said the clerk.

I was saved.

I zipped up my coat and dashed out the door, pushing through the Eighth Avenue hordes. Upstairs in the apartment, I collapsed on the bed. Cleo nursed. Afterward, she hung on to my breast for what seemed like hours. I sat transfixed before the television clutching the remote, volume at zero, gaping at Barney. That lascivious pear-shaped torso, that enormous purple bottom, swishy and sentimental, like some cartoon incarnation of Oscar Wilde, discriminating but deviant.

Wasn't Barney sexual, too?

The next day I decided to resume my quest for Dreft, the fabled baby clothes detergent I could never find. Every baby book I ever read made it inordinately clear that I would defile my baby's complexion if I dared to wash her clothes in regular detergent, that Dreft was the only soap gentle enough for her skin. But finding the stuff was like a hunt for El Dorado. No supermarkets carried it, and I had begun to wonder if Dreft were yet another fiction to distract new mothers from staring down the truth of their inalterable new state.

I strapped Cleo into the carrier and put on the parka.

Inside the pocket was a dollar bill. I was shocked.

How did it get there? I never put loose cash in my coat pockets, having been on two separate occasions the victim of a pickpocket.

There was only one possibility.

The clerk. It was his dollar, the dollar I'd given him for change. He had slipped it in my pocket when I wasn't looking.

I had to return it as it was against my principles of unfailing self-reliance ever to owe anything to anybody. Besides, as long as I had that bill in my pocket—in Richard's pocket, that is—I felt contaminated.

I hurried in a daze. I swore I wouldn't stay. I'd give back the dollar, turn around, and run. I'd bring antibacterial soap. I'd wear gloves. Afterward, I'd stroll to the Park and meet some new moms.

If only I could meet some new moms, I was sure I could put this all behind me.

I was just a few steps from the door when I saw the police. They were standing in front, two of them, sipping coffee and chuckling in their ill-fitting uniforms. I recognized one of them. They were from my precinct. This was their beat. I stopped dead, my thoughts lurching into overdrive. I stood at the corner in panic, a swarm of people rushing by. This was it. They would arrest me. They would haul me into the precinct—Cleo, too—and book me for child abuse. I wondered what my feminist mother would do under the circumstances. Wasn't it a question of equality? What were my constitutional rights?

On the other hand, I was just settling a debt.

Cleo was asleep. I forged ahead, looking down to avoid eye contact. But just as my hands landed on the door to push it open, Cleo let out a squawk. The cops did a double take. I froze. One of the cops was a woman, and her eyes looked ready for blastoff. My mind flashed back on my mom and on the ERA.

If this isn't my equal right, then what is?

I barreled through the door and into the nearest booth. The saloon doors slammed against each other as I fell against the inside wall. I was shaken, but inside a piece of me was thrilled.

This was victory.

Then came the fear.

They would come after me. They would take my baby. They would put her in foster care. I was sick, an unfit mother—there had to be a statute against women hauling their children into sex palaces. In a Snugli, no less. If the clientele weren't bad enough, there was the air, the smutty toxified air which could only be ripe with germs, germs for diseases, not just sexually transmitted diseases, but all of them: cholera, tuberculosis, leprosy. I pictured Cleo's tiny fingers snapping off like pretzel sticks. My breath was shallow. My legs, weak. Cleo whimpered. I wanted to return the dollar and bolt but in my flight from justice I hadn't seen if my creditor was even there. Only then did I realize I was stuck. The cops hadn't chased after me, but they were probably expecting me any minute to step outside. It was a stakeout. I pictured them on the other side of the door, the man ready with the cuffs, the woman with the gun. All I could do was wait and hope for a murder somewhere in the neighborhood to distract them. Cleo's lips were searching for food. I opened one side of the carrier, undid my shirt and bra, and aimed my nipple inside her mouth. Then I reached into my jeans pocket for change. I pulled out my hand and studied my catch. Quarters—three of them. With one hand propping up Cleo to nurse, the other hand shaking, I dropped one coin down the slot. Then the next, and the next.

Across my shoulders and up and down my spine I could feel the relief. I felt lighter. Restored. And I was no longer afraid of what awaited me outside, as if the exploits of the film had instilled in me a kind of provisional faith.

Cleo nursed herself to sleep.

Next she was snoring. I remembered my purpose and stepped outside the booth.

"I thought that was you," said a voice.

Looking up, I saw the clerk.

"Here." I set the bill on the counter. "I found it in my pocket."

He didn't look at it.

"What's your name?"

I went blank.

"What's your name?" he tried again. "I'm Rodman."

I shuddered. Why did so many men have names that mean *penis*?

"Is something wrong?"

I shook my head. "It's just—that name—I never heard it before."

"It was my father's name. What is your name?"

I began to panic.

"If you don't tell me your name, I'll make one up."

An alias, I thought, *my kingdom for an alias.*

"All the regulars get nicknames."

"I'm *hardly* a regular." I was piqued, curious. I patted Cleo's bottom for comfort. "What would you make up?"

"I'll think of something." He paused. "We get a few ladies here. But not *babies.*"

There was a silence, as if he thought I might explain. I felt my degradation engulf me like a carapace.

"For me," he went on, "it's a job. In another two years, I get my degree. Then I go back."

"Back where?"

"To Ghana."

I nodded like I knew. I didn't. West Africa, East Africa, weren't they both east from here? He kept talking. He was an engineering student at Baruch. He lived in the Bronx. He wasn't married to his girlfriend, but they were engaged. Her name was Joelle. I pictured the cortex of my brain peeling away from the rest like the skin of an orange, and a voice in my head hollered: *Chatting up the clerk—do you think that's respectable?*

Then I remembered. The night before, at eleven o'clock, in the quiet lull before the frenzied midnight feed, I was dozing undressed on the sofa and Richard went on a mission to the all-night drugstore. Our Pampers reserve was down to one.

He had worn this parka. *His* parka.

The dollar was his.

"I have to go."

Rodman folded his arms across his chest and smiled. He was like the jolly green giant, I thought, only black. Peas. I pictured a vast sunken valley of oversized green peas as big as beach balls and me reeling backward on them. I felt a kick in my ribs, then a poke.

I grabbed the dollar.

I ran.

I became desperate. For three weeks I did everything I could not to go back. I tried shopping, foraging in every Gap and Ann Taylor, putting together entire spring wardrobes not just for me but for my unmarried sister-in-law, and lugging them over my shoulder into the changing room, locking the door behind me. Then I'd sit on the floor in the corner and nurse. I went to classes: Mommy and Me, Gymboree, baby massage, baby yoga. The wheels on the bus were spinning, my brain besieged by the entire animal population of Old MacDonald's Farm. I found a photographer who took lush portraits of mothers and babies—nude. I convinced Richard that five hundred dollars was a good price to invest in such an heirloom (who cares that we'd been married five years and still hadn't had our wedding pictures printed). But when the contact sheets came back, I buried them behind the bookcase. I hated them. All that naked flesh in shadowed tones of black and white, not just mine but Cleo's, too. They seemed pornographic. The one thing I didn't consider was going to a therapist. I doubted they had a *DSM-IV* diagnosis for new mothers self-medicating with porn.

I found the notice about the mothers' group in a sheaf of documents we had taken home after the birth: discharge papers and instructions for baby care at home, none of which I had ever read. The group met at the hospital.

More and more, I was beginning to think that was what I needed. Something medical.

I told Richard I was planning to go. We had just had dinner. Take-out Indian. I was worried about the spices—I had read that they could contaminate a mother's milk supply and make the baby refuse to nurse. Of course I didn't remember this until after I had finished eating. I pictured a red dot growing in the center of Cleo's forehead and I felt a slight but growing concern for the entire population of nursing babies on the Indian subcontinent. Richard was standing in the doorway, shuffling absently through the day's mail. By some miracle Cleo was asleep in the bassinet.

"A mothers' group—why would you go to such a thing?" he asked.

"Why not?"

"Are you lonely?" He dropped the mail on the table and joined me on the sofa.

"No," I answered truthfully and then I corrected myself. "Actually—

yes. I mean, I thought I could make some new friends."

"Somehow I don't picture you there." He put a hand on my thigh.

"Why not?" I shifted my legs and his hand fell away. I knew I was beyond his help.

"I don't know. I just can't picture you there."

"What do you mean? Is there somewhere else you picture me instead?"

"It's just—do you think you'll fit in?"

"Of course I'll fit in. There's only one requirement. You have to be a mother with a baby. I *am* a mother, and I *have* a baby."

"I know. But still."

For a moment I panicked that he'd got a call from Child Welfare Services. Maybe this was the time to confess.

He laughed, as if he thought I was making a joke.

"I don't know. I just don't see you in a coffee klatch with a bunch of new moms."

I went with a vengeance. I packed a diaper bag and a large decaf cappuccino. I wore my diamond studs. I brought a fistful of wipes.

The room was a windowless space in the interior of the hospital. It was easy to find by the din. Entering, I saw the women. They were seated in a circle like a tribe and they were almost uniformly big, with big hair and big shirts over big breasts, and even bigger attitudes, some of them sprawled on two chairs, loaded with gear, legs apart and spandexed in fuchsia and black. On a blanket on the floor lay the adored heirs, squirming on their backs like beached fish. Girls wore pink, the bows around their heads like gift wrap. Boys wore football jerseys and Yankees caps, announcing their early interest in sports.

Cleo was wearing green.

At least a dozen babies were wailing.

This was the second meeting. Everyone knew each other. Already I felt left out. There were no more chairs. I found a desk in the corner and hoisted myself on that.

The leader stood up and introduced herself. Ronnie. She wore large tinted glasses and short sleeves, and she had stretch marks on her arms. She worked in the hospital's outreach department and had three teenage boys. "Believe me, ladies, I've been there, and I have seen it *all*," she said. Then she opened a pack of gum, dropped her jaw, and laid a stick on her tongue.

"For those of you who did not have the opportunity to attend last week," she shot me a look, "let me repeat the format. Every week we have our speaker. Afterward, we do the Q and A. Fees are on the sheet." She passed a yellow handout in my direction.

I considered crawling under the desk.

"Ladies, we have a fabulous lineup. Today we'll be talking about getting those tummies flat again. Next week we have the fourth-trimester fashion show."

There were groans and laughter and a collective shift of weight.

"The week after, because I know how hard it is—I mean, tell me about it—we have a couples therapist."

Silence.

I was about to slide off the desk and hit the floor when a pain shot up my leg. *Sciatica.* It was supposed to have gone by now but like so many pregnancy ailments—hemorrhoids, indigestion—it lingered. Cleo was mewling. I hauled out my breast and nursed. Everyone was doing it. The room had morphed into a giant stationary milk truck.

Today's speaker was late so Ronnie opened the floor to questions. A woman in a track suit waved her hand.

"I have a question," she said. Everyone turned. "It's about my son. He's six weeks," she paused, "and my husband says he's small." She paused again. *"Down there."*

There was a collective gasp.

"Like it's supposed to be big already."

"Mine said the exact same thing," murmured a blonde in the back. The room was abuzz. Ronnie put her hands on her hips. Her voice took on a godlike authority.

"Ladies, birth size is no predictor of mature length or girth." She laid another stick of Freedent on her tongue, then clapped her hands like the chaperone on a fifth-grade field trip. "Next?"

There was a show of hands. Ronnie pointed to a beak-nosed woman sitting on the floor. She was so thin you could hardly believe she'd been pregnant. She opened her mouth, but nothing came out. She blushed, then clasped her head. The room fell silent.

"My hair!" she whispered. "It's *falling out!*"

Everyone gasped. I touched my own crowning mane, lusty and thick after nine months of do-it-yourself hormone treatment. This was the one compensation for swallowing brewer's yeast every day. Never in my life had my hair been so beautiful and lush.

Ronnie was matter-of-fact.

"The progesterone drops big time. Get yourself a haircut."

The next woman didn't wait to be called on. She was like a bull breaking out of the pen. It was as if the previous question had removed all shame and the rules no longer applied. Her voice was agitated and shrill. She thrust her hands into the air like the ruined heroine of a Greek tragedy, shaking her fists, exclaiming.

"What about the growth spurts? I'm worried about the growth spurts!"

Having read about this phenomenon in books, she feared her son might at any moment visibly double in mass and size, bursting the seams of his onesie like an infant Superman. Would she be ready? I slipped a hand into my pocket and found a solitary coin. I scratched at the edge with my nail. It was a quarter. I pictured it in my head: Washington's profile, his ponytail, his double chin. The word LIBERTY stamped over his head. The father of our country, honest to a fault. I tried to reconstruct how that coin had found its way in there. Was it some kind of fate? I listed in my head all the ways I could spend that quarter.

I could call Richard.

I could buy some chocolate.

I could give it to the homeless man who lived on our block.

I could—

The speaker bounded in. She was a fitness entrepreneur promising physical and spiritual rehabilitation through lunges and squats while pushing our strollers though Central Park. It was a sales pitch.

I snapped Cleo into the carrier for takeoff, gathered up the diaper bag, and fled.

The rest was a blackout.

I was at the hospital and then I wasn't. I was in the booth. But how? Taxi? Bus? My legs ached; maybe I had run. I was terrified. An hour of my life had passed and I had no memory of how I got there, what I saw, or anything about Cleo. Usually I was aware moment to moment of her moods and needs. But that day, on that afternoon, how we ended up in the Pussy Cat Palace, I had no idea. It was like the time I was in college and my Iranian roommate convinced me to go with her on a booze cruise around Boston harbor. I woke up the next morning on a sticky water bed without my tights in the lounge of a freshman dorm.

Only I wasn't a freshman.

And the dorm was at B.U.

But I didn't go to B.U., and I didn't know anyone who did.

The coin hung suspended halfway in the slot, pressed between my finger and thumb. Cleo clung to my chest, and I knew that however great my will, it was nothing to the force that had brought me here. Flouting every indicator that my mental faculties were failing, I felt a guilty release. This was for me the only real moment, the screen about to flicker. By then I could admit a smug satisfaction watching the men portrayed there, as if they proved the violence of their sex. But the truth was that I was watching those encounters for the women, scrutinizing their every moan and move, since I could no longer imagine ever wanting to engage again in such acts myself.

Cleo woke up, snorting like a truffle pig. The noise startled me, and by mistake I let the quarter slip from my fingers. It fell to the floor.

With one arm wrapped around Cleo, I squatted down to retrieve my quarter. It bounced twice, twirled, then skittered across the floor of the booth. When at last the coin stopped, it was heads up and nearly in the corner, in the dead center of a thick glossy puddle, which at first I thought was spit. I leaned forward and reached my hand to reclaim the escaped silver piece.

There was a certain smell. Briny. Familiar.

My fingers recoiled.

I tasted vomit. Cleo let out a scream, as if she'd tasted it, too.

I backed out of the booth and headed for the door.

Behind me a voice shouted, "Wait!"

I kept my pace, not looking back. The poster on the door was new: two giant breasts as big as wine casks and ready to burst, nipples the size and thrust of Cleo's fists. No arms, no face, only a woman's torso, gleaming and disembodied.

I was almost at the door.

"Hey, you!"

It was Rodman.

"Hey, Porno Girl!"

I froze.

He came loping over. I felt his hand land on the back of my shoulder. I flinched.

"I have something to show you."

I turned. "I'm sorry. I think I'm sick."

"You have to see this. Over here." He grabbed my arm through the sleeve of my parka and pulled me to the far side of the counter. We went up the two steps. He took out a key and unlocked the wooden gate that kept out customers. It was painted white, like a New England picket fence. He pulled open the gate.

"Look," he said, gesturing in front of us. Spread on the floor of this filthy, cramped enclosure was a pink Tweety Bird blanket. In the center of that blanket, propped against a cushion with a rattle at her feet and a plush yellow bunny, was a wide-eyed, brown-skinned baby with a tuft of curly black hair.

"Is that yours?"

He nodded, beaming.

"That's my baby, Olivia."

"What is she doing *here?*"

"Joelle took her father to the hospital. Kidney stones. So Olivia came with me."

"She's beautiful."

"She is the face of her mother."

I studied Olivia's face. "She also looks like you. I see the resemblance. The eyes."

He nodded. He was pleased. My head was pounding. Between my physical agitation and Rodman's candied aroma, I thought if I died here and now, that just might be for the best.

"Put yours down there, too."

I clasped instinctively at the lump on my chest.

"Go on," he said. "Put her down."

He had to be insane.

"Put her down next to Olivia. She'll be okay."

Slowly, I unzipped the parka. It was all I could do to follow orders, but it was liberating. For weeks I'd been taking orders from a person who couldn't even talk, and all along I had felt grossly unqualified to the task. What a relief to be no longer in charge.

I opened my coat and unsnapped the Snugli to lift Cleo out. She was quiet, alert. I looked into her eyes as if to say, *I know this is crazy, but what have we got to lose?* I dropped down on one knee and laid her on her back beside Olivia.

They looked like a Benetton ad.

They were beautiful.

Slowly, I stood up. My legs felt weak.

Even at the birth, when I saw that brave head emerge from between my legs, I didn't shed one tear. The doctor wrapped her in flannel, set her on my stomach, and I lay there gaping, dumbstruck with love. Rodman had that look now, too, like he was floating on some faraway cloud of euphoria and awe.

I leaned against the fence for support. My eyes welled up with tears, and I began to cry. Not so much from exhaustion, but from joy.

We stood there crouched before a wall of dildos, two of us, new moms.

THE NANNY TRAP

Eight months pregnant, I lay on the examining table, legs apart like pruning shears, the doctor's fingers probing the walls of my vaginal canal.

I felt the dull grip of a Braxton-Hicks.

I had gone to great lengths to get pregnant—six months of Clomid injected daily in two buttocks, three extractions from my ovaries, and sleeping every night with a crystal between my knees—but I was having this baby for no ordinary reason. I had one child already, Eliza, three years old, infinitely adorable with corkscrew curls like fusilli pasta. I could have stopped there, but I did not.

I *could* not.

Nola.

I was having a second baby because of Nola, the *nanny*, so she wouldn't leave. So she would stay in the job for another two years or three at least, because finally I had everything arranged in a way that I could handle: my job, my child, my marriage, and if not for Nola, the precarious arrangement that comprised my life could instantly collapse.

I felt a red hot pain beneath my ribs.

"That was me," said Jan, one hand on my pubic bone, the other burrowing. "Cramping. A normal reaction to pressure."

I forced a smile. Sometime after the birth of Eliza, Jan had come out as a lesbian and ever since, I'd been uneasy. There was a reason I had chosen a female obstetrician. I needed to be sure all that rummaging about down there was strictly business.

That all now seemed petty. I was eight months pregnant with a child I was having *for someone else.*

I was a surrogate mother.

Jan peeled off the latex gloves and threw them onto the heap. Besides delivering babies, she ran triathlons and flew a Piper Cub.

"Relax. Everything looks great." She said good-bye and vanished behind the door, leaving me to dress myself. That was no small challenge. It wasn't the same, this pregnancy, as the first. Everything had erupted sooner. I was bigger at four months than I had previously been at six, and the only reason I could possibly imagine was that mastodonic dose of testosterone—it was a boy. I couldn't see my toes. I couldn't bend my waist. And all my joints were soft and puffy like rotting spuds. Inside was worse, as if the floodgates had burst. My bladder had declared itself an independent state with its own free will. I was like the Nile Delta in the Fertile Crescent, gushing from every orifice.

I shuffled home hoping for Eliza's big hello. The lights in the apartment were on, but the place was silent. I opened the hall closet to hang my coat. Inside a thick curtain of quilted parkas gently rustled, as if a wind had passed through. From behind the coats came a voice.

"*Shhhhhhh!*"

Eliza, invisible.

"We're playing hide-and-seek. Go away."

I shut the door. She seemed already an adolescent. She had taken to throwing vast imaginary tea parties alone in her room with the door shut, refusing me entry. It was a complete inversion of power, though in her bare feet she stood only thirty-eight inches tall, her entire spoken vocabulary maybe a thousand words. I threw my coat on the bench and waddled toward the half-dark bedroom hallway. I needed to lie down.

I was carrying a child I did not want.

Then came Nola, surefooted as always and taller than I, now that I was restricted to flats. She was fearless and upstanding, with an encyclopedic knowledge of nursery rhymes, none of which I knew. She had impeccable posture, as if a shining silver cord connected the crown of her head to the heavens, and she looked half her age. She paused before me on the red kilim runner, poised and commanding, wielding in her hand a red Tinker Toy rod. She was large but not fat, her body soft and pliant where mine was angular and hard. I wore a size six, present circumstances notwithstanding, and it had not escaped my consideration that hers was perhaps the more natural anatomy or the more appealing to a child seeking comfort.

I scanned her lofty cheekbones and the dark ridge of her brow.

Here she is, the mother of my second child.

"I saw her in the coat closet."

Nola looked at me as if I had spoken to her in Turkoman. She opened the linen closet.

"I said, she's in the *coat closet*. Near the *front door*."

"We're playing hide-and-seek," she said in her lush West Indian trill. "It's a game."

Here she is, the mother of my son, and she plays games.

I needed to sit. Except for solitaire, which back in college I played tournament-style in bed for days, I had never liked games. All that competition and uncertainty—the roll of the dice, the spin of the dial, everything up to chance—it gave me migraines. Board games were worse, with their tedious turn-taking, their contrived outcomes. I had gone to some length already in obstructing Eliza's discovery of such onerous pastimes, but I dreaded the future, when some unsuspecting visitor would expose her to Candy Land, Parchesi.

"Right. So if you want to find her, she's in the other closet."

"Missus, it's *pretend*," she said, smiling, and I felt myself shrink. Nola had just enough of a British inflection to make me feel intimidated. She opened the closet door.

"Liza! Are you in here?" she called inside, peering into the darkness, and waited for an answer. It was like call and response in church, with an undeniable playfulness that was beyond me to muster, but the only reply was the smell of cedar.

That nickname—*Liza*—I hated it. It had not been my intention to name my child after a substance-abusing show-business personality. But Nola had taken to calling her that, and I hadn't the nerve to stop her. Worse, Eliza seemed to like it.

My bladder beckoned. I squeezed by Nola and down the hall to the toilet, my sixth visit since lunch.

I caught up with them in the kitchen. Nola was setting food on a plate, one tofu hot dog with ketchup, baby-sized carrots, and two pitted prunes, my daughter's set piece of a diet, as variable as liturgical text. Eliza lined up her appetizer on the dining table: ten cheddar cheese goldfish crackers, her ration, arranged for execution. I sat down beside her. She seemed not to notice.

"What did you do today?" I asked boldly.

She popped a victim in her mouth.

"Tell your mother what we did today," said Nola, caressing Eliza's head, coaxing.

No answer. She popped another victim.

Nola gave me a look as if to say, *try another tack.* I ransacked my brain for another topic of conversation.

"Did you go to the Park?"

She looked at me, her face an empty moonscape, dropped open her jaw, and showcased the pulpy orange paste.

"Tell your mother, *Liza.* We went to Tildy's house."

Tildy, Tildy, who was Tildy? I speed-dialed every name in my head. Had I met Tildy? Was she even a girl? You couldn't be sure. Casey, Annabel, Felidia, these names I knew. Nola took Eliza to their houses for play dates, these children I never had met. Nor had I met their parents. She took my child to play with strangers whose parents were strangers, too. Every day my daughter entered the apartments of strangers and I did nothing to protect her. They could be sociopaths, for all I knew. Sociopathic parents with sociopathic children.

"Then we stopped by Jane's for snack," added Nola.

This was too much. I should have laid down the law with Nola when I hired her, but like so many consequences of my childcare arrangement, this had not occurred to me until it was in full swing. Other moms set limits with their nannies, so that despite leaving their child ten hours each day with a person they hardly knew, they still felt in charge. One mother I knew didn't let her nanny bathe her son because she feared the woman might accidentally drown him in the tub. Another mother forbade playgrounds because of the rats, which admittedly were everywhere, no longer politely restricting themselves to the garbage bins. Fool that I was, I had given Nola carte blanche to go anywhere, do anything, and now I was paying the price. I had handed her my power, and I had no idea how to reclaim it. If I asked her to stop the play dates she would say I was depriving her of a social life and she might threaten to quit— she was friends with the other nannies, and play dates were fun for them, too. So I shut my mouth and justified the situation with what I read in a mounting stash of childcare books, all of them wildly contradictory. One point they agreed on, though, was that regular interaction with same-aged children was good for Eliza's development. Who cares that most of it resulted in fistfights and tears? Didn't I want her *socialized*?

Nola set the Big Bird plate on the table.

"Baby-sized pieces!" cried Eliza. "I want baby-sized pieces!"

"I'll do it," I said.

"No!" she shouted and slammed her fist on my forearm. Nola called out from the kitchen, asking what happened.

"Nothing," I said, hoping to conceal the extent to which my own daughter could abuse me, now that she knew I was only weeks away from ruining her life.

"Nola do it! I WANT NOLA!" She shook her head in defiance, her two perfect pigtails swinging frantically back and forth. Those luscious amber ringlets—usually I looked upon them with joy, but it occurred to me now that what she wanted was to slap me in the face with them. Maybe I deserved it, considering the trauma I would soon inflict upon her. She was color-coordinated, too, the elastic hair bands matching her

T-shirt and leggings, lavender and pink. On this there was no doubt. I could never dress Eliza as well as Nola did.

I got a knife from the cutlery drawer and stalked back to the table.

"Let me cut it for you, honey," I said.

I was determined to slice that frank if my life depended on it.

I sectioned the hot dog. Eliza shrieked. Her face was scarlet.

"Mommy does it wrong!"

She thrust her arm across the plate. The hot dog flew from the table, hit the top rung of a chair, and bounced on the rug. I wanted to crawl into bed. If this was how I handled one child, how would I manage with two?

Desperate, I turned to Nola, who remained unfazed. She took the plate, picked up the lint-infested runaway weenie from the floor, and carried the mess back to the kitchen. When she returned the hot dog was fuzz-free and reduced to pieces no bigger than a thimble, each one identical except for the one scrappy trapezoid I had slaughtered in haste. Eliza quieted and started eating, dipping the fleshy stubs in the ruby-red dollop.

My tongue touched the inside of my cheek, which was as rough as burlap. I'd been gnashing for months. Nola spoke first. I was grateful that she changed the subject. I took it as an act of charity.

"I called Dr. Kasen's office," she said. "They gave me an appointment for next Friday."

"Good."

Dr. Kasen was my dentist. I had given Nola his number and insisted that she call because the quack she had seen in Flatbush wanted to pull two of her back teeth. They'd been aching for weeks. I suspected all she needed was a crown. Moreover, I had told her (as I had told my dentist) that I would pay the bill. Michael thought I was being magnanimous, but in truth my motives were purely selfish. I didn't want Nola to miss a single day's work.

In the meantime, more than anything I wanted Eliza's attention.

"Guess where I went today?" I said, my voice possessed by some alien falsetto.

No answer.

"I went to the doctor!"

"Did you get a shot?"

"No, silly. It was a checkup. *For the baby.*"

Eliza's face fell into a grotesque contortion and she stuck out her tongue.

"Stinky baby!" she cried out and set to humming. I should have expected that response. Two weeks earlier we had given her a life-sized newborn baby doll as a kind of introduction. She ripped off the blue onesie and dangled it upside down over the open toilet. She said it was making pee-pee.

Nola asked, "What did the doctor say?"

Eliza hummed even louder.

"Fine. She said everything was fine."

Nola smiled.

"I hate babies!" Eliza declared. "I only like big girls like me and Nola." She was like the dictator of a small island nation, her power disproportionate to her size. I cowered. Unlike me, however, Nola could ignore her.

"You remind me of me when I was expecting my second," Nola said, once again changing the subject. "I think I was more nervous the second time than the first."

I hated when she volunteered her own experience. As if I were perennially the novice. I tried a smile, but I suspect it looked more like a smirk.

"The second time is always easier. You'll see."

Among the many missteps I had made with Nola was that I had let it be known what those first few months with Eliza had really been like, before she came to work for us.

"Besides, this time you have help."

She knows, I thought.

She knows this baby is hers.

Strangely, I felt relief. At times it seemed Nola was the only person interested in this poor unwitting fetus, other than me. Eliza certainly wasn't interested except to say that if it were a boy we would have to call the FedEx man and send him back. As for Michael, I had come to believe that his perfunctory statements of confidence in me were in fact proof of his disengagement. He was humoring me. Like it or not, it was Nola to whom I turned for support and approbation. It was as if we were paired, she and I, in some strange new kinship, as though it were her joy and her gratitude that I craved for carrying this baby to term with such infinitely good care.

As for how I knew it was a boy, despite not having taken advantage of the various methods available for proof, let me explain.

I remember the circumstances of his conception exactly, not for any romantic reasons, but because I had kept a log of every coitus on the PETA fund-raising calendar tacked on the refrigerator, target days highlighted in pink. It was June and the featured photograph showed three brindle pug puppies nestled on bales of hay, which was how I knew to expect a boy. Michael had an 8:00 A.M. meeting at a construction site in Queens and he was on his way out but I blocked his exit at the door and made him undress, because for that month's egg hunt, 8:00 A.M. was the zero hour. Not to mention the astrology, Ares pressing on my moon. I was drowning in maleness.

Nola was loading the dishwasher.

"You can go home, Nola."

"It's only five, missus. I didn't pick up her room."

"Yes, but *I said*. You can go."

Against my objections Nola rinsed out the sink. How many times had I told her not to clean the kitchen, it was not part of the job description, but she did so anyway and I wondered if it wasn't part of her strategy to wrack me with guilt.

Nola hugged Eliza good-bye and left, though not before Eliza chased after her to the door with a dozen kisses. When finally she returned to the table, it seemed it was only the food that had drawn her back, not me. I watched Eliza eat. You would think she was an early practitioner of Zen. She could take an hour to eat six pieces of ziti. I asked what she ate for lunch, but she kept humming.

"Did you eat at home or did you go out?"

"Out."

"Where did you go?" There were a few neighborhood spots where Nola sometimes took her—the coffee shop, the bagel store, the dingy, nefarious corner bodega where I'd never step foot myself. I'd never given Nola permission to take Eliza to any of these places, but how could I stop her?

"I don't know."

"What did you eat?"

"French fries." She smiled.

"Did you go to the diner?"

She shook her head.

"Where did you go?" The expression on her face was blank.

"All done!" She wiped her hands on her shirt.

"Where did you have the french fries?" I needed to know. Michael and I did not approve of fast food, and I had told Nola that.

"Let's go play in my room!" she shouted and slid off her chair. Then she took off in little thuds upon the floor.

I got up to follow, but it took me longer just to stand. I heard the door slam and then her crazed coloratura giggle. Crossing through the foyer, I saw the stroller parked by the door. That was a problem unto itself. I hated pushing that thing, and I had been trying for months to wean Eliza from it, but Nola insisted on using it. The mesh string carryall hanging in back was empty except for some trash stuffed to the bottom. Inching closer, I saw the cardboard backside of a child-sized paper crown.

Napkins and wrappers.

A logo in red and yellow print.

Burger King.

That night I told Michael we should hire a new sitter. It was ten o'clock and I was propped on the bed in my usual slant. He was sitting in the club chair, reading. Eliza had gone to sleep early so we had actually sat at the table for dinner instead of standing at the counter, picking like thieves. I thought the inroads were safe.

"You mean for the baby? Like we need two?"

"No, I mean someone new. Instead of Nola."

He put down his book and looked at me as if I had unhooked my maternity bra and pulled out a mouse. The book was a huge volume on the history of clocks and clock making. It was his latest obsession, the history of time, the idea of measuring the immeasurable. I didn't pretend to understand, and who knows if he did either, but I took it as further evidence of his tactical evasion of reality. He was the sort of person who was comfortable only with abstractions, and this book was the latest proof.

"Why are you reading that thing, anyway?" I asked.

"It's interesting," he said.

"Why's it so interesting?"

"It keeps my mind busy."

"I can't imagine having to make such an effort just to keep your mind busy."

"No," he said, looking at me. "That's not one of your problems."

I couldn't help but take that personally. "That's not very nice."

"Sorry," he said and closed the book. "Okay. Tell me, what's wrong with Nola?"

"I just thought with the new baby we should get a new nanny."

"But you like Nola. Eliza likes her. She's attached."

I heard the diagnosis in his voice: estrogen-induced dementia. Morning sickness, the mental kind. I shrugged. Any moment now he would ask if I had been seeing my therapist. I saw his hands inch across the dust jacket of his book. He'd had enough of this already. He was ready to check out.

"I thought you hired her because you knew she would stay. Wasn't that the point?"

It was true. When I hired Nola she fit all my requirements. She was a native English speaker; she was churchgoing. She came from the same island where we had spent our honeymoon, which I thought would give us a bond. She was not so young as to be irresponsible and not so old to be sedentary. She had children herself, but they were grown and out of the house so they would not compete for her affection, and she was past childbearing age. One nanny I knew had the nerve to get pregnant and ask for maternity leave. Nola had experience, and she had stayed at her last job for seven years. Or so she claimed, assuming her references were honest. It's true that at two of her previous jobs she worked under a different name, Jeanne Marie, but that, she said, was a nickname.

The mother of my son has an alias.

I drew the covers over my belly and sank down into the mattress.

"I thought maybe we've given her too much rope." She worked a four-day week (I stayed home Fridays), though we paid her for five. In return, she baby-sat two nights a month. But we had long ago stopped going out, maybe because we could no longer stand to be alone together, but also because secretly I had made a decision. I didn't want to leave Eliza with Nola any more than necessary. Even before I became pregnant, I had begun to think they were becoming too close.

"But you said we should treat her well to make sure she'd stay." Sometimes he was like a parrot, spitting back my words exactly. Unfortunately, I had no control over when.

I hadn't the energy to talk any further.

I turned off the light and arranged the pillows under and around my body like landscaping for sleep.

That night I dreamt I gave birth to a baby boy who was the spitting image of Nola. Brown skin and full lips, his hair braided like hers in cornrows around his head. I offered him my breast but he arched his back and turned away. He spoke to me in a voice like Bob Marley's and said he wanted curried goat. My waistline was thin and my hair was blond and cropped short like a boy's. Michael had that haunted John Cassavetes look.

It was *Rosemary's Baby.*

We were LIVING *Rosemary's Baby.*

As luck would have it, however, we did not have the apartment in the Dakota. I woke up in a sweat, my bladder leaking as I half ran, half waddled down the hall.

Sunday we took Eliza to the Central Park Zoo. The bulging recta of the rhesus monkeys nauseated me so we went to the children's section. Despite the chill, Eliza had insisted on wearing her tutu and spent much of the time prying quarters from Michael to buy grain pellets to feed the cow. That poor cow, idle and forlorn on the cold midwinter concrete, only a stone wall separating her from the din and grime of the Sixty-fifth Street transverse. The only cow on the island of Manhattan, only I felt like a cow myself, a gravid cow roaming the streets of New York, except that cows didn't have nannies. They managed without. I fell into a fugue state recalling the *old* children's zoo: Noah's ark; Jonah and the whale, the playhouse cottages of the three little pigs. All that was gone. Michael had never known that zoo, having grown up in Cleveland, and given his unbridled antipathy toward anything religious, he no doubt preferred this secular version with its benign lessons on ecozones and habitats. But Michael didn't bear on his arm the sad palette that colored my everyday life: the gray and purple misfortunes, the yellow pangs for the past or what the past was not. I could not walk six blocks in this town without being reminded of some childhood loss or sad occasion. I had had to train myself by force of will not to notice the hidden prompts crouched behind every next street corner. This was the great unforeseen accomplishment of my first pregnancy, when I could no longer afford to dwell on old sorrows, as they sent me into early contractions. I'd be plodding down Madison Avenue and suddenly remember here was the shoe store where my mother left me, aged three, waiting outside an hour because she didn't like me knowing how much money she could drop in one session. Then there were the taverns on Third Avenue where she'd park me in a booth with a cheeseburger and a Word Search book while she sat at the bar trying to find dates. Or worse: in my ninth month, when I could barely walk, five times I found myself on the corner where I said my last good-bye to my father, that week before he died. It was not even in my neighborhood. Each time I buckled, hands braced against a street lamp, expecting to see the baby fall out headfirst between my legs on the pavement in front of Duane Reade.

I learned at last to let the thoughts come and let them pass, watching my memories as a passenger on a train watches the landscape: in a blur, slightly sedated, eyes focused on nothing.

Look but don't stare, I told myself.

So why was I staring at Nola?

Eliza had meanwhile grown bored with the cow and moved on to an enormous spiderweb, as big as a king-sized mattress, with thick nautical ropes for filaments, hung at an angle to the ground. It was a sort of trampoline. Up and down she jumped, her tutu adding a strange effect: the *Nutcracker* staged in an insect colony. I thought of the spider: feared and unloved, solitary and self-sufficient.

I wanted to be self-sufficient.

"I had an idea," I told Michael, shifting my prodigious weight, as I could no longer stand for very long in one position. "What if I quit my job and took care of the kids myself?"

"Just you?"

"Who else? I *am* the mother, you know."

"But why?"

Michael walked to the vendor and bought a bag of peanuts.

What could I say? That I wanted to be a spider? Or that I could no longer stand taking Eliza to the playground on Fridays, because roaming there on the pavement were dozens and dozens of abandoned children. It was a kind of ghetto, the children well-dressed and warehoused. Inside the tall iron fence, crowding the benches, were the jailers, a legion of nannies, all of them black, and all of them West Indian, with a downward sliding scale of vigilance and care. There were exceptions to this profile, like Scottish nursemaids or French au pairs, but only on the East Side, where fair-skinned childcare had become yet another status symbol. On the West Side, with its last gasps at informality and vestigial liberal values, the nannies were uniformly black. They sat in clusters gossiping and sharing food, casting the occasional desultory glance at their charges when the poor tykes crashed into each other. As for their immigration status, that was dubious at best. In any playground, the mere appearance of an INS officer could have launched a stampede.

And if they ran, where would they go? They lived in the farthest recesses of Brooklyn, as even the best paid nannies, those with green cards, could not afford to live in Manhattan, though that was where they worked. Some of them traveled two hours each way on the D or the F to work for white people, raising their children.

"Apartheid," I mumbled. "It's like apartheid."

Michael looked at me, bewildered.

"The nannies. It's like they live in Soweto," I explained, "and we live in Johannesburg."

"Are you okay?"

"Just answer the question."

"Which was?"

"What if I take care of the kids myself?"

"Impossible."

"Why?"

"Maybe if we had started out that way, if you had stayed home with Eliza, before we bought the apartment. But we have too many expenses. We have a mortgage."

"What if I cut my hours to two days a week?" Doubtful, I knew. The firm where I worked imported in-home tranquility gear, like table-top waterfalls and miniature standing stone fountains. Right before I got pregnant, I had won at last the promotion I'd been vying for: executive vice president for sales. Volume was up like crazy. People were desperate for serenity.

Michael shook his head.

"Don't you remember what you were like when you weren't working? *That nightgown?*"

"What about it?"

"You didn't take it off for weeks."

"That was different." He cracked open a peanut and let the shell fragments fall to the ground. It was like him, not to consider the workers who would have to clean up. Yet another example of how he had been spoiled by his mother.

"What about when you spent the whole day riding back and forth on the Staten Island ferry?"

"That was Eliza. She wanted a boat ride."

"She was only three months old."

"What do you know? Newborn babies have a special relationship to water."

"Yes, but later you said you were doing it for yourself. You said you thought being on water would lift your depression."

"What are you saying—that I'm unfit for motherhood?"

"No—but staying home is out of the question."

The smell of peanuts was making me gag.

Now was the time.

"I had this premonition."

He smiled. "You're supposed to. You're pregnant."

"This was different. This was about Nola."

"Don't go worrying about Nola. She can take care of herself."

"You don't understand. It was about Nola and the baby."

He ate the last peanut and crumpled the bag in his fist.

"What about the baby?"

"I had this premonition that this baby I'm supposedly having—I'm having it for her."

Silence.

"I don't know what you're talking about."

"I'm saying that this baby is hers," I said.

"Don't be silly."

"You don't understand. I'm saying that she's the mother. This is Nola's baby."

He looked at me like I was crazy.

"Michael, I'm telling you, *it's either her or me.*"

I felt a punch in the ribs, as if the baby had done a back hand spring.

I clutched at my side and screamed.

Michael grabbed my arm.

"Are you okay? We'd better go home."

In the taxi, Eliza sat between us threatening to ingest her last grain pellet from the zoo. She kept brushing it against her mouth like lipstick, while I botched every attempt at confiscation. Michael talked over her head.

"Have you seen your therapist?"

I should have seen that coming. I shook my head.

"Why not?"

How could I explain?

"Pregnancy is no time for self-examination. Like combat."

His eyes narrowed. His mouth turned down, deflated, and I saw those droopy little bulges under his eyes, soft like melted wax. I saw the sadness in his face. He looked old. He looked helpless, and I knew the minute we got home he would pick up that enormous treatise on tickers and bury himself behind the pages.

"If that's your choice—" he said.

He turned away. I had disappointed him again. Maybe the solution was a world without men. A tribe of urban Amazons fending for themselves. I pictured myself among them, a battalion of women draped in black wool crepe, briefcases like quivers across their severed breasts. I read somewhere about a trend in Westchester, about moms sleeping with their nannies. Maybe that was the solution.

The one thing I knew was this: The topic of Nola was closed.

That night I thought of making a formal study, exploring all reasons remotely possible for having a second child. Unfortunately, the data pool for my research was severely restricted, as (for reasons perhaps obvious) I couldn't comfortably pose the question to anyone but myself. So I made up the answers, and what I decided was that people had two children not because they wanted two but because they didn't want to have just one. Because they thought only children were freaks. Because they wanted a playmate for the first. Because they believed in siblings, no matter how much they despised their own. Because they wanted proof to the world the first child was not a mistake.

That night I had another dream.

I came home from work and found Nola seated on the edge of the tub giving Eliza a bath. Only when she turned around it wasn't Nola, but my mother back from the grave. She was wearing a wrap dress printed with blazing yellow poppies, her long legs crossed above the knee, smoking, as usual, and reading out loud from a magazine. The magazine was *New York*, and she was reading the short reviews and synopses of current films. It was the seventies, and movies could be taken seriously. Eliza stood ankle-deep in the water, waving her arms overhead like a castaway on a deserted isle sighting a plane, desperately screaming, "Help! Help! I'm drowning!" I stood outside the bathroom door desperate to save her but I could not cross the threshold. My feet were blocks of lead. The more I tried to lift them from the floor, the more they stuck.

I woke up in terror.

In the sleepless hours that followed, I struck on a plan.

It was not yet ten o'clock Monday morning when I walked into the distinguished offices of the Spence-Chapin Adoption Service. They were not expecting me but who can turn away a woman with a seventy-three-inch waistline lurching breathlessly? I took my seat opposite a Mrs. Farquhar, who sported a pair of pert blue Belgian shoes and an equestrian-motif silk scarf. It draped across her shoulders as if she had flung it effortlessly, but I suspected more artfulness than that. She threw me a battery of questions about my health, my prenatal care. I told her my due date, the name of my obstetrician, and name of the hospital where I planned to deliver, which was the New York Presbyterian Hospital at Weill Cornell, and her mouth dropped open. She asked if I had been pregnant before, if I had carried that baby to term.

"Was it a live birth?"

"Very much."

"And that child—was that also placed?"

"No. She's at home with the sitter."

Mrs. Farquhar took a candy from a Chinese porcelain bowl on her desk and untwisted the wrapper. It made a racket strangely loud for its size, like a newborn baby crying. She cleared her throat and paused, candy naked in hand. I got a whiff from across the desk. Spearmint. I tasted vomit.

"Are you married?"

She placed the candy in her mouth and, with a drop of her wrist, gestured that I help myself. It was a move she had perfected at a lifetime of dinner parties. I shook my head. She repeated the question.

"No," I said. "Not."

"Not—?" Her head tilted and up went an eyebrow as if completing her sentence.

"Not married." I figured a single mom would be given an advantage. Lucky for me, my wedding band hadn't crossed my knuckle since the end of the first trimester.

"The children," I added, "they have different fathers."

She studied my face. I felt the urge to urinate. She glanced at my belly, then back at my face. Maybe she suspected. Maybe she thought me demented. If she did, maybe she would punish my son with an inferior placement. She reached into a drawer and pulled out a sheaf of papers.

"Here," she said. "Take these home and read them. If you're still interested, call me and we'll make an appointment."

I could have kissed the very bows on her shoes. That day and all the next I felt drunk knowing I had spared myself the horror of the double stroller. Already I had in my head a photo portrait Bachrach-style of the happy couple who would adopt my son. I pictured a serious Park Avenue family with fourteen rooms and an eat-in kitchen, not to mention a house in Litchfield. I was giving up my son, but I was doing it for his own good.

I kept it a secret.

Wednesday I came home early and sent Nola home. It was four o'clock and Eliza was napping in her bedroom, the walls hand-stenciled by yours truly in classic Pooh. She had kicked off her blanket.

I tiptoed over to replace it.

It was then that I saw.

The smudge.

It loomed over her brow like a dark cloud, a shapeless foreboding blot on her forehead. I tried wiping it off.

She awoke.

"No!" She pushed me away.

"There's dirt on your face. I'm cleaning it."

"That's not dirt!"

"Honey, it's dirt. Let me clean it."

"No!" She kicked my protruding stomach. The pain was excruciating.

"Leave it alone! It's *ash*!"

Ash? Where had Nola taken her to play now, the dump?

Then I remembered. Ash. Ash Wednesday. It was today. Nola had taken Eliza to mass at the church and now her face was marked with penitence and death. Only she loved it; the smudge was like a sticker, and even in the tub that night she refused to wash it off. I had to sneak into her room after she was asleep to erase it. I might have overlooked it, as I had so many other Nola incidents, but Michael could not.

"I don't want my daughter going to church," he said.

I was stunned. It never occurred to me that he would care about anything regarding Nola, but on this Michael was indignant. He was Jewish, though only in the technical sense. He was what he liked to call a *nominal* Jew—every year he baked a *buche de noel*. Yet the mere sight of that smudge on his daughter's otherwise flawless forehead kindled in him some dormant speck of identity, ethnic or otherwise, that I had never before witnessed.

The smudge disturbed me, too, but for different reasons.

Nola had exposed me for what I was.

Godless.

Heathen.

I made a note to call Mrs. Farquhar. I wanted to insist that my son's parents be tithing Episcopalians.

In the meantime, Michael demanded I bring up Eliza's ash mark with Nola.

The next morning, I confronted her straight on.

"Did you by any chance happen to take Eliza to church yesterday?"

"No, Missus."

"Then why did she have that mark on her forehead?"

"What mark on her forehead?"

"She had a mark. Here." I touched my forehead as if that alone were proof.

"I have no idea, Missus," she said. She looked genuinely baffled.

"But she had that mark. On her forehead. You had one, too."

"But I didn't take her to church. I went to services in Flatbush. Before work."

I was skeptical, but I didn't know what else to say.

"Besides, Missus, they don't put ash on the little ones." Her cheek was swollen slightly. I remembered her tooth. I felt horrendous guilt.

"Then where did she get it?"

Nola shrugged. "Maybe she put it there herself."

"Come on."

"Why not?" Nola smiled. Clearly she was not concerned. "Maybe she used chalk. She's very creative."

I resented this assessment, as if Nola knew my daughter's talents more intimately than I. Whether or not it was meant as a compliment, I had no idea. I chose to ignore it.

I dragged myself to Eliza's room. "Was that chalk on your face yesterday?"

She shook her head imperiously. "I told you. *Ash*."

I gave up. I wanted to go to work and forget all this. It was more a problem for Michael than for me, so why did I bother? Why was I wasting my time trying to protect him? I stalked to the door and was halfway to the elevator when I heard Nola calling after me.

"Missus!" She opened the door and stuck out her head. "Your appointments book! You left it!"

I felt a wave of embarrassment. As Nola knew very well, I couldn't get through the day without those pages in hand, yet I left it at home on more occasions that I could count. And every time she came to my rescue. Once she delivered it to my office before I even noticed it was missing.

I took the book as graciously as I could, though I could barely look her in the eye.

"Thank you, Nola."

Out of her sight, though, my mind reverted to Eliza's telltale ash. How did it get there? Whom should I believe? It occurred to me that perhaps my problems would all be resolved if Nola would quit. I reverted to making bargains with God if she would just go away. I promised next Christmas under the tree I would set up an entire miniature crèche. Or the epidural—I would deliver the baby without it. No matter I was an avowed agnostic.

That night Michael was incensed.

"Nola is lying," he said in the kitchen after Eliza was safely in bed.

"You mean you trust the word of a child? Since when do three-year-olds get called to the witness stand?"

He shook his head. "She's lying. Fire her."

His face was flush with rage.

"I just can't believe you changed your tune."

"This is different."

"What's different about it?"

"I don't want my daughter getting sucked into a lot of hocus-pocus." He curled his lip as if he had smelled something bad.

"Hocus-pocus?"

"You know, confessions and crucifixions."

He had become observant.

He reached in the refrigerator for a beer, opened it.

"What—have you decided to raise her as a Jew?"

"No, but that doesn't mean I want her to be Catholic."

I was ready to sign her up at the convent if it would resolve my problem with Nola, but I wasn't about to say so.

"I'm not so sure a little spirituality is so bad," I ventured.

"Yes, except I'm not Catholic, and neither are you, remember?"

I let out a stilted, careless laugh. In fact my mother had been Catholic, but perhaps he had forgotten.

"It's also a question of trust. How can you trust her, knowing that she lies?"

"Who says she's lying? There isn't any evidence. Besides, since when do you care?"

"I've always cared." He lifted the bottle to his lips as if in defiance.

"Cared about what? Not the nanny situation, that's for sure."

"I don't want my daughter getting indoctrinated into the Catholic Church."

As far as I was concerned, of course, the problem with Nola had nothing to do with religion and nothing to do with trust. I started to say he was completely offtrack, but he interrupted.

"I've told you what I think," he said. "Fire her."

My resentment was blistering, its causes twofold. There was his Johnny-come-lately change of heart; firing Nola had been my idea and here he was, acting as if it were his. Secondly, I resented his assumption that the hatchet man would be me, as if the job were beneath him. So much for his management savvy. Little did he know I had been proving myself lackluster at that task all along. But in a way, his ignorance was a relief, and I decided I would keep Nola, if only as an act of spite against Michael. Nola would stay. We would keep the status quo. Thus I recommitted myself to my secret destiny with Mrs. Farquhar. Adoption was the only possible solution.

Nothing prepared me for what happened next.

Monday night I came home at the usual time. I hung up my coat. Bobbing toward me from the hall came a diminutive, runty form, unrecognizable, smiling.

The body was familiar. The head was not.

Eliza's hair—those honey-streaked curls, luminous and fine, hair that had never been profaned by scissors—it was gone.

Was this my daughter?

She was shorn.

She was maimed.

I screamed. The baby felt the trauma, propelling himself into what felt like a classic breach. I buckled to the floor. Eliza shrieked. Nola appeared, the tea towel on her arm like a hero's hammered shield.

"Is it time?" she asked, eyes lit with excitement. "Is the baby coming *now*?"

She squatted on the floor, her hands extended, palms turned up, ready this minute to catch the baby herself.

I composed myself, clutching my belly as if to keep it intact. Eliza sidled up to Nola and parked herself on Nola's hip.

Nola offered me a hand. I refused.

"WHAT DID YOU DO TO HER HAIR?!"

Nola turned to Eliza and ran her dispassionate fingers through what was left of her locks. "She had lice. All her friends had lice."

"BUT WHY DID YOU CUT IT?"

"Missus, I called the doctor and she said take off the tangles, because they hide the eggs."

"WHY DIDN'T YOU CALL ME?"

"I did. You weren't there. They said you had left."

I had gone out for lunch and never returned, shuffling instead to the library to look up actuarial tables on adopted children, their odds for success in life. All that time I had sat staring at a computer screen in the steely quiet of the mid-Manhattan branch of the New York Public Library, while without my knowing, Nola was knifing my daughter's hair. I gaped at the stubby endpoints, each mutilated shaft unerringly straight. Not a wave or a bounce left. I was ready to dilate. Eliza was calm, resting her cropped head against Nola's capacious breast.

"Caroline, Tildy, Jane, they all had lice. Head lice. They all got a washing. I stripped the beds and laundered everything. And everything in the linen closet. Seven loads."

"Did you save any curls? A single lock?"

"Missus, they was crawling with lice. I saw them myself, nasty little creatures."

I pushed myself up, furious. I had trusted this woman with my daughter and she had gone and defaced her. Skinned knees and elbow bruises I could tolerate, but not discretionary dismemberment.

Eliza had been butchered.

She looked like a boy.

Now I'd have two.

"It was only an inch or two," offered Nola as a kind of apology.

"More like *five*." My heart accelerated, a race car on a death crash. "You're *fired*."

"What?"

I covered my eyes and pressed my fingertips into the sockets. I wanted to be liberated from this. I wanted to be rescued. I wanted to be anywhere but in my own apartment in my own life talking to this woman who under the guise of usefulness had delivered me instead to anguish and catastrophe.

I lifted my hands from my eyes.

I looked at her holding my daughter. Rather, what was left of my daughter.

Was I nuts?

I couldn't fire Nola.

I panicked.

"I said—all that laundry, you must be *tired*. And aren't you having your dental work soon? Why don't you take off the rest of the week? Why don't you take two?" I paused. *"I'll pay you."*

I couldn't believe my words. I couldn't look Nola in the eye, but I couldn't live without her. She had become a kind of adjunct mother, not just to Eliza but to me. If it takes a village, Nola was the entire population. I was stuck. It would do no good to replace her. I'd just rally my prejudices and obsessions and foist them on someone new, someone else from Jamaica or Guyana or Trinidad. No matter who succeeded Nola, I would again measure my mothering skills against hers, and I would again rank inferior.

She set Eliza down on the carpet. Eliza clung to her knee.

"Are you sure you can manage?"

I nodded, weakly, and in that moment I knew I would not call Mrs. Farquhar again.

Eliza was smiling.

DON GIOVANNI IN THE TUB

She was waiting as long she could. She told herself that as long as Jordan didn't know, it wasn't actually happening, as if by telling him she would make it fact. But it was fact; they were separating. Lawson hadn't been home in sixteen days, unless you counted the jaunty afternoon visit to refill his suitcase with clothes and back issues of *Foreign Policy*. Frances couldn't bear seeing him strutting about the home he had deserted, so she took Jordan to the zoo, where she started weeping for the penguins, shading her eyes to hide tears. She couldn't face Lawson, though when he first announced he was leaving, his voice measured and intent, it was all she could do to stare at him, incredulous, her mouth hanging agape.

He had seated her on the love seat and brought her a beer. She didn't touch it. He talked, pacing the floor, one hand turning magisterially in the air, the other deep in his front trouser pocket.

"You have to admit that things have not been good between us for a while," he said. "So it stands to reason that this is a change we can both be happy with."

Frances was dumbfounded. In truth, she had not noticed anything at all different between them, or if she had, that information was tucked away in a part of her brain to which she had no immediate access, a kind of emotional demilitarized zone where she dared not set foot. But he kept confessing, pressing out the details and circumstances of his affair like pus from a wound. If only he would stop his jabber and say it was all a joke. But he kept talking, as if the honesty of his disclosure could give legitimacy to his actions. If he would just stand still, thought Frances, maybe she could kindle in him some spark of shame for what he was doing to her, doing to their son. But he kept moving, making a tour of the living room, touching the furniture as if saying good-bye to the camelback sofa, the stenciled shade on the cast-iron lamp. It was as if he were giving one of his lectures—he was talking nonstop—and she were some hapless, second-rate student slouched in the back row. With every turn he took on the carpet, she felt herself being erased.

By the time he finished, Frances had dissociated completely: Though she was seated on the sofa, she no longer felt its cushioned mass beneath her; her mind was detached, floating upward, hypervigilant. She had had these out-of-body experiences before in situations of extreme danger: once, years ago, when she was mugged, and more recently, three years past, at Jordan's birth, an emergency C-section late in the night. In retrospect, on each occasion, the splitting off remained in her memory more frightening than the actual circumstances that preceded it. It was a defensive reaction, self-protective and completely involuntary, but it was terrifying both because she was unable to reverse it and because, when it happened, she felt herself drifting unmoored into a gap in the universe, connected to nothing and to no one.

Upward she went, rising toward the northwest corner of the ceiling, where it seemed she could curl her back against the wall. Gazing down from her perch, she was amazed at how small everything looked. Even Lawson, even herself. She began to panic: the sudden dizziness, the shortness of breath. She needed to make it stop. She knew, from experience, that the best chance of reclaiming herself was to stand up and walk.

"Excuse me," she said, though inside her head she heard a voice telling her that manners at this moment were ridiculous.

She made her way down the hall, talking herself through every senseless step. Left foot, right foot, left; this was her best hope for piecing herself together. She made it to the bathroom and the voice in her head said, *This is the part where you're supposed to throw up.* She leaned over the seat. Two minutes passed, then three, but nothing came up. So she splashed water on her face, dried off with a towel, and touched at her reflection in the mirror.

She had seen this story before, though always it had happened to *other people.*

"It's happening," she whispered, "and it's happening to *you.*"

Then she opened the bathroom cabinet, took out a small vial of tablets, broke one in half, and swallowed it. Xanax.

She returned to the living room and told Lawson immediately to leave.

Since that day, they had not spoken once. All communication, New York to New Haven, was transmitted by fax, which suited Frances fine. But now, in his absence, Frances found that looking at Jordan was like looking at Lawson. The boy's face was his father's in miniature: the angular cheek, the quickening eyes. At times she had to look away.

She sat in the room behind the kitchen, bent over the desk. It had three overstuffed drawers stacked left and right, leaving in the middle a hollow for her legs. Jordan called that space "the cave" and built LEGO kingdoms there. In the two hours since he had gone to the park, Frances had marked only three papers. The last paper, a poorly organized attack on object relations, had made her cry, as if the student's artless criticism had been directed at her.

A key scratched in the front door.

"Momma!"

Jordan careened down the hallway, pummeling the blond wood floors. Nina's voice called out from the door.

"Frances, I have to go."

Frances stood up. The baby-sitter had the day off, and Frances had called her sister for backup. She knew where Nina was rushing, to her fourth-year medical student with plans for a residency in surgery. He wanted to specialize in hand injuries, to rebuild shattered digits and lacerated tendons. Nina had reported every detail of their romance and Frances, six years older, had been glad to listen. But in the last sixteen days the doctor had gone unmentioned, as if Nina were ashamed to boast of her amorous good fortune when it seemed that Frances's life had been laid waste.

" 'Bye," Nina called out. The door slammed and Jordan appeared. He stood straddling the threshold in his coat and hat, arms overhead, his slender limbs just long enough to touch both sides of the door frame. His body was the shape of a star. His lips were ringed with dirt, and he needed a haircut. She thought of Lawson.

Should that have been a clue? The way in the past few months he'd grown his hair so long he could tie it back in a ponytail, as if he were adopting a new self-image?

"Why are you sitting in the dark?" Jordan asked.

She couldn't answer that so she redirected the conversation.

"How was the park?"

"Someone pushed me down the slide."

She bent down and kissed his brow. Then she unlooped the small counterfeit tusks running down the front of his duffel coat. He gave first one arm then the next, his small sudden movements like a bird's. *My son*, she thought, the soft wool mantle coming away in her hand, *at times it seems he could burst into some iridescent plumage, beat his arms, and fly away.*

He yanked off his hat, threw it on the floor, and scurried down the hall. Stopping at the front door, he checked the double-bolt lock, a recent tic, as if he thought their home were no longer safe.

Frances wandered into the living room and surveyed the mess: Jordan's panda slippers and Batman pajama bottoms; yesterday's Sunday *Times*; a box of doughnut holes (three left); the sword and scabbard of Jordan's pirate costume. Lawson would look at this mess, drum his upper lip with his three middle fingers, and relate it to some theory of national sovereignty or the collapse of statehood. It was as if he could experience even the most banal everyday stuff of life only in terms of political theory. Then he would insist on immediately cleaning it up.

Frances sighed. Jordan raced back down the hallway and crept between her legs.

"Where's my castle?" he asked.

"Right where you left it. Do you think I would touch it after all that?"

"Where is it?"

She pointed. "There."

He showed no recognition, his body completely still. Even his eyes were motionless. She took his hand and walked him to the castle, laid out beside the club chair by the window. It was an impregnable fortress, with turrets and lookouts and a carriageway bridging the moat. The moat itself, the steaming waters and the crocodiles therein, was imaginary, but on every other count, stone for stone, parapet by parapet, the edifice was fully realized, a refuge made of one thousand tiny pieces carefully locked together, intricately authentic and medieval. Lawson had bought him the kit for Christmas, and they assembled it together. Since then, however, the population of its inhabitants had become anachronistic and diverse—*multicultural,* Lawson would say cynically—as so many other toy figures had been mixed in. Jordan fell to his knees and began searching among them: palm-sized facsimiles of knights in armor but also cowboys and native chiefs, here and there a pirate. As he searched, he pushed them farther and farther beyond his reach: under the furniture, across the room. She had known all those bits and pieces would end up scattered. She still couldn't believe Lawson bought the set in the first place, as he had little patience for toys that ate up any floor space. But beneath his fastidiousness, Lawson held a secret predilection for boyish pleasures—he was seven years younger than Frances, after all—and he had loved building that castle as much as Jordan did.

At last Jordan found what he wanted: a blond, feather-capped Pocahontas. He carried her to his lips and gave her a loud, smacking kiss. Frances took a seat on the camelback sofa. Jordan followed.

"I thought you were playing with the castle," she said.

"I want to do something else."

"Like what?"

He placed his hands on her knees, opening and closing her legs like a bellows. She saw the tension on the backs of his hands, the tiny tendons rise and stiffen under faultless skin. He was deep in concentration. For a moment she felt she was his puppet. A buckle rose between his brows. His father had that, too, when he focused.

She felt something hard under the cushion and fished it out. A book. One of Lawson's, by some colleague at another university. *Game Theory and the National Security Dilemma.* Frances had studied game theory herself, back in graduate school, but she had never been drawn to it in the way that Lawson had been. He had won his tenure writing about it. She found it somehow atavistic, the idea of predicting human behavior based on strategies for gain, winning the biggest victories to inflict the greatest possible damage. In the wrong context, it could be too easily used against people. At times she felt in a way it had been used against her, as if her marriage had become a piece of game theory in action, with Lawson the zero-sum winner.

She let the book drop to the floor. Jordan was pinching her kneecaps. "That hurts. Honey, why don't you turn on a video?"

"No." His lips were parted slightly, the primrose tongue overriding his bottom incisors, still his baby set.

"Weren't you watching *Don Giovanni* this morning? What about that?" He was standing with both feet perched on hers, gazing at her. Her sneakers cushioned his weight. It was Monday, Washington's birthday, and the weekend had been interminable. She welcomed returning to work, though lately she was not up to the task. She should have told Jordan about the separation yesterday, but the two times she tried, her mind went blank and she found herself swimming for words.

"Let's play airplane," he said, grinning. The expression on his face— it was like Lawson's looking to make love.

"No."

"Please, Momma, can't we play?"

"I'm tired."

"Please? Just once? Lift your feet. Please?" He was whining. He had whined all weekend. Lawson's voice sounded that way, too, nasal and sharp—whenever someone asked how was his commute back and forth to New Haven.

Frances relented and took Jordan's hands for the game, though immediately after she felt regret. It seemed as if her whole life ahead would be a succession of surrenders, if not to Lawson, then to Jordan. She pulled in her chin to deepen her register.

"Lock your elbows for takeoff, Captain."

She straightened her legs and lifted her feet, his diminutive sneakers piggyback on hers, and up he went, all his weight on her hands and feet. His body hung suspended almost parallel to the floor, his small buttocks perched behind him as a fulcrum, his tawny hair cascading before his face.

"I'm floating!" he cried with glee, eyes drunk with delight, the tickle in his laugh like a waterfall. He was transported. Frances had to laugh. She kissed his nose—their faces were that close—and brought him down.

"Do it again!"

"I'm tired."

"Please, Momma, please! Again! Again!" His voice turned slightly shrill, as if shrillness were the necessary underside to mirth. She thought perhaps it was. They were like neighbors, his anguish and his glee, only they shared a door, and lately to enter one you had to travel through the other.

"One more time, Momma, *please!* Daddy always does it more than once!"

She felt the squall inside her begin to blow. She didn't want to hear about Lawson. She didn't want to hear his *name.* But Jordan was desperate. She thought, *Maybe he knows already.* Frances breathed in deep through her nose and out through pursed lips, a trick from Smokenders, and quelled her emotions. Not once had he seen her cry.

"Okay. One more time, but that's it." Her feet rose faster because she wanted to be done with it. It was easier, under the circumstances, to move the body than still the heart. She had been sleeping less than five hours a night, and rather than lie awake in bed, she had scrubbed inside the kitchen cabinets and organized the linen closet. It was as if she were making room for someone moving in, but with Lawson gone the apartment had a surplus of space. She could let herself sprawl.

On those first nights when sleep evaded her, she spent the hours into dawn studying old photos. There was one picture taken soon after Jordan was born where Lawson was literally clinging to her waist, and it confirmed what she knew. Lawson was the one to fear abandonment; his mother had died when he was ten, and he was sent soon after to live with an aunt. Back in graduate school when they first were dating, he had teased Frances, calling her a homebody, because her apartment was larger and well-furnished, if only because of her mother. The truth was that his own apartment was roach-infested and decrepit, but Frances didn't say so, and it wasn't long before Lawson simply moved in with her. Like a child, he had almost no possessions of his own—no household possessions, that is, but a lot of books. In those first weeks of living together, he put on an almost groveling display of gratitude. But she had liked making him a home, welcoming him in. Home, it seemed, was what he wanted, until he walked out. Looking back, Frances saw that as perhaps another clue. It seemed the very thing about her that had attracted him terrified him once he got it. Or worse, this: That what drove him out in fact was Jordan, that Lawson could no longer stand sharing his wife with his son. That was the more devastating explanation, and the rage beneath it might explain why he had turned so nasty, as if the only way he could wriggle out of their life together was to denigrate it. She could see through the meanness, but it stung nonetheless. When he told her he was leaving, he said it was because they were too *cozy*. "You *smother* your students," he said, "and you're *smothering* me."

Frances felt smothered herself right now, with Jordan's spritely body pressing on top of her.

"Once more! Please, Momma, please?" He tugged at her hands, his fingernails cutting into her flesh.

"Your hands are filthy," she said with disgust.

He smiled.

"What did you do with them?"

"Nothing."

"Did you drag them along the sidewalk the length of the way home?"

He laughed. She had that over Lawson for sure, the ability to make Jordan laugh. It was perhaps the only trait of her son that she could with confidence attribute exclusively to her, as if she and Jordan shared a funny bone, though lately she was not in the mood for laughter.

He licked his soiled fingers, then mewed like a cat. Until she had Jordan, Frances had never imagined that a boy would act this way. It was so *feminine*. But now, three years into motherhood, she hardly knew what was boys' behavior and what was not.

In the weeks after Jordan was born, Frances was stunned that she had carried inside her the body of a man—miniature but anatomically complete, including a penis. It seemed horrifying, freakish.

She'd been married to a man and she was mother to a son, but she found the opposite sex more inscrutable than ever.

"Wash those hands right now, and I'll turn on the video." He could run the VCR himself, but in the last few days, that skill, too, he had unlearned. He darted to the bathroom. She slid the cassette into the machine, the wedding of Masetto and Zerlina, a familiar scene, the lech leading the bride astray. Frances thought of the times she might have been led away herself (that Kleinian at the Boulder conference, the dad in Jordan's first play group). She wondered why she hadn't followed those leads, except that she had believed in marriage, especially *her marriage*, as much as she had been blind to all the changes within it. Changes like this: the way Lawson had lately insisted they go out more frequently alone. She had interpreted that as a wish for greater intimacy. Now she knew it was because he was bored at home, restless, looking elsewhere for sanctuary and distraction. Or his recent wardrobe changes—she had taken the new dress shirts and jackets as a sign of Lawson developing his own taste. Rather it was the discovery that he could be attractive to someone else.

The water in the bathroom sink was running full force. Jordan cried out.

"Almost done!"

Frances stepped into the kitchen. The telephone rang. She stood beside it and listened for the caller's voice on the answering machine before picking up.

"How are things going?" It was Nina.

"Okay." Frances was breathless, standing still. She couldn't adjust to her younger sister acting as caretaker; it felt unnatural. She preferred playing that role herself, much as she had been caretaker for Lawson. It gave her a sense of power, though she realized now that was only an illusion.

"Sorry I had to leave. I thought Robbie's rounds were finished." She was calling from his apartment.

"Of course."

Jordan raced down the hall into the living room shouting, "Finished!"

"Did you get any work done?" asked Nina.

"Some."

"Did you tell Jordan?"

Frances turned her back to the door so Jordan couldn't hear. "He's totally regressed. He won't even get himself dressed. I can't stand it."

"Did you tell him?" Nina was the only person who knew about the separation, and she was sworn to secrecy, but Frances now wished she had kept the news to herself. She opened the refrigerator and began foraging for dinner.

"Tell him what?"

"*Frances*. I thought you were telling him today." Frances wanted to groan. In the family mythology, Nina had been pegged the free spirit. By the age of twenty-seven, she had broken two engagements. Today Frances found her dogmatic.

"Maybe. Maybe later. After his bath."

"You said you were going to tell him this weekend."

"So? It's a long weekend. It's not over yet."

"Frances, just because it feels like the end of *your* world doesn't mean it has to be the end of *his*."

Frances scanned the shelves of the refrigerator: peanut butter, tuna salad, half a chicken cutlet, that mound of baloney encased in plastic like a school bus headlight. She lifted it out.

"At some point, you're going to have to tell Mom."

Perhaps worse than telling Jordan was the prospect of telling her mother, who had been the first to say three years ago that commuting marriages never worked. They were close, Frances and her mother, but when Frances moved back to New York, she had had to cultivate between them a necessary distance. It didn't help that as a fellow at a psychoanalytic institute, Frances was in analysis herself and thus she had to spend a fair amount of time talking about the woman, about the extent to which she had ever separated from her. Frances had never been adept at leaving home, and with so much of her furniture from her family of origin, she had in some ways carried her past with her. She had come to the conclusion, though, that her mother's compulsive generosity was merely a compensation, conscious or not, for historical neglect. Regardless of the motive, however, Frances had begun to take note that Lawson was jealous. And not just of her mother's generosity; he was jealous of her mother being alive. Perhaps he had arranged their lives so that he now had everything he wanted: Frances could be his mother, and his mistress could be his wife.

"I don't expect Mom to be very sympathetic."

"You don't know until you give her a chance."

"She's had a lot of chances."

"It won't help to be stuck in the past."

Frances wanted to get off the phone. She pictured herself shoving the mound of baloney into her sister's mouth. Her mother's take on this she knew would be difficult if only because of her own marital history. For the past seventeen years, her mother and father had inhabited adjacent apartments with separate entrances, neither married nor divorced. They bought the second apartment after Nina left for college, claiming it was for tax purposes, but everyone knew the truth, that *that* was the only way they could live.

There was a pause on the line.

"Frances, are you drinking?"

"What kind of question is that?"

"You told me what you drank over the weekend," defended Nina. Frances sniffed the baloney for spoilage.

"Well, if I weren't drinking now, I certainly would want to start after your quizzing me."

"It's just—"

"I'm cooking dinner," Frances interrupted. "I have to go."

She hung up.

She heard a sound emanating from the living room. Jordan. He was singing along with the video. He didn't know the libretto but he knew the melodies. He knew Don Giovanni was a brute, and he recognized the distress of the women, so he made up the words.

I'm the evil Giovanni,
The meanest man I swear,
Ladies better hurry
Or I'll steal your underwear.

Frances poured couscous into a pan with water, threw in a few baby carrots, then peeled off five baloney slices. Five would be too many, but she would eat whatever Jordan didn't. She was glad she had hung up before Nina, who was fanatically macrobiotic, asked what she was cooking. She felt guilty enough.

She rolled the flimsy circles into tubes and arranged them on a plate, radiating from the center like a five-pointed star. Jordan appeared with a black vinyl cape draped over his shoulders and an eye patch, his right hand brandishing a sword.

"I *am* Don Giovanni!"

"Okay, Don Giovanni. Sit down *per mangiare.*" The table, one side flush against the wall, could seat only three. Jordan took his seat in the tall cane-seated chair he claimed as his, and she passed the plate, pushing aside the markers and the dozen or so valentines he had received that month in nursery school. Mostly they were store-bought, forty-eight to a box with puppies and kittens, protestations of friendship floating above their heads in cartoon balloons. Some were crudely homemade, hearts cut from construction paper, three reds, two pinks, signed with love. Jordan unrolled a baloney slice, spooned couscous into the center, and folded the meat like a crepe.

"What are we going to do with your valentines, Jordie?"

He hummed the minuet and shrugged.

"How about we throw them out?"

"No!" He raised the baloney tube to his mouth and took a bite, spilling the delicate white granules of couscous.

"Use the spoon, honey, please." She pushed it toward him.

"Momma, can we play tic-tac-toe?" he asked, swinging his legs wildly under the table. Wrangling the spoon, he uncurled the next roll of baloney. *He is relentless*, she thought, *looking for treasure inside every concealing receptacle.*

She wondered what he would find if he looked inside her.

"Tic-tac-toe, Momma, *please?*"

"Later, maybe. Eat."

He stared at her and chewed. She reached over and took a piece of baloney herself, inserting it lengthwise in her mouth. It was like a second tongue, fleshy and pendent; if only she could talk to the boy and speak the truth. She was hungry. She reached for the bag of carrots. They were thumb-sized and dwarfed, scraped clean and blunted like stumps. The bag said *JACK RABBIT CLASSIC*. Once, the summer after sophomore year, her mother had called her a rabbit because she had stayed overnight at her boyfriend's house. That was the last time anyone had accused her of being promiscuous. The only rabbit now was Lawson.

"When we play tic-tac-toe, I'll be X, and I'll go first." He watched her face for approval. She said nothing. "X is best. X goes in the middle. That's how you win. Daddy *said*." He reached for his juice cup, knocking a trail of couscous from his plate.

"Jordan—" Her anger mounted; she squashed it. "Be careful, please." He nodded, chewing, his mouth open and shut, open and shut. She deplored his manners and she blamed herself, but she felt helpless to improve them. Lawson's manners weren't much better, despite his being neat-obsessed. Why had she tolerated that?

The food on his tongue was gray and pink. She caught sight of it and felt repulsed. She stood up.

Jordan cried out. "Where are you going?"

"Nowhere."

She found her way to the door of the hall closet and opened it. Standing before the wine rack, she chose a merlot. She gripped the bottle in her hands and felt a rushing thrill, knowing she was depleting Lawson's precious cellar. Returning to the kitchen, she found that Jordan was no longer eating. He had turned one of the homemade valentines on its back, crimson construction paper cut in the shape of a heart, and drawn a grid. It hung in the swelling upper right-hand arc of the heart, a green oversized number sign, only the lines were neither parallel nor straight but wayward and shaky.

"Momma—can we play?"

"Later, Jordan. Finish your dinner."

"I like playing with you because when we play, I always win."

"And with Daddy?"

"He always wins."

"How do you know I'm not just letting you win?" Conversation was beginning to exhaust her.

"Because I know. Besides, Daddy says you're easy to beat. He told me he beats you every time."

She stared him down, a tactic she disliked, though it worked. Lawson called it a cheap trick from a clinical psychologist, and hearing his voice in her head, Frances felt supremely outnumbered, knowing her son by no fault of his own would one day grow into a junior replica of Lawson, and he would also one day leave her. She would serve and please him as she had his father until he found someone to replace her.

He could leave her now, by taking Lawson's side.

She uncorked the bottle, poured a glass, took a long sip. Reclaiming her seat, she capped the pen. Jordan drove a carrot into his mouth through pursed lips.

Frances gazed into her glass. A tiny wisp of dust floated on the murrey-red surface, no longer than the white of her fingernail. It was an infinitesimal thread of lint, finer than the eyelash of a baby. She remembered a book Lawson once had, photographs of household goods seen through the lens of an electron microscope. Every kitchen sponge is a nursery for microorganisms, the bed sheets feast for vermin. Lawson was fascinated. The pictures seemed to turn him on. Frances hated those pictures: mites like raccoons, bacteria like elephants. Why did he like seeing microbes and parasites in his own home? Was it fascination or was it fear? Perhaps those pictures just confirmed for him what he already believed, that home is a place that is innately contaminated. Perhaps even then he was looking for an excuse to leave.

"Momma?"

"Uh-huh?"

"When is Daddy coming home?"

She lifted the glass. She could tell him now. He had asked before and she had skirted the truth, but she could tell him now. She looked at him hard. He had bitten two holes in a ring of baloney and draped the meat on his face, peering at her through the vacancies. It was like a mask, and he was hiding behind. She wondered how he felt on the other side. His father was a man who lived for ideas, not people. What could she tell his child, why he had left?

She had seen a lot of patients. They asked her to explain the chaos in their lives, to find causality for their suffering, and usually she could. She told herself she should do the same for Jordan, but everything she thought of saying would belie the void she felt herself.

Perhaps she had let her professional role leech into her marriage. Lawson frequently had quipped that he didn't need a therapist; he had her. But how could she resist? Before he met her, he had never given a thought to how his childhood losses had informed his character. The day he left, he used the insights he had gained as a weapon against her.

"As long as we're together, I will never be myself," he announced, just as she began her out-of-body ascent.

Jordan pulled at her sleeve.

"Momma! When's he coming home?"

Frances refilled the glass and straightened her back.

"Daddy's working in New Haven. He's working very, very hard, and he hasn't been able to come home." She paused to measure his reaction but saw only his eyes in shadow through the mask. "But he loves you very much, even when he's away." She took a long sip, the oaky dryness numbing her cheek. She closed her eyes to swallow. When she opened them, Jordan was pressing the baloney against the point of his nose, forcing a hole like a vent through which to breathe. The baloney was streaked with green.

"Jordan! What are you doing?" She grabbed his hand and the slip of meat collapsed limp onto the table. His hands were green, also the underside of his wrist. He had played a game of tic-tac-toe on his skin. Frances pushed back her chair and stood up.

"You're going in the tub *now*!"

Her voice echoed down the hallway. The apartment had felt so empty these last two weeks, as if cloaked in sadness. She stared him down again. He was frightened, the small cushion of his chin dimpled and stiff. Rage was not going to help her. It would only make him behave worse. She needed an exit. She topped off her glass, walked down the hall to the bathroom, and ran the tub.

When she returned, Jordan was squatting on his chair, his plate pushed aside. He leaned over the table as if deep in study, already the curmudgeon scholar, a shrunken, time-warped reproduction of his father. Before him lay the red paper heart, a purple marker in his fist. He had drawn another two grids for tic-tac-toe, making three altogether, enough for a match, but they remained unused. It was as if he were trying to construct his own playing field, where the rules would all be his.

If only life could be so neatly played out on a grid, she thought, *or plotted on a graph.* She pictured a chart in her head, the two lines perpendicular and infinite, one pointing upward, the other to the right. Inside the coordinates were obvious: Lawson's life could be illustrated with one string of dots curving upward for his career while another string, a mirror image, sloped downward, infinitely approaching zero. The second string of dots was their marriage.

The intersection of those lines was Jordan.

"It's bath time," she said, clearing the table with feverish energy. "Take off your clothes." She emptied the glass and turned to the sink, loaded with two days of unwashed dishes. She ran the hot water, pushed up her sleeves, and began scrubbing. Meanwhile, Jordan slid down from his seat and crawled under the table and out the other side. Standing barefoot on the unswept floor, his shirt untucked and stained, he tugged at her sleeve.

"Can't we just play *one* game of tic-tac-toe?"

She turned. His face looked so small. Even the tousled crown of his head, his caramel hair yet another inheritance from Lawson, was no match in height to the top rung of the chair. She reached out to touch him, her hands soapy and wet. They dripped on the floor. She pulled them back. She felt terribly stunted, inadequate to the tasks of mothering him.

"Okay. We'll play after your bath." She refilled her glass. She wanted to avert a panic. "Why don't you go check the tub, if it's full?"

He turned and left.

She finished the dishes and reached for the glass. It was lighter than she expected. She returned it to the counter—the stem nearly slipping from her fingers, sudsy and slick. She had better check on Jordan, she thought, pouring.

All the rooms were off a central hall, with Jordan's at the rear. Frances stopped in the bathroom to check the tub. It was about half-full, maybe more. She tested the temperature.

"Jordan! It's ready!" No answer. Frances set her glass on the rim of the white pedestal sink, the wine's ruby glow strangely dark. She felt alarmed. "Jordie! Bath time!" She waited one moment and then another, but he did not appear.

She went looking.

His room was almost impossible to enter. Toys and books lay everywhere like snares for defense: the rocking horse that had been hers, the tractor, the jolly worm he refused to ride. Not once in sixteen days had she asked Jordan to tidy his room. Here was the result.

In her head she heard Lawson's familiar complaint that Jordan's toys were too many. That with so much choice he would never learn to focus. Maybe he was right.

Jordan himself was out of sight. Half under the covers, on the shadowed, bottom bunk of his bed, he had surrounded himself with a crowd of stuffed animals: the elephant, the giraffe, the hen, three teddy bears, his owl. Through the menagerie, Frances for a moment could not single out her son's face.

"Are you getting in the tub?"

He shook his head, pouting.

She took a few steps, stepping on a Matchbox car and nearly taking a fall. She cursed under her breath.

"It's halfway full, Jordie, the way you like it. Not hot."

He shook his head again, his bottom lip protruding like a monkey's. She bent down beside him, tucking her head to clear the top bunk.

"Would you *please* come to the bath?"

He said nothing, his eyes glazed on her. She was at a loss. She thought of giving up and getting in the bath herself. He was so mercurial. If only Jordan would pick one mood and stick with it, maybe she could find the mettle in herself and behave accordingly. She hated him like this.

"If you don't take off your clothes, you'll have to wear them in the tub." Expecting to call his bluff, she scooped him up like a baby and carried him out of the room. His lightness startled her, as if his bones were hollow. He giggled and shrieked, kicking her waist, but she ignored him. It gave Frances the feeling, finally, of control.

"Are you taking off your clothes or not?"

Jordan gasped. "No!"

They crossed into the bathroom, past the standing sink, the mirrored medicine cabinet, its door swung ajar. The walls were tiled and white, each ceramic brick as old as the building itself and intricately crackled. A towel hung over the shower rail; the wineglass idled on the sink. The water in the tub was still and beckoning, a smooth, translucent bower in a porcelain shell. Standing over it, her son cradled in her arms, Frances was at the brink.

"Last chance. Either you take off your clothes or you get dunked. Clothes and all."

His body convulsed with laughter, his face mottled yellow and pink like the flesh of a sturgeon. He was like something not quite human. He tried to speak, but he couldn't get out the words. He squirmed, thrashing his legs and arms, perspiration shining his brow. She had turned this into a test. Better yet, a competition. Maybe this one she could win. She didn't think of consequences.

"Jordan, this is it."

He was hysterical.

She lowered him in slowly, feet first. The strain on her back was enormous—she might pull a muscle—but she felt peculiar strength. He was screaming, but just as his feet touched water he fell silent, as one does upon entering a church. She saw the water seep into the denim at the hem of his jeans, coursing upward with ominous speed, darkening the fabric.

"MY PANTS! THEY'RE WET!"

He was in past his knees. He stared at his jeans as if they were ruined, as if all those tiny untold cotton threads would never again be dry. His breath was shallow and quick, his limbs and torso stiff. She could see the heat on his face, his small cheeks flush with panic. She froze. The boy was half in the water but his clothes were nearly saturated. He was on the verge of tears, his mouth open in shock. She could stop now, but she felt invigorated. For the first time in sixteen days she felt empowered. She felt herself. After all those years playing caretaker to Lawson, now she would be caretaker to her son. She rotated him belly side down and lowered him into the tub.

"IT'S COLD!"

His words broke at the surface of the water, his eyes rimmed with terror. He coughed. If he cried now, she would not necessarily know, his tears merging with the bathwater. She forced a smile and lowered him farther.

"Swim, Jordie, swim!"

He remained immobile.

"Be a reptile!" she cried out. Among the nicknames Lawson had coined for him was Gator and at last she saw why. Jordan was genuinely lizardlike, facedown, his body half-curled below the water, elbows bent, his scaly hands drawn close to his cheeks like forepaws. "Come on, Jordie! Swim! Like you're in the pool!"

He didn't move.

"JORDIE, SWIM!"

She felt infuriated. She wanted to be through with this. She pictured the rest of her life a bleak desert wasteland of nagging reminders and corrections. Already she felt the resentment for having to attend to him every day on her own. Better not to have kids at all than to have to raise them alone. She remembered thinking that years ago. This was like a Greek myth, like Oedipus; the very thing she had wanted most to avoid, and she had walked right into it. She wanted to be out of there. She wanted her glass. She wanted to give Jordan a bath, to dress him for bed, to say what she had to say, and to be done, until it occurred to her, long in coming like the dim light of a faraway train, that for some time the boy had not uttered a sound.

He hadn't moved.

Jordan was facedown in the water. He was completely submerged.

She jerked into action. Rousing every muscle in her arms and across her back, she pulled him out and turned over his body.

Jordan was soaking wet.

His eyes were shut, his sodden body weighted and still. His mouth was ajar, his tongue dangling limp. It seemed like hours since he had made a sound.

"JORDAN!"

No answer.

She shook him furiously.

"JORDIE! ARE YOU OKAY?"

His eyes opened to slits.

Her heart was pounding. She felt herself beginning to split away. She tried to stop it by feeling the fear. She had so many feelings she wanted to hide.

Inside her head the voice shouted, *He could have drowned!*

Had he any idea? She forced a laugh.

"Jordie, isn't this *fun*?"

He blinked, dumbfounded, staring at her. He made a sound like a gurgle, a waft of stale air rising deep from his lungs. The sound was hesitant and coarse, breaking on his slippery lips in a shimmering transparent bubble. He made the noise again, louder. It could be a preamble to laughter, though it sounded like a death rattle.

"Jordie, it's a *game*. Think of it like a *game*." Her voice was high and shrill. He gave up a brief desperate laugh, unsure of the joke. He hadn't moved a limb. But she had to go through with this. She turned the ivory top of the drain pipe to reduce the water level and lowered him back in, holding his back to ensure he sat up.

"Jordie, don't you like wearing clothes in the tub?" She took one of his hands in hers and grazed the surface of the water, splashing. A few drops spattered her face. She knocked one of his toys into the tub, a blue plastic frog. It went under headfirst but righted itself and floated. It made a groaning sound. Frances smiled. Jordan laughed again—she saw the rise and fall of his belly with each small expulsion of sound. He splashed the water himself. She offered him the bar of soap.

"Wash your hands."

He cupped his hands around the bar, pressed them together, and began to lather. The foam was soon thick. He looked up with shy determination.

"Is this okay?" he asked.

"Plenty."

He rubbed harder. The lather became extravagant and rich.

"I can make it suds *more*."

She shook her head. She was about to say *that's enough already*, but then she saw his expression: urgent, hopeful. He wanted desperately to please her. She didn't have the heart to deny him. Someday, for some woman, he would be a persistent, needful lover. Lawson was needy, too. It was part of his charm. But the flip side to that need was scorn, and scorn was what she felt when he left.

She noticed a twitch developing below Jordan's left eye. Lawson used to get one at the corner of his lip. She had stopped remarking on it because that always made it worse. In the hollow of her chest she felt a gaping sadness.

She straightened her back and stood up, her knees creaking. She pictured Jordan after the bath, wrapped in his enormous hooded towel.

He was her swaddled Don Giovanni.

But for now he was hers completely.

DAUGHTERS

WHAT MARCIA WANTED

Many years before their marriage broke up, before anyone could say openly that Frank was gay, the Dresdens threw a lot of parties. People came all the way from Boston and New York, doubling up in the guest cottage and the annex, sometimes staying through Monday. Sometimes the Dresdens had more guests than beds. I used to count.

During the week, when Frank was in town and the house was quiet, Marcia herself was continually drunk. Or maybe it was her posture. She could never stand still but was always swaying. She was drunk the time she made us camp out on the widow's walk. The roof was slant, and when she slipped she was two inches from impaling her leg on a lightning rod. For Marcia, any excuse would do for mixing drinks in pitchers with long, twirled-glass stirrers—the last new shingle on the barn, the flash of the Pleiades, or a hurricane that was only limping its way to Buzzards Bay. Sometimes she had no excuse at all, but endless gin and tonics and cases of Almaden in bottom-weighted jugs designed, it seemed, for long journeys on merchant ships. She let her sons drink, too.

They had two, Nick and Colin, each a year older than Lally and me. But that summer they kept a low profile from everyone, especially from their mom. Maybe it was because Marcia, who my mother said was compensating for her tight-lipped Indiana roots, had started pouring them wine at lunch. She said it was better if young people drank in the open. She let me and Lally drink, too. I sipped my first martini on the blue patio swing. It made my head swirl, and I felt the wind rush inside my skirt, soft as chinchilla. The Dresdens' house was like a speakeasy, where age was no excuse for sobriety. It made my mother, who had never really felt at ease there, stop going. It couldn't have pleased her to see us spending so much time there ourselves, but she never told us not to. Even if she herself felt intimidated by the Dresdens' largesse, I think she got a certain satisfaction knowing her daughters were comfortable with it. It made her feel good.

Nick and Colin were teetotalers. Nick was too much the All-American, and Colin was too much an observer, or rather too introverted, perhaps because he had just got his leg brace. He spent a good part of that summer in his room building an entire miniature village with only matchsticks. When he wanted to get wasted, he smoked pot.

I was fourteen that summer, and by then I had known the Dresdens more than half my life. More than anything I wanted to be one of them. I thought they were normal, though I thought so about any family but mine, ever since my dad died. Lally found him in the claw-foot tub, floating almost. Naked. He used pills. I saw the trail of water from the bathroom down the stairs and out the front door after they took him away. They zipped him in a bag that leaked. I was ten. Marcia said it proved how sensitive he was, that he chose to use pills. Like a woman, she said. But it never seemed sensitive to me. The day after the funeral I cut holes in his Sulka shirts. Three years later my mother married Jerome.

When we were little, Marcia took us to the carnival every year in New Bedford. She went on the Dervish, which was how we knew she didn't wear underpants. She took us clamming on the marsh, and one year, the summer my dad died, she got us a booth at the village art show. We sold rocks we'd painted, Colin, Nick, Lally, and me, and the Murray kids from the next cove up, but they sold their house the next summer and moved away. Marcia was like a good teacher who keeps your interest from simply her smile, like she's got a secret that she's just about to tell. I'd have done anything for her. The Dresdens had a secret, but it wasn't one I expected.

They had by this point the only enduring first-time marriage on Clarey's Neck. Everyone else was divorced and remarried, as if wives and husbands could be recycled as easily as tin. Even my parents, before my father died, had talked of separating, my mother told us later, as if that would make us feel better. But Frank and Marcia hung fast, perhaps because of Marcia's midwestern values, or perhaps because of all the families on the Neck they were the richest, and it took that much longer for all they had amassed to come apart.

My mother, meanwhile, was at it all hours of the night. You could hear them through the second-floor landing wall, the groans of the box spring and Jerome's raspy breaths. I slept in the third-floor attic room to get out of earshot. Lally was also at it (monkey see, monkey do) with Nick, though she was more discreet, fumbling home from the Dresdens' pool house at 3:00 A.M. Once I got up the nerve to ask how far they went.

"None of your business," she said. She was seventeen.

I took up gardening. At the start of the summer, Marcia announced plans for a Victory Garden. "Like we had in Vincennes," she said, speaking of her hometown, as if there were still a war on. The garden became her project. She had one every year—one project, that is—and every year her project was different. The year before she bought a pair of peacocks and trained them to fetch like dogs. Before that, there was shingling the barn.

That June she arrived at the Neck with a stack of gardening books two feet high. Until then I'd never thought of her as much of a reader. The only book I'd ever seen in her hands before was *Passages*.

At first, she took it for granted that the boys would help. After all, Nick had swept the peacock shit flung about the yard the year before and dumped it behind the shed. Someone told her it made rich compost.

But with Lally nearly stitched to his back pocket, Nick was not available. Marcia had only to say *mulch*, and he would skulk off, muttering he had to water the courts or check the tire pressure on the Willys. She had better luck with Colin, at least when he was stoned.

By mid-July the tomato plants were blooming in tiny yellow stars but hobbling, their unstaked stalks parallel to the ground, the cabbages were the size of softballs and riddled with bugs, and weeds were rampant. Standing alone in the chalky dirt, Marcia looked desperate, her curry red hair wrapped turban-style in a leopard scarf, a menthol Lark dangling from her lips, glass in hand. Her uniform during the week was a string bikini top and a pair of low-slung khaki shorts with a gazillion pockets, something you'd wear to cross the desert. She was a skinny drunk, as if everything she poured in poured right out. She hated being alone; with all her projects, her real motivation was to assemble a crowd.

I still loved Marcia then. She would talk about my dad—how handsome he was, how he founded the Pequod Society. They met, members only, for five o'clock commodores in the red canoe.

When I turned my head a certain way and lifted her glass the way she told me, Marcia said I looked just like him. It set my heart thumping.

"Your mother's in love with Jerome in a way she wasn't with Hal," Marcia said one day out of the blue while I mulched the squash. I froze. "She was in awe of his mind. But with her, he was too detached." She stood barefoot on the loose soil, her painted toenails like cinnamon Red Hots beneath the dirt. It was morning, and the tumbler which she had said was filled with orange juice was empty. She said my dad would probably have been happier with someone else.

"Your mom didn't have the tools to love a man as brilliant as Hal," she said.

I stopped mulching and looked up at her, agape.

"A marriage has to be stoked every minute like a fire, or—*poof!*—" she said, "it goes out."

———

Early one Friday in July my mother sat Lally and me down in the sunroom with Jerome. She plumped up a throw pillow and wedged it behind her back.

"We have some news," she said, turning to Jerome, smiling.

There were things I couldn't get used to, like the puddles of skin beneath his eyes as if he were always tired. Or the way he combed his few strands of hair across the top of his head, as if hair grew sideways.

"What is it?" asked Lally. "You're making me late." She was cashier at the boat club snack bar, the only teenager working there who wasn't a member. We weren't members. The Dresdens were. Nick was a sailing instructor. He got her the job.

My mother giggled, her hand poised nervously before her mouth. She looked at Jerome one more time and then she said, "We're having a baby."

There was a long silence, the kind that seems to go on forever. At first I wasn't sure I had heard right. I thought maybe they were talking about me, since when I was little my parents liked calling me "the Baby Eve," after some old movie. Actually, it was mostly my dad who called me that. He loved old movies. We used to watch them together weekend afternoons on the green velvet sofa.

We're having a baby.

I ran the words several times through my head. Eventually they stuck. I shuddered.

"A baby girl," said Jerome. His face was soft and ribbed like a cruller. He didn't have kids of his own. For nine years of his life he'd been a Catholic priest. "We considered adoption, but then we got lucky. The doctor says not to worry."

"You'll have a baby sister," said my mother. Her eyes lit up as if she were surprised herself.

"I already have a baby sister," Lally answered back.

I couldn't believe she remembered. I wanted to jump up and give her a hug.

Jerome cleared his throat. "You'll have two."

"Aren't you too old?" I ventured. My mother let out a nervous laugh. Jerome answered.

"They say she'll be fine."

I wondered why she hadn't answered the question herself. Was there something she wanted to hide? There seemed to be so many more secrets since she married Jerome. It wasn't the first time I felt betrayed. I felt them all at once now, each and every instance.

I thought maybe my mother would stop the conversation and shout, *April Fools'!* It seemed unnatural, like a lady with a beard or bodies rising from the dead. I felt sick. She must not have loved us anymore or maybe she'd just given up, as if we had gone so wrong she had no choice but to start over again with a number three. Either way, from then on I knew that whatever was left of my family was gone.

"Who's going to take care of it?" asked Lally.

"Of *her*," Jerome corrected. "We're working on that. She's not due until January twenty-first. God willing."

I could vomit. Our father, who was Unitarian, said there was no God, or if there was, it was a God that failed.

"Which is almost your birthday, Lally," my mother added, smiling.

"So?"

"Another Aquarius," my mother said proudly.

"Where's it going to sleep?" asked Lally.

"In the parrot room," said my mother, meaning the room at home in Concord with the stuffed bird. It perched, glued to a twig in a wedding-cake birdcage my father had found at an estate sale. The parrot room had been my father's den, where he used to smoke his pipe and do the Sunday crossword—the *Times*, not the *Globe*. Lally let out a painful snort and gathered her Bolivian hemp shoulder bag. It was her first summer with a pocketbook. I wanted one, too. I wanted something to hold on to. I thought she would stay and ask more questions, but she stood up.

"I'm out of here." She stomped out the door to her bike.

"Me, too."

I had to leave. There was nothing I could say.

Behind me the door slammed. Outside in the soft ocean air and the smell of privet, I could at least breathe. I ran to the opening in the hedge and crawled through.

Someone was in the garden.

"Nick!"

I hurried over.

I recognized the sweater, the way it tied around his waist. He was kneeling in the dirt, touching at the peppers. On the rare occasions he was away from Lally, he would sometimes flirt with me.

"Can I give you a garden tour?" I asked.

He stood up, brushed off his pants, and turned around, only it wasn't Nick. It was Frank. He looked at me. My knees went soft like paste.

"It's fabulous," he said.

I wanted to do a one-eighty for the beach. I couldn't look him in the eye on account of what my mother called his movie-star good looks. Something about the way he talked made me want to stare at his mouth, how he moved his lips. It was fascinating, but embarrassing, too, so I tried focusing on his chin. He made me feel dirty, like he could see inside my head and read my thoughts. I mumbled thanks. "Really, it's all Marcia's doing."

"Your thumb is so green," he went on, "it must glow." I shoved my hands into my pockets. He pulled one out.

"I see it here," he said, opening my palm. His touch was soft, his fingertips stained yellow from tobacco. He smiled and his eyes took on a downward slope that looked like heartache.

"See what?"

"The lines of fertility." He laughed through his nose, his mouth shut. It seemed like a private joke. I looked at my palm, mottled from nerves, then stammered something about the spade and took off for the shed. Glancing back, I watched him stroll off. You would never have known he'd been crouching in dirt.

My mother spent the rest of the summer in bed. We hardly saw her. Donna, who'd gone to the local high school, helped around the house.

She had a roving eye and Lally said she was so dumb the only reason she graduated was because her dad was vice principal. She also said Mom was puking nonstop. I asked Lally how she knew, but she only smirked. She was hardly around herself, having all but moved in with Nick. She'd come home in the mornings to shower and change as if our house were the locker room to a gym. Or she did her laundry, though that was Donna's job. I found her in the basement one day in August. It was our first time alone in weeks. I thought maybe we could talk like we had the summer before, maybe have a laugh. Watching her, I realized how much I had missed her.

"I hope *you're* not having a baby," I said.

She rolled her eyes.

"But you and Nick, you're practically married."

"Who asked for your opinion?"

There was a pause. She was folding her underpants, fourteen pairs. I never imagined she had so many.

"Marcia says she takes it as a compliment. She says she and Frank are your role models."

"Is that what you and Marcia spend your time talking about? About *us?*"

"No," I said defensively. "We talk about a lot of things. We talk about Dad, for instance."

Her eyes turned hard and distant. Dad was the last thing Lally would want to talk about. It was as if she had laid down an unwritten law between us never to speak of him. And not just him and how he died, but his likes and dislikes, the little things he did.

"I wouldn't consider Marcia an authority on anything."

"She says you and Nick are just like her and Frank when they were young."

"I can't imagine we have anything in common with *them.*"

"I'm just repeating."

"Anyway, do you expect me to take that as a compliment?"

I shrugged.

"Why would I want to be anything like Marcia?"

"I don't know. Why not?" Until that summer, in everything I had ever done with Marcia, all the projects and adventures, Lally had been there, too, and she seemed to have enjoyed them as much as I. What had changed?

She scooped up her laundry, ready to leave.

"Unless you're training to become a parakeet, I suggest you shut up."

Later that week, I was watering tomatoes when the hose split. I told Marcia we needed a new one, but it was Wednesday and she had yoga, so she had Colin take me in the Willys. He didn't have a license, but she let him drive it anyway. The whole time, he leaned forward with his nose over the wheel, like he could barely see, and he drove fast, maybe because with his brace his walk was so slow. Every bump in the road lifted me two inches off the seat. There weren't any doors, so I held on to the roof, laughing from fright. We got the hose at Pearson's, and then he said he had to make another stop. We took a left down the road where the carnival was setting up and into one of the developments where the houses all look the same. He parked the Jeep in the drive and went inside. After a few minutes I poked around at the clutter above the dash: the registration (expired), a braided boat bracelet, a bottle opener, a piece of blue sea glass, some stones from the beach. One of them caught my eye. Slate gray and smooth as glass, it was flat like a disk but oval, sized just right for the palm of my hand. Lengthwise down the middle was a white chalk stripe, as if long ago by some sudden titanic force two rocks had crashed and merged. It was like nothing I'd ever seen. I took the stone in hand and closed my fingers over it. It was warm from the sun. It slipped into the pocket of my jeans.

Colin emerged from the house and approached the Jeep. Between the hem of his jeans and the top of his Adidas, the metal back shaft of his brace flashed against the sun. He got in, turned the ignition, and drove a quarter mile without saying a word.

"Wanna get high?"

I felt my throat clutch.

"*Do* you?" he pressed.

I shrugged. "Okay. Let's."

We drove in silence following the route home until he took a turn down Hatch Road to the old Cronin place. Their house burned down years ago and the field was empty. He parked the Willys and we cut through knee-high weeds to the skittering dock. When we were little Lally and I used to catch blowfish there, puncture their cheeks and watch them die. He pulled out a pipe and filled it.

The first two puffs made me gag, but I kept at it. Soon it seemed I could hear wildlife whispering on the bay: the gulls in their dialect, the tadpoles quibbling, crickets, the squawk of gulls. For the longest time I stared at the Donovan house across the bay. I swear I saw a man standing naked there on the roof, signing for the deaf. Who knows—maybe he was signing for me. Colin took my hand.

"Let's sit in the grass."

I giggled. Colin had a chicken pox scar at the corner of his lips. I could hardly believe it, but in all those years I knew him, I had never noticed. I followed him to a soft spot of grass above the bank and he pulled me down beside him. He brushed his mouth against my brow and lifted my chin to his face. It was all in slow motion. His kisses came in little bites as though from hunger. I kissed him back and inside I felt some kind of humming, like some marvelous wind-up toy. He lapped at my mouth and pulled at my tongue until my shirt was off and then he stopped.

He pulled himself away. His eyes were so nearly shut I thought maybe he was asleep. Inside me, I felt something taking root, seeds of panic and regret. What had I done wrong?

"Why are you always hanging out with my mother?"

"What do you mean?"

"You spend so much time with her. Nobody else does."

"So?"

"What is it? Do you feel sorry for her?"

I'd never thought about Marcia that way.

"*Do* you?" he persisted.

"No."

I wasn't sure how much that was true. I decided to throw the question back.

"Do *you*?"

"Do I what?"

He rolled onto his stomach and started pulling up blades of grass and splitting them lengthwise. I thought of the hose, which was what got us there, and how so much of everything was happenstance. I was beginning to wonder if anyone liked Marcia but me.

"Do *you* feel sorry for her?"

He took a wooden matchstick from his pocket and gnawed at it. After a while I could see he wasn't going to answer.

"Is that why you get stoned all the time?" I said.

The look on his face made me regret my words. His cheeks and eyes turned suddenly hollow, as if beneath the skin he had no bones at all, just a flimsy scaffolding. He stood up and peeled off his jeans. His swim trunks were underneath. I saw the brace, all of it, from the sole of his foot to the crown of his knee and above. It struck me as inhumane, a trap set for a hunted animal. I saw the shape of his ribs against the sky. They stuck out as if he didn't get enough to eat.

"I'm going in," he said.

I put on my shirt and watched as he walked down the dock. Even with the brace, his left foot dragged a little, you could tell. He perched at the end, hands overhead, and dove in. It was more like a fall than a dive, without a lot of spring or momentum. He disappeared under the dark water with hardly a splash on the surface. Without him, the place was silent. When he at last came up for air, he was a good ways out toward the center of the inlet, his head so small and far into the distance. I had the sense he wanted me to watch him, to be his audience, and I obliged.

Besides, I needed the ride home.

Saturday after dinner my mother appeared downstairs with paint chips in her hand. She held them to the light and for the first time I saw her belly starting to show. She said the parrot room had to be painted soon so that the fumes would disperse before the baby came. Just talking about it seemed to make her giddy. She taped the chips to the dining room wall. They were greens and blues, but they had names like Oceana and Tiburon. She was under the impression that I was interested.

"Which do you like?" Her smile was beaming.

I sat on the windowsill and drew my knees to my chest. Behind me the window was open and a breeze tickled my neck. From over the hedge I heard music, the bounce and thwack of tennis.

"Tell me, which one?" she pressed.

"Why do you want my opinion?"

"I always want your opinion."

"Then what if I tell you I hate them both?"

She frowned slightly. Just then Jerome called her into the kitchen.

I grabbed my red hooded sweatshirt and headed for the music.

The light above the Dresdens' patio was a swirling silver haze, all aglow, as if the stars themselves were stepping down to dance. There were lights out on the lawn, too: brown paper lunch bags filled with sand, each with the glimmer of a candle lit inside, illuminating the curving paths to the pool and the guest house. That was Marcia's touch, a spectacle which enchanted me, and I wondered how she'd set it all up, who had helped her, since it hadn't been me. I was close enough now to make out the words to the song booming from the outdoor speakers.

Here I go and I don't know why . . .

That was Marcia's choice. Some guest that summer had turned her on to Patti Smith, and she was playing it all the time. Frank preferred jazz and standards. Not just the obvious ones, but covers by obscure vocalists that even my dad didn't always know.

I peered beyond the patio to the tennis court. There was a doubles match going. I recognized Frank at the serving line; the others I didn't know.

My plan was to sneak through the back door into the kitchen and up the back stairs to the third floor.

I had just landed my hand on the doorknob when I heard a woman's voice, gaudy and familiar.

"If it isn't my own little Evie!"

Marcia.

I was caught.

"Come here right now, Red Riding Hood, you!"

I turned and saw her. She was rocking back and forth on the patio swing, her legs bent at the knees and tucked under her slim-fitting skirt. Clustered around the table in front of her were three other people: a woman in a caftan and two men, one in tennis whites and another who was extremely short. Another woman, who I assumed was asleep, lay stretched out on the chaise, a scarf across her eyes like a blindfold. The only light was candlelight—little votives on the table, the sconces on the wall, those six-foot cast-iron candlestands Marcia had got at a church auction. Against the flickering shadows, Marcia and her guests took on an otherworldly splendor.

"I'm winning!" Marcia cried out.

They were playing backgammon. I knew the game well. It was the usual cork and leather board, the kind that opens and closes on a hinge like a briefcase. But stacked up and down the points, instead of the usual pearly green and white discs, were shotglasses. It was my father's invention. You scored a piece, then you drank the contents. He was the all-time champ.

I felt a pinch on my arm. Marcia erupted in a shrill, staccato laugh, then leaned into my ear.

"We're a little tipsy," she whispered loudly.

"Some of us are, some of us are not," said the tennis man. From his build I could see he was not your average weekend athlete. His body was too sculpted, his muscles too pronounced. The short man let out a deep belly laugh. He had a mustache, and when he grinned, it stretched across his face like a ferret.

"Evie, dear, you must stay and join the party," Marcia cooed. "Monty's friend Shaina is giving everyone massages. *Shih tzu*. Like the dog."

"Shi-*a*-tsu," corrected the woman on the chaise. She was apparently awake.

"Shi-*a*-tsu. Shi-*a*-tsu, shi-*a*-tsu, shi-*a*-tsu," the priestess in the caftan incanted. She reached for an olive and against the dim light, in the shifting gauze folds of her dress, I could see her panties and bra. It was a matching set in fur, light brown spotted with white, like Bambi.

Next thing Frank comes walking toward us, his long strides cutting across the lawn. Marcia caught sight of him first; she had an invisible antenna tracking all his whereabouts and doings. I saw the joy light up her eyes.

"Frank, darling, join us. *Please*." She scooted over on the swing to make room.

He shook his head.

"Bill pulled a muscle," said Frank, fixing his gaze on the man in white. "We need someone to fill in."

Marcia let out an exaggerated sigh and turned to the woman who was supine.

"Men and their games," she said.

"And what do you call this?" jeered Frank, pointing to the decked-out backgammon board.

"This is hardly a game!" Marcia said, defending herself. "This is living!"

Frank pursed his lips as if he were about to say something else, but he didn't. Then he laughed through his nose and flashed his automatic smile. I remembered what Lally had said about them, Marcia and Frank, and I began to wonder.

Frank turned back to the man in white.

"Do you want to play?" The man seemed flattered.

"I'll get my racket."

"Honey," Marcia cooed to Frank, "why don't you send Bill over here? Shaina can give him a massage. She's a massage *therapist.*"

"I'll mention it," Frank said absently.

"What about you? Can I give you a massage?" Marcia was practically pleading.

"Thanks," he said. "I'm saving my tension for the tennis ball."

Marcia was crestfallen.

"Come back and tell us who wins."

He turned and made his way back toward the court.

Someone took my hand. The ferret.

"Would *you* like a massage?" he asked. I flinched.

"I'm looking for Lally."

Marcia let out a moan and threw back her head. She sucked on a cigarette, smoke billowing from the corners of her mouth like tiny storm clouds.

"Sad-eyed Lally of the lowlands," she croaked. She paused for a response from the guests, only there wasn't one; they didn't get the reference. She straightened herself up.

"If you see my son Nick," she said, casting anger in her voice, "tell him that his mother is hoping to have a word with him before Labor Day."

Colin's room was on the third floor. The door was open and I walked in. He was picking at an acoustic guitar. Somewhere in the room I heard a radio, but so quiet I couldn't make anything out. He strummed a few bars, then looked up.

"That stash is played."

"Oh?"

"You probably think I'm some big ass supplier, but basically I get enough for myself. Sorry to disappoint."

Maybe he had to be stoned to be nice. He plucked at the guitar, each string sounding its peculiar delicacy. I saw the matchstick village on a table in the corner. It was amazing. He'd seen one in Val d'Isere the winter before when they went skiing and he'd been given a kit, but this was all his own, more New England than alpine. One of the houses, white with black shutters, was just like ours. I realized the whole thing was a representation in miniature of all the houses on Clarey's Neck.

"That's so beautiful," I said.

"It's not finished."

"I didn't come for the reason you think."

"Then why did you?"

I didn't have an answer to that, so I let it drop.

"Did you see the crowd downstairs?"

I nodded.

"What do you think of them?"

"They seem okay." It was a lie. I didn't expect him to believe it.

"How'd you get past them?"

"I didn't. Your mother saw me."

"Speaking of mothers, I heard about yours."

"What about?"

"That she's having a baby."

I forced my face into a smile. Then I picked up a jar of roasted peanuts on the desk and poured some into my hand.

"What's that like for you?"

"Why don't you ask Lally?"

"I'm asking you."

I thought of telling the truth: that from now on we were like orphans, Lally and I, that I felt an emptiness, that my mother was no longer my mother.

"I try not to think about it."

"Who knows. You might like it. It might get your mother off your back."

"She's never really on my back."

"Then maybe you'll like having someone to boss around. I know my mom for sure would be happier if she had another one, not that I think it'll happen."

I was relieved to change the subject. "Why doesn't she?"

He started strumming.

I gave up and started toward the door.

"I've got some Colombian coming Sunday, in case you're interested."

"Who?"

The next day Marcia found me on all fours picking aphids off the tomatoes with rubbing alcohol and Q-tips. Her hair was loose, and she grabbed at her pockets. Her juice glass was empty.

"It has come to my attention that my son Colin is smoking marijuana." With the sun behind her, her untamed hair looked ignited. I thought if I kept quiet she'd shut up.

"It has come to my attention that he smokes every day."

Hadn't she known all along? She'd told me herself back in June about the joint she'd found in the Willys; she'd wanted to smoke it with Frank but he refused. "But your dad," she had said with a dreamy smile, "he would have said yes in a minute. He would have smoked that joint with me. And that's one more reason we miss him so very much."

She loomed over me, casting me in shadow. From her hip pocket she fished out her Jackie sunglasses and slid them up her nose. They seemed to renew her energy.

"Do you think he's a pothead?" She was swaying in a catch-me-if-you-can sort of way.

"I don't know."

The hell you don't!" She edged toward me, stomping her feet, flat-footing an eggplant, but she took no notice. She set a Lark on her bottom lip and kept talking, wagging her cigarette at me like a finger. I shrank back.

"I'll tell you this: Colin can have all the dope he wants—Christ, I'll buy it for him—"

She snatched the unlit cigarette from her lip.

"—so long as he's no *faggot!*" She flicked her lighter and the flame shot so high it would have seared her eyebrows, but for her sunglasses. For a moment I saw her eyes through the darkened lenses, eerie and surreal.

My neck was stiff from looking up.

"Do me a favor," she went on, pointing her Lark at me. "Make sure he's no faggot. Because that's what his father is. A faggot."

She turned with two attempts, as the first one didn't spin her enough to point her home. I stood up and knocked over the bottle of rubbing alcohol. It spilled, disappearing into the dirt, but the smell lingered, stinging my nose. My knees were shaking, and I watched as she made her way zigzag to the patio. The glass slipped from her hand and crashed on the brick. She never looked.

Three days later I ran into Colin coming back from town. I was riding my bike on Red Kettle Lane when he pulled up in the Willys and offered me a lift. Only we couldn't fit the bike in the backseat.

"I got that payload I told you about," he said. "Come and check it out."

I wasn't sure what he meant, but I went over that night anyway, this time making it to his room unseen. He unlocked the door and the smell hit me like a truck. I'd heard it was sweet but so much at once made my lungs weak, like they'd been crushed. The room looked like he'd decamped for days: dirty plates on the floor, clothes piled on the bed, and right beside the door where I stood, his swim trunks and beach towel, sopping wet, like he'd come straight from the pool and dumped them there. In the center of the floor was a big Chinese porcelain bowl from Marcia's sideboard, brimming with pot.

"I made some money, so I'm celebrating," he said and sat on the floor. I sat down, too. He was wearing a pair of cutoff fatigues. The brace was off his leg, and for the first time I saw how slender his left calf was next to his right, the muscle almost atrophied. It looked un-loved. He pointed to the bowl, grinning, and said, "That's reserve."

He lit up a pipe and passed it. I only half inhaled. When the pipe was out he slid over on the floor and put his hand on my shoulder and we kissed. The taste was hollow and dry. His hands went up the back of my shirt and down in front and I felt some part of me loosen inside, like maybe this was what I had come for. We kissed again and stretched on the rug, my body rendered weightless and heavy both at once. He stroked my arms and my neck and took off my shirt, and I had to wonder.

Is this what Marcia wanted?

He got up and slid the bolt on the door.

"Okay?"

I nodded slowly.

He unbuttoned his shirt and stepped out of his shorts, naked. Then he knelt down beside me, feeling around for the buttons on my jeans. He undressed me, caressing my stomach and my breasts, then climbed over my legs, and again I'm thinking.

Is this *what Marcia wanted?*

He entered me and I was shocked. To be so suddenly connected to another human being, it was terrifying. Freakish. I told myself it was only physical, this joining, but that wasn't the whole of it. I felt Colin was telling me something that couldn't be put in words. Or he was taking me someplace new, someplace I had never been. I made myself immeasurably quiet and watchful. I tried to silence the chatter in my head. I thought if I could curb my thoughts I would get a vision of what this was about. But the only picture I got in my head was a big white room filled with longing and forgiveness. I didn't know what for. I wanted to enter that room and find out.

He finished and it was over.

Lying there afterward, I thought of Marcia. Somehow I knew she would find out about this by Labor Day, if not sooner. She would just look at my face and she would know. I thought about all the things I had yet to do that summer, as if summer were already over. It was never in my plan to have gone and done this. But I couldn't help thinking about babies. How the easy part must be making one—that two people could hardly know each other and make a third. How everything difficult came later. I thought about my new sister, what she'd be like. If she'd be anything like me.

I fell asleep.

When I woke up it was nearly four. Even if Lally were in Nick's room next door stretched naked on a rack, I knew I had to get myself home.

"Can I walk you?" Colin asked.

I shook my head. I pulled on my jeans and slid my hands into the pockets to straighten them. I found something inside.

That stone. There it was. Seamless. Cool.

I lifted it out.

"That's pretty," said Colin.

"Thanks."

He didn't realize it was his.

"Can I walk you to the hedge?"

I shook my head and grabbed my shoes and sweatshirt.

"I'll be okay."

Outside the sky was bright with stars, the moon only a sliver. The Dresdens' lawn was soft underfoot, not like ours, which was rough with chickweed. I made my way in the half dark, marking the guideposts: the bird-bath, the toolshed, the barn. By accident I bumped into the rider mower Marcia had left for Colin and banged my knee. I stopped to inspect the injury, and when I straightened up I saw something move in the clearing past the garden by the hedge. I thought it was a shadow, until it split in two, dividing like a cell.

It was two people embracing. I knew exactly who.

"Lally!" I cried out.

I wanted to show her that I could stay out late, too. That she wasn't the only one. But they merged again, she and Nick, making one solid mass against the dark, and she didn't hear. I called her name again and started running over, thinking for once I had the last laugh. I was laughing already.

I was halfway there when she finally turned to look. Only it wasn't Lally. It was a man, and the guy wasn't Nick. It was Frank.

It was Frank kissing a man.

I made a dash for the hedge, only I was nowhere near the hole, and my face and arms got scratched going through. The cuts stung on my cheek but I kept running. By the time I got to the back door I was panting and I could see the welts on my arms beading up blood. The lights were on. I got to the kitchen thinking I was safe, thinking this could all be sorted out, only who's standing at the sink but my mother, topping off a glass of milk with a shot of brandy. She set the bottle on the counter.

"Evelyn, do you have any idea what time it is?"

I shoved my hand in my pocket and closed my fingers around the stone. What could I say? She was looking less like my mother and more like some sublime mutation, like some portrait hung in a museum, a bejeweled lady with bees and cherubs humming over her head. She downed the glass and wiped her mouth with a crumpled paper towel.

"You girls," she said, shaking her head. "I'll sure be glad when this summer is over."

She leaned toward me, picked a twig from my hair, and dropped it into the sink. Then she patted her stomach and turned toward the stairs.

WAITING TO DISCOVER ELECTRICITY

He dressed quickly, lank fingers buttoning his blue pin-striped shirt. He pulled on his trousers and zipped the fly, the two vertical creases rising up his pant legs like wires. His hair fell flat against his head, his cheeks no longer flush. I knew why he was hurrying. He had dinner waiting.

"Are you coming Thursday?"

I nodded. There was that smell again, of Brooks Brothers and sweat. I wrangled my feet one at a time inside the leather flip-flops I bought at the beach the summer before. I thought maybe if I moved in slow motion, so would he.

"Did she say what time?"

I dawdled before answering, like I hadn't exactly heard. "Seven."

He groped around on the floor and found his shoes under the dresser where I'd kicked them. He slipped them on.

"Seven?" His brows pressed together, a tiny volcanic peak. It drew attention to his hairline, how far it had receded. That always surprised me, how old he must be, but I pretended not to notice. I knew from Carolyn he didn't like talking about his hair.

"That's right," he said and I nodded. He didn't always remember what his wife had planned. I didn't know that in the beginning, but I figured it out along the way.

His arms steered through jacket sleeves, and I saw the glinty flash of turquoise satin lining. The only piece missing now was the tie, which hung on the back of my chair. It was part of a set, chair and desk, lemon yellow with powder blue trim, my mother's attempt at decorating when I was nine. The tie had red diagonal stripes, the skinny end in front pointing down like a road sign to nowhere. We lived on the fourteenth floor, my mother and me, though because of her job she wasn't around much. Most of her clients were companies in the Midwest and as much as she said she hated all that travel, we never discussed the possibility of her getting a new job, so I had come to the conclusion that in fact she must have liked it. In any case, it paid well and she said we needed the money. Her being away was what I was used to.

Actually, we lived on thirteen, but they didn't call it that for fear of bad luck.

He picked up his briefcase. It wasn't exactly planned, this time. He had caught me going up the elevator. I was getting the laundry from the basement—mine and my mother's. The elevator opened on the first floor and he got on, coming home from work. The Turkins lived on twenty, one floor down from the penthouse, in the front of the building where the apartments are twice as big and have a river view. From the white sectional sofa in their living room, you could watch tugboats hauling barges of trash downriver to be dumped in the sea. I sat there sometimes when the kids were asleep. I'd press my chest and elbows into the back of the sofa, knees deep in tapestry cushions, and wait, watching the lights of the vessels sneak across the vast black water.

The elevator door rolled shut, and we lifted upward. The hum of the motor beneath the floor was like wind. He slid his hand under my chin and cupped it like an egg. He didn't have far to bend; he wasn't that much taller, five-eleven, maybe. His hands were always clean—the smell like a pinewood forest. His face drew close to mine, his thin dun lips widening into a smile. I closed my eyes. I felt vaguely dizzy. He kissed me. I never looked. His tongue was spongy and sweet against the smell of Tide.

I opened my eyes. We passed seven, then eight, and a pair of skin-color pantyhose got brushed to the floor. They were my mom's, and the sight of them there made me wonder, *What would she do if she knew?*

He picked up the pantyhose and held it by the stiff elastic waistband, dangling it forefinger to thumb high over the basket. He was like the snake charmer on cartoons, the pantyhose the cobra rising from the basket.

I was ready to be entranced.

He dropped the pantyhose on the laundry pile. It collapsed, a useless membrane. The basket in my arms felt suddenly heavy. He asked if I needed help but before I could answer, I saw the number fourteen articulated at the top of the button panel in flaming segments. The door opened, I stepped out, and he followed. My mom was on a plane to Cincinnati. She would never know. By then, I could no longer count the times we'd done it.

It wasn't like I was a virgin. There was Doug Sandler. He was a senior. At school everyone thought he was mature because he had sideburns. For his eighteenth birthday, his father, who lived on a houseboat in Miami, gave him a credit card and a room booked at the St. Regis. We stayed two nights. We did it three times more after that in his room at home late my junior year, but each time I liked it less. He kissed the undersides of my breasts, which to be honest made me squirm. Once he was inside, it seemed he forgot I was even there. He was fast, and his fingernails were always dirty, like he worked in soil, though mostly he played computer games, building imaginary cities only to raze them, headphones on his head like an alien, the sound of Metallica leaking out. He didn't talk much. I found out later that during that same period he was sleeping with Dina Pittman.

I had worked for the Turkins since the end of ninth grade. Twice I spent the month of August at their shingled house on Fire Island, watching their kids on the beach, a girl and a boy, and carting groceries home in a wagon. He began by giving me presents. Carolyn had given me stuff, too, mostly track suits and gear she got for free from the company where she worked before she had Jesse, before she stayed home full-time with the kids. It was different with him. He had waited, he told me later, until I got accepted into college and got my track scholarship before initiating things between us. He said our relationship would perforce be different, though I didn't exactly know what "perforce" meant. When I asked him to explain, he said what he meant was that our relationship was transitional, and I should think of it as such, helping me through the period between living at home and going away. Just like Jesse still held on to his old crib blanket when he started walking, he said, I could have him.

The presents started my junior year. First was a video on cross-training. Next was a book on Grete Waitz. Then in May, he said he wanted to start running himself and he asked me to help him train. I said sure, only I was a sprinter, and at his age he'd probably want endurance more than speed. He should know; he was a doctor, only he wasn't that kind of doctor. He was the kind people told secrets to, pulling Kleenexes from the box and shredding them.

I went to one myself when I was six, after my dad left. My mother made me go, but I didn't talk. He had a beard, and I could swear I saw something moving in it. Hung on his wall were carved wooden masks he had bought in Peru, mouths gaping as if in shock, as if they could somehow hear day after day the sad confessions of the patients who drifted in and out. His office was high up, hanging over the rushing traffic of the FDR Drive like a dresser drawer extended too far. Down below us was the East River. The shrink said it wasn't a river at all, but I didn't believe him. He took out a set of colored boxes in graduated sizes, one as small as a spool of thread, the biggest the size of a toaster, spread them across the carpet, and asked me to play with them. They were smooth, with the smell of a woodshed. I wanted to stack them one on top of each other in two piles and stand on them like they were stilts and make myself a giant. But somehow I got the suspicion that I was supposed to do something else, or that whatever I might think of doing with those boxes would be wrong, so for a long while I did nothing but stare at them, now and then glancing at his face for a clue. I never got one. In the end it seemed I had better just clean up, so I put the boxes away, fitting one inside the other like Russian dolls, all in perfect order, until they were all contained inside the biggest.

I went a few more times but I never really talked, and after a while my mother weighed my silence against the expense.

In August, he gave me a bikini. It was cotton boucle and yellow, the color of French's mustard. Even my mother liked it. I told her I'd bought it myself. I liked it okay, only I hadn't worn a two-piece since I was nine. They exposed too much. There was that mole beside my belly button.

It was a late Sunday afternoon, the sky behind him like the flesh of a pink grapefruit. Against the glare of the sun, I could barely see his face, but he was smiling. We were on the patio at their house in Fair Harbor. Music and laughter floated up from a party next door. Carolyn was seated on a chaise, her slim, tired body wrapped in a giant gardenia-print scarf. She made me call her Carolyn. Him I called Dr. J. I still think the name Jeremy is ugly. Carolyn had been ranked seventh on the junior tennis circuit, and one season she played doubles at Forest Hills— you could tell from the musculature of her arms. She was drinking Campari; he had scotch. Emily and Jesse were inside watching a video. He handed me a small brown and white shopping bag from Bendels, white tissue spilling from the top like sea foam. Inside was the bikini. They watched as I lifted the two faltering pieces from the bag, the top half only a pair of triangles threaded on a string. Carolyn said, "Mmmmmmm," like it was food.

"It's from both of us," she went on, though later he claimed he chose it himself. When I didn't wear it for almost a week, she sat me down— just the two of us—and asked if I didn't like it.

"Schuyler," she said, her cool, fluttery hand landing on my knee, "you should *enjoy* your figure. Now. While you have one." I was wearing a sweatshirt and cutoffs, the bleached white threads hanging down my thighs like fringe. "Try it on." She insisted. We were in their bedroom.

The furniture was bamboo, the chairs upholstered in a print of para-keets. I changed in the bathroom and modeled the bikini for her. She lit a cigarette and I knew this would be one of our secrets—she never smoked in front of him. He was in the city seeing patients. Sometimes I smoked with her, something I loved doing, though I hated the taste. She threw one of those big flowery scarves at my head and draped it around my shoulders like a cape. She told me to push my hips forward and sway a little, to walk like my limbs were coming unscrewed. We were both of us laughing. I watched the smoke rise from her lips like a hazy film. She said the mole on my stomach was fetching. For the first time in my life, I felt pretty.

I thought maybe he would give me a present today, after following me off the elevator. I sat on the bed waiting, feet tucked under, knees together, my white Nike T-shirt pulled over my legs like a dress.

"Don't forget your tie," I said, pointing. Usually I tied the knot. "Aren't you putting it back on?"

"Who's to say I didn't take it off in the cab?"

He grabbed the necktie and shoved it in his pocket.

I turned away from him toward the bookcase. I should have gotten rid of those Madame Alexander dolls, but it wasn't the first time he saw them. He'd been in my room before. With a sigh, he pulled the tie from his pocket.

"Go ahead."

I kicked off my flip-flops in triumph and stood on the bed, still made from the morning. He didn't like getting under the covers.

"First one under, second one—"

"I *know*." The silk was smooth to touch, like rose petals. I looped the tie around his neck and under his collar, making the ends just so. The first time he let me try, it was like an initiation. I loved the science of it, how you started with the wide end way below the other. Do it right, and they even out. I pressed the finished knot high against his Adam's apple. In the small moment before letting go, it was as if I had him completely, lassoed like a horse.

"I did it!" I felt immensely satisfied. I crossed my arms on my chest.
"No one will ever know I took it off."

"Look in the mirror. I did an excellent job."

He reached forward and tucked my hair behind my ear. I was glad
I had washed it that morning.

"I have something for you," he said.

"What?" Standing on the bed, I was taller than him by at least a
head. I bent my knees to level the difference.

"I don't have it here." He stroked his necktie. "I didn't expect to
see you."

"Tell me what it is."

"Next time." He looked at his watch. "I'm late."

"What is it?"

"You'll see. It's a graduation present, a little early."

"What *is* it? Is it something to wear?" I looked at his briefcase. It
was cowhide, the kind that opens standing upright, the sides pleated like
an accordion. It could hold more than you'd think. He caught my gaze.

"I didn't bring it." He paused. "All right. It's something to wear all
right, but not for warmth." He laughed. "Now I'm going." He kissed
his fingertips and raised them in the air for good-bye. His palm was flat,
the skin no older looking than mine. He picked up his briefcase and
headed for the kitchen. I heard the back door click shut, but just barely.
He was careful that way, taking the stairs and not the elevator. I stepped
into the bathroom and studied my face in the mirror. The birthmark
above my brow had darkened. Sometimes that's the only way I can tell
I'm nervous.

Was that a sign of getting older?

I put on my gear and ran the two miles up to Grant's Tomb and
back. Those last two years of high school, that was the only way I could
feel clean, working up a sweat. I pictured the organs of my body purging
themselves of so many microbe toxins through the million glistening
pores of my skin. I saw my veins and arteries like the great dark Hudson
down below except in miniature, with so many accumulated layers of

trash and sewage lurking unseen. When I got home I ran a bath and soaked, scrubbing my arms and legs with the loofah. The dead gray skin rolled away like tiny elongated vermin.

Thursday night, once Emily and Jesse were asleep, I started my search. I thought I would know it as soon as I laid eyes on it, like it would have my name on it. I pictured a small wrapped box, square perhaps, maybe a box of chocolates, with a red satin ribbon.

I had a hunch it was a thong.

Inside their bedroom, the shades were pulled all the way up. Across the river, behind the scattered buildings, the sun had left a skimming glow. I thought of all the lives people lived over there and how none of them could see me. Opposite the bed was a chest of drawers, the oak grainy and dark like cinnamon sticks, as high as my chin. The mess on top was his: loose change and cuff links, the name card from a pharmacological conference in Phoenix, a brown paisley cummerbund. I picked it up and ran it by my nose; it had no smell at all. I knelt down to search the drawers. There were six of them, each one opening with resistance, dry wood grinding to dust.

The bottom drawer was the first one I searched. Folded inside were sweaters already sealed in plastic for summer, the smell of mothballs rising to my nostrils. I reached into the corners—nothing. By now I was sure it was underwear I was searching for. The next two drawers had dress shirts—stripes of every width in Popsicle colors, the collars fixed in place with pins and standing at attention. I pictured the gift—my thong—in the same shades. It could be a matching set, panties and bra, in red or black. Maybe a push-up.

Next were socks—dozens—matched in pairs and rolled together like giant sour balls. Carolyn did that. I had watched her sort laundry on Fire Island; she matched my socks that way, too. My hands roamed among them, brushing up against the sides of the drawer until something sharp drove under my fingernail. I pulled back my hand and saw blood filling the space beneath the nail. A splinter. I squeezed the skin around the puncture to make the sliver come to the surface and sucked at it. The culprit was shorter than I expected, no longer than a ladybug, but it left beneath the nail a hole so wide I could almost see into it.

I was determined.

Only the top drawer was left. I opened it. Inside were boxer shorts, pressed and folded. I groped inside until I felt something in the back corner. My heart was thumping. This had to be it.

It was an old handkerchief box. I opened it, but it was empty. I felt winded, like when I sprint too fast too soon without first warming up. Maybe someone could see me from across the river after all. I thought of giving up. I retreated to the bed, pushing aside a dress that lay there. It was white with black polka dots and silk. Carolyn must have considered wearing it before she went out. I never wore dresses, but I tried it on, as if the dress would tell me where to search next. The neckline was low and the waist loose, but with the belt, the dress fit like it was made for me.

I pressed my palm to my breastbone.

Naked.

I caught my reflection in the mirror behind the bathroom door. I turned my head a certain way like Carolyn does. She was beautiful in the way that only sportswomen can be, but most of them are not. My coach, for example. She was athletic-looking, but she wasn't feminine or pretty. Carolyn was all those things. I might have felt guilty for sleeping with her husband except that once, when he first suggested we do it, he made it seem as if she were having an affair herself. Someone from her office, I think. He said it was normal for two people who had been married as long as they had to pursue outside arrangements. He said they had an understanding, which made everything okay.

I studied my reflection. I drew a make-believe cigarette to my mouth, narrowing my eyes. I heard crying.

The two children shared a room. When I got there, Jesse was standing on his bed, pressing against the safety rail, his mouth turned down and quivering. He had just turned three. I picked him up and held him against my chest. The back of his head felt warm and damp. I stroked it lightly with my hand, like it was something that could shatter, a crystal globe. Sometimes I pretended we were orphans, Jesse and me, stranded together in a cabin in the woods. Sometimes I pretended I was his mother. He had been slow to talk, but once he started, it was as if he were making up for lost time. I asked him what happened.

"I had a bad dream," he said at full volume. "Bad guys came and robbed us." Emily was sleeping. I told him to whisper.

"What bad guys?"

"They looked like doormen. They took my fire truck. They knocked down the door."

I told him it was only a dream, that the door was locked, and his fire truck was on the shelf exactly where he had left it. "Go back to sleep," I said. "Besides, you know the doormen. They're your friends."

"What if they break in?"

"They can't. The doors are locked."

"Where's Mommy?" I laid him back down on the bed and tucked him in.

"They went out. They both did. Remember?"

"That's Mommy's dress."

"No, it isn't," I rebutted. It was a reflex, an impulsive and unthinking untruth. "It's mine. She just has one like it."

He lay on his stomach, knees bent, feet tucked under. I stroked his back, his breaths deepened, and his body relaxed into sleep.

I returned to his parents' bedroom. The room was dark; I hadn't touched the lights. My hands itched to resume my hunt; it seemed they had taken over my body and the rest of me was forced to follow inert, the back of my neck tingling, my fingers electric. I pulled open the drawer of one of the bedside tables. Inside, beneath newspaper clippings and a bus map, was a photograph of Carolyn and Dr. J at a party. She was dressed in a sleeveless black dress, holding in one hand a highball and a miniature French flag. Her other hand was draped on his shoulder and manicured, her fingernails like perfect opals. Her hair was longer, and she wore it loose, nearly to her waist, and she was laughing, her cheekbones set high like little plums. They were probably not yet married. She was looking into the camera. He was looking at her. She was beautiful.

Farther back in the drawer was a black lacquer box. The top lifted off. Inside was jewelry, all sterling—a set of bangles, a locket, a necklace made of silver mesh like some delicate antique chain mail. I opened the locket expecting some momentous find. My fingers came away tarnished. The locket was empty.

Then I saw the charms. There were four of them, hanging from a silver link bracelet, though there was easily room for more. A martini glass, a race car, a woman's pump, and a tiny Empire State Building. It seemed unfinished. The car was my favorite. I snapped the bracelet on my wrist.

The phone rang.

"It's me."

Carolyn. I stood up from the bed, smoothed the back of the dress. *Her* dress. I had forgotten she would call. She always did.

"They're asleep." The charms clattered against the receiver. I switched ears, left to right, wedged the handset in the crook of my neck and fingered the martini glass.

"This is a disaster," she said. I heard the long intake of a cigarette. "The dinner, I mean. Jeremy is going to kill me, dragging him along." They were meeting a former colleague of hers. She was angling to get her old merchandising job back. She talked and I studied the photograph. They looked so happy. What had changed? Why didn't they look happy now? I pictured her now, talking into the phone, standing somewhere private, like beside the door to the ladies', dressed as she was in the photograph, though she left that night wearing trousers. She asked if the kids ate dinner. Then she asked about me.

"There's a chicken leg in the fridge." She paused. "If you don't see anything you want, order in. There's money and menus in the kitchen drawer."

I thought of asking her about the photograph. I wanted to know where it was taken and when—how many years ago—and if she still had the dress. But then I'd have to explain how I found it and that was too uncomfortable—I would have to lie. We said good-bye and hung up.

By the time they came home, I had changed back into my jeans. I was sitting on the sofa, waiting, my search abandoned, calculus text open to a page of practice equations, none of them done. I heard the elevator door trundle open before the key turned in the lock. Carolyn appeared first, set down her black suede shoulder bag, and waved hello. She put forty dollars cash on the foyer table and kicked off her shoes. The money was for me. I was hoping she might come to the sofa and talk, but she went straight to the children's room. Something told me they had had a fight. I picked up my bag to leave.

"Everything go all right?" asked Dr. J. His voice was cheery, but the lines of concern crossing his brow betrayed him. More and more, that was how he looked at me when Carolyn was present: lips pressed shut and pickled, a certain abstracted affection in his eyes, detached and unquantifiable. I imagined that was his expression when he looked at his patients. It made me wonder what it would be like to be one of them, to meet in his office as a patient and talk only about me.

"Did everything go all right?" he repeated.

"Fine." I couldn't look at his face, so I looked at his shirt. It was rumpled. I recognized the stripe—there was another one like it in the drawer. His tie hung crooked. He kept staring. I felt myself blush. It seemed strange, in that moment, that he was the same person who had stood naked in my bedroom Monday. I thought of dropping my knapsack, throwing myself against him, and giving him an open-mouth kiss like it would prove something, only I didn't know what. I decided not to risk it. Besides, I didn't like kissing him enough to make the game worthwhile. The truth was lately I couldn't even talk to him in public. It was okay talking to Carolyn in front of him, but if I had to pay the slightest attention to him in front of her, I couldn't gather my thoughts, like his stubby fingers were all over them. On that count Carolyn had always been easier. There were times when I felt I could talk to her for days, especially on Fire Island, where we were often alone.

Sometimes I think that getting close to him was a way of getting close to her.

"Nice shirt," he said.

"Thanks."

I looked down to remember which one it was. A blue T-shirt with embroidery around the neck. I wanted to go home.

He strolled over to the table and touched at the cash Carolyn had left for me, checking the amount—he liked making fun of her math. There were two bills, twenties. He grimaced, reached into his pocket, and pulled out his billfold. With his hand cupped for discretion, or perhaps he was just hiding his indecision, he put down another bill. I didn't see how much. Then he gathered them up, all three, and pressed them into my hand. I could swear he was daring me to look, but I didn't.

"Aren't you curious how much that is?"

"I have to get home," I said and closed my hand into a fist. I called out "Good night" to Carolyn, though softly because of the kids.

I inched my way toward the door. He beat me to it, landing one hand on the knob. He opened the door. He could be chivalrous sometimes, too. I passed through, and his hand reached out and stroked the top of my head. That was one of the things he did that I liked. But I pretended not to notice and kept walking. He shut the door behind me.

I took the stairs down, taking big jumps at the bottom of every set. On the landing below seventeen, I stopped and opened my fist. Inside, on top of the two twenties, was a fifty-dollar bill.

It wasn't until I woke up in bed the next morning that I felt something jabbing my wrist.

A woman's silver pump.

The bracelet. I was wearing it.

I was a thief.

My head flooded with guilt.

I had to return it, but when? How? I needed a plan but I couldn't think of any. I didn't want my mother to find out.

I decided to tell Dr. J.

This was my idea: I'd bring the bracelet to his office, give it to him, and make him return it to Carolyn's box. I assumed he had given it to her as a gift when they were courting so he would be interested in reclaiming it. Once I was in his office, of course, I would lie on the couch and talk. We would have lots to discuss, and not just the bracelet. I pictured his office: the couch like an operating table, only lower to the floor, upholstered in black leather. I might feel comfortable with him there at last.

I found out later he didn't have a couch at all. His patients sat in a chair.

I called his office and got his machine. His voice on the tape was more gentle than usual and more deliberate, as if everyone who called him were in distress.

"It's me. Schuyler. It's an emergency. Call me at home."

Forty minutes later, he called back. I told him I had something to tell him, but I couldn't say over the phone.

"Can't this wait?" He was annoyed.

"I need to come to your office." He was silent. "Please?"

"Schuyler, what is this about?"

It was his tone of voice that made me tell. That and the way he said my name, with the terse exasperation of someone who has suffered one too many interruptions. The way he gets when Jesse can't stop whining. I told him the whole story. Three times I heard myself say, "I didn't mean it." I didn't want him to think me a thief. The surprise was that he could hardly have cared less. It was trivial, he said, and he said he couldn't believe I had called him about it. But when I asked if he would put the bracelet back in the box, he refused.

"Keep it until the next time you come, and return it yourself. In the meantime, wear it. Maybe you can enjoy it."

"But what if she sees it's missing?"

"She'll never notice. She never wears it."

I took that at face value and followed his instruction. After all, he had given me permission. The truth was, I *wanted* to wear it. I wanted someone to notice it and ask me where I got it, and when they did, I knew what I would say: That it was an early graduation present from my father in Baja. That was the postmark, the last time we heard from him.

Monday morning at school the next week, I clattered the bracelet against my locker. In classes, I let the charms clank against my desk. I was sure someone would notice.

Three days passed and no one did.

Finally, someone complimented it. The ceramics teacher.

"I bet someone really special gave that to you," she said.

I nodded obediently. Like a dog.

But the attention emboldened me, so I kept wearing it, and I decided to wear it not just at school but at home, in front of my mother. It was dangerous, I knew, but I was ready to lie. Sometimes, when she was around, she would show a sudden interest in my life, battering me with questions, as if loading up with facts to take with her the next time she left. It had long made me angry, that her interest in me was always on her time, not mine, but there wasn't much I could do about it. So I decided to make this a test of her observation skills, to see if she'd pass.

I wore the thing at home for three days in a row. She didn't notice. At first I was scared of her response, but as the days went by and nothing happened, what I felt was rage. At times I wished she would just catch sight of the thing and snatch it from my wrist. Finally, I took to my room, defeated. I took the bracelet off my wrist and stashed it in a box in my closet.

Things got worse. I stopped sleeping through the night. All that week and into the next, I felt possessed. I would find myself awake at 3:00 A.M., compelled to check the closet, making sure the bracelet was still there. I'd pour the links from one hand into the other, fingering the charms—so tiny they were, like dollhouse toys. I started to hate that bracelet. I tried running longer distances after school to knock myself out, as if that would help me sleep.

It didn't work.

The next Friday was the last day of school for seniors and I knew I had to take an action. I realized I never wanted that bracelet. It was a mistake. If there was anything of theirs I wished I had, it was the photograph. I loved that photograph. I wanted to take it to college with me in September and pin it on the wall above my desk in my dorm. I could pretend they were my parents. People would be impressed.

I walked home from school that day, and I could see that photograph in my head: the delicate turn of Carolyn's hand, the hand that combed through the tangles in Emily's hair and brushed the crumbs from Jesse's cheek. I never saw *him* doing those things. Maybe that was what marriage was about, or *their* marriage, at least: two people doing different things. Pursuing outside arrangements.

Is that what he meant when he said they had an understanding?

Two blocks from my house, I stopped myself dead.

What about *her* side of the story?

I felt like a jerk, but I had never thought of that. And she had been so kind.

I raced home, changed into gear, and took a run. Afterward, standing under the hot pulse of the shower, I devised an explanation. Then I hunted in the kitchen for a jar of silver polish and some paper towels, though the bracelet did not seem particularly soiled. Gingerly, I applied the polish to the bracelet. The towel turned black with tarnish. I applied more polish, and more tarnish appeared, though the bracelet by now was sparkling, with no hint of discoloration. Again I polished it. Once more the towel was blackened. The bracelet could abide an infinite amount of stain.

Enough.

I wrapped the bracelet in tissue and stuffed it in my pocket. Then I went upstairs and knocked on the door.

Carolyn let me in. She was alone with Jesse. I followed her into the kitchen. She offered me a Coke, but I said no thanks. We sat at two sides of the table, only a corner between us. Jesse stood next to her, pressing his small weight against her leg, sucking one pacifier, clutching another. My palms were damp. I placed the wadded bracelet on the table between us and began to cry.

"What's this?" she asked. I tried to answer but nothing came out. Meanwhile I'd broken into a sweat, my whole body flushed and damp. She unfolded the tissue.

"Oh, *that*." She lifted the bracelet from the makeshift wrapping. Jesse came to attention. He reached for the race car, but his mother preempted him, raising the bracelet over his head. It dangled from her fingers unclasped, a serpentine row of silver links, catching the light. "Where'd you find this?"

"I tried it on, and I forgot to take it off." I wiped my nose on the back of my hand and sniffled, only the sound came out like a snort. "It was a mistake."

"Of course, it was." She touched my shoulder, and I felt the warmth through my shirt. Jesse was laughing, as if he spied a happy ending. "Do you like this bracelet?" she asked.

"Well—"

"Do you?" She leaned closer toward me. I wiped my nose again and nodded.

It was a gift from a former fiancé, she said, a man she had met when she first came to New York. I was wrong again.

"I would have married him, but—I hate to say it—he was too nice." She laughed. "Jeremy hates it," she went on. "He says charm bracelets are for girls, not for women." She fingered the martini glass. She said she couldn't wear it in front of Jeremy.

"He gets terribly jealous."

"He does?"

She waved her hand and rolled her eyes as if to say she didn't want to talk about it, or perhaps she thought it too obvious to explain. She paused, and in the silence between us I thought maybe she was telling me something. I felt immensely stupid. I wanted to confess and be forgiven. I thought if I told her, she might still love me and nothing would be changed. I felt the words forming deep in my throat, but she started talking. The moment was lost.

"I was trying to think of a graduation present for you. What about this?"

She slipped the bracelet around my wrist and shut the clasp. The metal links were cool against my skin and lively. I felt split top down like a log, like I was two people at once, one of them me and the other someone else looking down on me, askance. I was a liar. I felt ashamed and unworthy, like I was nothing but emptiness, the mass and liquid of my body a shapeless sack of waste.

I wanted to be Jesse.

I wanted to crawl inside Carolyn's lap and weep.

Two weeks before graduation, I got a card from my dad. My mother said it was like him to send something conspicuously early or send nothing at all, as if waiting too long would make him forget. It was from California, and it was oblong, hinged on top. The picture on the front had party balloons and HAPPY BIRTHDAY in colored block letters. He had crossed them out and in tilting ballpoint script written "Congratu-lations" instead. Inside the card was a pocket for cash, with an oval cutout to show the face on the bill: Ben Franklin, his hair as long as mine and set in curls. I pictured him standing buoyant with his kite and key in the rainy dark, waiting to discover electricity. There wasn't a single other thing I knew about him, though junior year in U.S. history I'd made a B.

My mother snatched the card from my hands. "This goes straight to the bank," she said.

I snatched it back.

"You put that in the bank," I growled, "and it might as well be any other hundred-dollar bill."

I stashed the card and the cash in my jewelry box with the charm bracelet and my race medals.

The next time I saw Dr. J alone was the Thursday before Memorial Day. We were in their apartment. He had never given me the gift he promised, and I was still curious, so that night, when he invited me, I went. Carolyn had gone to Fire Island a day early with the kids to open up the house. It was her last summer not working, she said, though she no longer counted on getting back her old job. She planned to spend July and August at the beach, and she had asked me to go with her and help out. I would tell her no, though I didn't yet know how.

We were sitting, he and I, across from each other at the glass dining table, waiting for pizza. The long wall opposite the window was lined with bookcases, hardcovers mostly, some of them medical texts. It was eight o'clock. I had let him kiss me, but that was all. I didn't miss the sex. I was hungry, and the pizza was late. Part of me felt like picking a fight.

"If I were one of your patients," I asked, "how would you psychoanalyze me?" He pulled back in his seat, his mouth slightly ajar.

"I don't understand what you mean."

I said it again. He wriggled in his chair, as if finding his balance.

"It's not exactly appropriate, is it?"

"But what if you *had* to, like for evidence in a trial?"

"Whatever gave you that idea?" He folded his hands on the table. His forehead broke out in lines, first two, then many, ribs of skin on skin. He looked as if he'd swallowed a bug.

"What would you do?"

"What do you mean, *what would I do?*"

"You know what I mean." He was playing dumb.

"Do you *want* to be psychoanalyzed?"

I stared at him. I tried to imagine how it would be, going to his office for consolation and advice, hoping to be saved, as if he knew every available truth in the world and he could dispense them to me, all of them, one by one like jewels. He leaned closer. "Do you want to see someone?"

He meant a psychiatrist. I thought of making a joke—how I was seeing one already and what I wanted was to give him the heave. But I guess I did want someone. I wanted a confessor, but not a stranger; I wanted to spill my secrets to someone I knew.

I must have not answered him soon enough. By the time he spoke again, he had changed the topic.

"Maybe it's time I gave you your graduation gift. What do you think?"

Almost three weeks had passed since he mentioned that thing I'd gone crazy searching for. With all that business about the charm bracelet, I stopped thinking about it. I was wearing the bracelet now—I had made a point of doing so—and I fingered nervously at the charms. I wanted to keep after him about psychoanalyzing me, but he was already up and out of his chair. He left the room, shirttail hanging in back. He had the walk of a nonathlete. He never did train, though he bought the gear and asked me a million questions.

He reappeared with a small turquoise box. I wondered where he'd kept it hid.

I untied the white satin bow and lifted the top. Inside was a slim gold-link bracelet with a diamond set in the center.

"I got it before," he said, and he made a kind of smirk.

"Before what?"

"Before she gave you *that*." He nodded at the charm bracelet. "You'll like this one better. It's worth more."

He snapped the new bracelet on my wrist. It was feminine and delicate, each link intimately knotted with those beside it. The round diamond was its showpiece, and at different angles it loomed larger than it was, flashing and multifaceted, as if cut for deception. But he was wrong. I liked the bracelet that Carolyn gave me better.

The pizza arrived, extra cheese with green peppers, but my appetite was gone. He started talking about summer. I kept wanting to ask about being his patient, but he talked so much I couldn't cut in. I remembered what Carolyn said once about him being what she called Type A, that he was destined for a heart attack. He ate his pizza fast, first one slice, then another, and a third, and between hurried bites he said he didn't want me stuck at the beach with Carolyn. He said I was old enough to get a job that wasn't baby-sitting, and he wanted me here, in the city. His words were pressured, as if someone had clicked a stopwatch and he was being timed.

"If you stay in the city," he said, "we could do things."

"What things?"

"Whatever you want."

He sponged his lips with a napkin, then sipped his Coke. He never drank booze alone with me. He said I was underage. I wondered what he would say if he knew last summer Carolyn had served me Chianti.

He pushed away his plate and leaned forward. I saw his reflection in the dark glass of the table, his face swelling as he neared me, lips and nose distended.

"You don't need a job," he went on. "I can take care of you."

I felt sick.

"I'm going to the bathroom." I got up and started walking. I didn't need the toilet; I had to get away. When I found myself in their bedroom, I was not surprised.

I walked across the room straight to Carolyn's night table. I opened the drawer. The lacquer box was exactly where I saw it last. And the photograph. I thought of taking it after all, but then I knew. I no longer wanted that picture. It would only make me sad.

They had been a sort of family to me, and I was separating from them.

I was separating from Carolyn. Already I felt the loss.

I lifted the lid of the box, my heart hammering against my chest like it does before a race. Inside, the silver bangles flashed with light. I unsnapped the exquisite gold bracelet from my wrist and dropped it inside. It slid, gemstone first, then each articulated link, beneath the baubles and trinkets, and disappeared.

SAVE YOURSELF

There we were in the toy store on Eighty-third and Madison, and Meredith, sinking fast into a giant tomato beanbag chair, said she needed a psychiatrist. I was checking out stocking stuffers. We were too old for that stuff, Beanie Babies and Barbies. We went just to look. Of course I'd be dead if anyone found out.

"I absolutely *hate* my life." She rolled up her sleeve. I saw the cuts on her arm, but even without them, I could tell. Something was up.

She pushed her hips deeper into the plump red sack and as she sank down farther, I heard a thousand tiny plastic pellets encircling her butt. She was a lesson in gravity—hair down to her waist, oversized jeans, nose rings—everything about her was drooping and slack. I wanted to be just like her. We'd taken a pledge to wear nothing but black. Until then I knew all her secrets, like the name of her parents' sex therapist, and the potion she took for cramps. Equal parts vodka and Sprite.

That was the first time I'd ever seen those cuts.

I should have been the last person to have to ask Meredith what was wrong. But she wanted me to. It was my job.

"I can't talk here," she said, her eyes darting sideways. "We have to evacuate."

In my hand was a blue metal windup whale. I turned the key, and the mouth creaked open. Inside was a tiny bearded man. *Jonah.* I knew the story from that year of Hebrew school when my mom tried reconnecting with Judaism. He got swallowed because he lacked faith, and the point, I was told, was how God granted His mercy to people of all faiths, not only to the Jews. I turned the key one last time, reluctant to let go. Meredith gave me her hand to help her up. She's so skinny she hardly weighs a thing, though you wouldn't know from her clothes. We got our packs at the front of the store.

"Let's go to the Park," she said. I checked my watch. It wasn't like I had to be home. There wasn't anyone there except Foley, though I had to walk him by five or he'd do it on the rug. We left the store and headed toward Fifth.

"Is this about Milo Biederman?" I asked.

She groaned.

"Milo Biederman is *history.*"

Two weekends before, Milo Biederman had grabbed her hand at a party and shoved it down the front of his pants. When she pulled out her hand, it was sticky and wet. She went home and crouched under the shower for an hour and a half. "This is *bigger* than Milo Biederman."

We crossed Fifth. I veered toward a bench to sit down but she grabbed my pea coat.

"We're going to Alice."

Central Park was empty except for some nannies with strollers hurrying to leave and a man in a cardboard tepee asleep on a bench. The sky was a kind of purpling gray. I loved being in the Park at that hour, on the cusp between day and night. It felt dangerous. We were coasting downhill and I had to brace my legs to stop them from speeding ahead. We got to the dell where the Alice statue rises in gleaming bronze. Meredith leaned against the Mad Hatter, fingering the studs in her ear: two on the left, three on the right, diamonds all. She cleared her throat.

"You have to swear."

"I swear."

"On what?"

"On whatever."

She inched closer. We were nose to nose. "On Foley's grave."

I lifted my right hand, wincing. "On Foley's grave."

She dumped her pack on the ground with a thud and offered me a sour ball. I passed, but she took one herself. "You know that woman?"

"What woman?"

"That one I told you about. She lives in my building. In the back."

Meredith was always starting conversations like that—you know that person or you know that thing I told you—and half the time I didn't know what she was talking about. Only it didn't matter because she'd tell the story from the beginning anyway. Even if I could recite every imaginable detail, like which pair of underwear she wore and what she'd had for lunch, she'd tell the story all over again and I would have no choice but to listen.

"You remember," she said, squeezing my arm. "The one I can see through my bedroom window."

"The woman with the giant mirror?"

She nodded eerily. "Yup. It covers the whole wall," she said, leaning close, the warm fog of her breath rising before me with the hint of sour lime. "I figured it out. She's my *birth mother*."

I'd been through a lot with Meredith, like the weekend she made me watch the entire Henry VIII series three times because she said she was Anne Boleyn. She taped a sixth finger to her left hand to prove it. She wore it for two weeks until Mrs. Gilles, the history teacher, made her take it off during a test because it kept thumping on the desk. Meredith pulled off the black electrical tape that attached it to her hand and tore off the top layers of her skin. The nurse took her to Lenox Hill, but before she left, she stood in front of the class, waved her bloody hand, and cried out, "Long live the King!"

"What makes you think she's your mother?"

"For one thing, she's got that mirror."

"So?"

"And the *barre*. She's a *dancer*. My birth mother was a *dancer*. That's why she couldn't keep me. Gil said." Gil was her mother, her adoptive mother. Since when did Meredith call her by name? It made me wonder if I should do that with my mom.

"There's probably a million dancers in New York," I said.

She shook her head. "It's her. I know it's her. Not only is she a dancer, she looks like me. Plus she doesn't have kids. Besides, I always knew my mother was a Jew."

Until then, I didn't know Meredith was interested in her birth mother. Her being adopted had always been the one thing she refused to discuss. The one time I tried asking about it, I got the message the subject was off-limits. "Butt out," she'd said.

I supposed the woman *could* be living in New York—but in the same building?

As for Meredith being Jewish, I didn't know that was ever an issue. Even my mother, who was always fiercely interested in who was a Jew and who was not, had never floated the question. Meredith was so obviously not.

She brushed the hair from her face. She had dyed it so often I wouldn't know her natural color if I saw it in a lineup. "She's not in good shape."

"What do you mean?"

"They have a lot of fights."

"Who?"

"She and her husband."

"How do you know?"

She smiled, resting her chin on the smooth top of the Hatter's hat. *"You snooped."*

"The back stairs," she said, words tumbling out of her. "Behind the kitchen. You can hear *everything*."

I wondered if anyone had been listening to the fights in our house. They were loud enough, though since the summer they had subsided somewhat.

"What do they fight about?" She looked at me like I was as dumb as driftwood.

"The usual. Money. Sex." She chomped on her sour ball and shattered it. Then she whispered. "She wants a *divorce*."

The way she said that reminded me of eighth grade when I was obsessed with soaps. Every day before school I set the VCR to *Another World* and *Days of Our Lives*. Amnesiacs, orphans, and sex addicts. I couldn't get enough. I watched when I got home. This was before I started hanging out with Meredith. My parents didn't come home until seven, and half the time they weren't talking. The lives on those shows were so filled with disaster. They made me feel steady.

"Why does she want a divorce?"

"I don't know. But if you ask me, he cheats." We started walking uphill. Behind us, the boat pond was darkening and still. Meredith was quiet. There was more, I could tell. The temperature had dropped. I had no gloves, so I shoved my hands in my pockets. A black squirrel scurried up a tree. It was the only tree with any leaves still hanging. Meredith linked her arm through mine and pulled me closer. That was her way, drawing you into her dramas like they were yours, too. I had to admit I liked that. Her life was a perpetual crisis.

"We have to do something to help," she said.

"What do you mean?"

She searched my face, sizing me up.

"We have to save their marriage."

That night my father said we needed a new routine. Dinners three nights a week, if only takeout. My mother, who was onto another round of self improvement classes, wasn't yet home. I wondered how much she knew about this latest plan, if they had even discussed it. I suspected it was all his doing, and not so much for its own sake but in response to something else, something he felt guilty about. He wouldn't come out and say. I got the feeling he wanted me to ask, but I went to my room instead.

My mother came home about an hour later. She breezed down the hall and stopped by the door of my room and waved hello. She said her martial arts class had been especially strenuous and she needed to soak. It was nearly eight o'clock. My father ordered Chinese and set the table for three.

We waited almost thirty minutes before the food came. My mother was still in the tub. I called to her through the bathroom door but she said not to wait. I ate with my dad, both of us starved. He told a couple of jokes, one of which I already knew. I could tell he was nervous. When we finished, he took two fortune cookies and loped down the hall to their bedroom. By then she was out of the tub. His voice was low, but even from the dining room I could hear their exchange. He offered her a cookie. I heard her raspy laugh. When she spoke, I heard the sting in her voice.

"You've got to be desperate, taking advice from a cookie."

I left the table and went to my room.

Over the next few weeks, Meredith became obsessed with ballet. She'd started lessons that fall and she'd been walking funny ever since, toes pointed out. Sometime in October she pasted together a wall-sized collage of ballerinas and hung it in her room. Then there was the day we went to Capezio. She bought five hundred dollars' worth of warm-ups and tights. Plus a sequined tutu. By Halloween she had started in on my posture, saying it was crooked, which is something my mother used to say until she gave up. Since my brother went to college in Colorado, she gave up on a lot of things, like she couldn't be bothered. Maybe I'd never noticed that about her because when my brother was home, Phillip, he'd been a sort of buffer. Maybe she was depressed. Except that in my family no one would admit to being depressed. Things were different in Meredith's family, where even Bogart, their yellow-spotted corgi, had been to a therapist. She said he had attachment issues and put him on Zoloft to stop him from humping everybody's leg. As for Meredith, she *wasn't* depressed as long as I went along with her plan. Or at least she didn't seem so. And as long as I went along with her plan, the marks on her arm would disappear.

There was one thing I didn't get. If she really believed the woman in that apartment was her mother, why wasn't she happy? Finally I asked her.

"Are you asking why am I depressed?"

I nodded.

A tear slid down her cheek. I knew from her days as Anne Boleyn that Meredith could summon tears at will, but this one seemed real. She looked to the window. The curtains were drawn, but she lifted them slightly, peeking through. She turned back, and she was smiling.

"Who wouldn't be depressed? All your life you think your mother's Darci Kistler or Heather Watts. And here she is. Some lady pumped up with Botox, trailing a Chihuahua."

The next day at school, I was dredging my locker for math notes when I felt a poke. I looked up and saw Meredith.

"Here." She handed me a copy of *Redbook*. Not the kind of periodical you will find in our school library, where half the teachers are women's libbers from the seventies and the other half are lesbians. It's a girls' school.

"Page one twenty-one. *Read it*," she said and left. We were tracked differently for math. I took the magazine to class and camouflaged it with my book. I read the whole thing uninterrupted—Miss Dyson was that oblivious. She was the algebra teacher. The week before, Emma Blincoe ate an entire Happy Meal in that class and Miss Dyson never noticed. I turned to page 121: Ten Sexed-Up Reasons Never to Cheat. Meredith was standing outside the classroom door waiting for me at the end of the period.

"It's for my mother," she said.

This threw me for a sec—I thought she meant Gil. But she meant the woman in 11D, the apartment across the way. Mrs. Weisgall. Or Ava, as she called her.

"What do you think? Does it get the message across?" She looked at me, searching.

"I guess."

"So you'll help?"

Her eyes were welling up. She was about to cry.

"Okay." Her face lit up in an enormous smile. Then she clasped my head in her hands and kissed my cheek. Pleasing her was so easy sometimes. Maybe that was all she wanted. It never occurred to me that I wanted something, too.

We went to her house after school.

"We have to go straight to work," she said. I thought she meant the history test we had the next day. I followed her to her room and she shut the door behind us. Then she closed the curtains and pulled out that magazine. Next thing, I saw in her hand a single-edged razor.

I froze.

I swear I thought she was going to put the blade to her arm and start cutting. I pictured a line of blood blooming across her wrist, spilling to the carpet. I thought of grabbing the razor from her hand, knowing that if I did I would probably slice up my own hand, as well.

She opened the magazine to the article, Ten Sexed-Up Reasons, set the razor against the spine, and began cutting out pages. I felt relief, though a little deflated. She rolled the pages lengthwise into a tube the way they did in kindergarten when I brought home my artwork. She tied the tube with a red satin ribbon. It looked like something ceremonial, a school diploma.

"This," she said, "is the first of our offerings."

I looked at her quizzically.

"To tell her we're here. That we're watching out for her. Like guardian angels." She put on her slippers. "Let's go."

Her plan was to leave Ten Sexed-Up Reasons at the woman's doorstep. I said I had to go walk Foley, but she gave me that look, that if I left her now I was leaving her for dead. We took the elevator down to the lobby and snuck around to the back of the building and back up. Only we couldn't take the elevator. She said it was indiscreet. We took the stairs.

I followed her up eleven flights, lagging behind, gasping for breath, my leg muscles in shock. Except for the mezuzah, the door of 11D looked exactly like the door to Meredith's apartment. She bent down and set the rolled-up article on the hemp mat with utmost care, as if it might break apart like an egg. She straightened up, briefly glancing back.

I thought we were done.

Without warning, she pressed her finger to the pearly round doorbell button.

The buzzer sounded.

From the other side of the door, I heard the yap-yap-yap of a tiny dog. Next the clicking footsteps of a woman, closer and closer.

Meredith turned to me with a wild smile. Then she ran down the stairs.

I panicked and followed, trailing behind.

At lunch the next day Meredith was so excited she didn't eat, her breath shallow like a bird's. She said she was going to Barnes & Noble after school. She wanted me to come.

"I need you."

I wondered what she was up to now. She wasn't a big reader; we were in different English sections, too. Actually, our only classes together were art, which was an elective, and history, which they didn't track because they figured facts were facts and they couldn't be fudged.

I said I would come, but I wasn't making any more home deliveries.

We walked to the bookstore after school. The sky was threatening rain, and here and there a drop fell on my head as a warning. We had no umbrella. I followed her into the store to the aisle marked self-help. I crossed my fingers that I wouldn't be seen by anyone I knew.

"This one," she said with authority and reached for a pink paperback spine. It was a guide, it said, "for couples who have survived adultery."

"What do you want that for?"

"It's for my *mom*."

This time at least I knew who she meant.

"Have you read it?" I asked.

"No. I don't have to. "I saw it on *Ricki Lake*."

She bought the book with a fifty-dollar bill and shoved the change in her pocket.

"You're the best," she said, crushing me with a colossal hug.

As for how I felt, what can I say? That she made me feel special. But her singling me out was a little scary, as if right now everything in her life depended on me.

We walked out of the store. Outside the rain was beginning to fall.

"If she's really your mom," I dared asking, "why don't you just go and introduce yourself?"

Meredith scowled.

"I have a *plan*."

"What's the plan?"

"I told you. They have to stay married."

"But that's not really any of your business."

"It is my business, and I'll tell you, but you have to swear."

Poor Foley. Forsworn again. Better he had been a cat.

"If they don't stay married, she'll move out and I'll lose her for good." She paused, eyes narrowed on me. "Besides, you wouldn't want *your* parents getting divorced, would you?"

"No, obviously," I said, though last summer Phillip said that's where they were headed. Meredith had hit a nerve. It made me wish I hadn't told her what happened last July, when my mother moved into the Yale Club for two weeks. No one told me why. She came home a few times briefly after dinner to tuck me in, or so she said. Then she went back.

The rain was coming hard and steady. Meredith picked up the pace and called out over her shoulder.

"So, *there*."

"But they're not your parents." I was right behind her.

"Look," she said, her voice faltering. "If they get divorced, they won't have any kids. And if they don't have any kids, I'll never have sisters."

There was nothing I could say. Meredith was an only child who would never have sisters. But neither did I. I wanted to say, *I'll be your sister—aren't we sisters already?* Instead, I felt a lump rise in my throat. I felt suddenly exhausted, as if faced with a task that was infinitely beyond my ability. We raced across the street to her block. By now we were drenched. She sprinted ahead to the broad canopy of her building.

Then she turned to me and waved. As if by magic, the gilded glass doors of her building slid open.

She went inside and vanished, the doors closing behind her.

She started another collage. The theme this time was matrimony. Armed with a yellow legal pad and a stack of back issues of *Us* and *People*, she said she wanted examples. I asked her what she meant.

"Couples," she said imperiously, as if it were obvious. "Like Romeo and Juliet, but not doomed. I don't want doomed. I want happy."

"Like who?"

"That's the problem. I don't know." She scooped Bogart into her lap and buried her nose in his belly.

I searched my brain, but all I could think of were stories from the Children's Bible my mother had made me read. Jacob and Leah, Abraham and Sarah, Samson and Delilah. My mother said there wasn't one marriage in the whole book you could wish for; they were liars and cheaters all. Maybe that was why she quit the Jewish renewal class at the Y.

"Can't you think of any?" She pulled a bag of M&M's from her rucksack and offered me some.

"I'm trying."

She hugged Bogart like a baby. "Think of it as a research project," she said. She pushed the magazines in my direction. "If you have to, use these."

Sunday night we had dinner, the three of us. It was the first time in over a week that we all ate together, despite my father's plan. He cooked pasta, but he forgot to salt the water. I could taste the absence. I ate it anyway. They weren't talking, which in itself was nothing unusual, but the silence was smothering, like a sodden blanket. My father tried shaking it off by asking questions, though only to me.

Have you done your homework?

Do you have any tests coming up?

When at last my mother spoke, it seemed she hadn't been listening at all.

"I ran into Marianne Brody. She said Ellie loves boarding school."

There was a pause, as if I was supposed to say something, and then my mother resumed.

"Remember how much you wanted to go?"

I let out a small grunt. It was a Meredith thing, that sound.

"It made me start to think," she continued. "Do you still want to?"

I couldn't believe she'd asked. All last year, the year my brother went away, I wanted to go away, too. Half the girls in my class were applying to boarding school, and I thought it would be a solution, but my parents refused to consider it. I must have mentioned it one hundred times, and every time I did, they laughed, as if they had zero confidence that I could ever take care of myself on my own. It was one of the few times I ever saw them agree. Not long after, I started hanging around with Meredith, taking care of her.

My mother repeated the question. "Do you still want to go?"

I shook my head. "No." I wondered, *Was she trying to get rid of me?*

From the corner of my eye, I saw my father's glance shift to my mother. He looked sad.

"Did you change your mind?" my mother asked.

I nodded.

"Why?"

I couldn't think of going away—I couldn't leave Meredith—but I wasn't about to say so.

I shrugged. I was desperate to change the subject.

"Meredith and I are doing a project."

"On what?" my father asked.

"On marriage."

My mother's mouth shrunk to the size of a cherry pit. She looked horrified.

"Whatever for?"

I panicked. "For art. She needs examples of married couples. Happy ones."

Silence. My mother went into the kitchen and set the kettle on the stove. I heard her clattering about in the sink, tidying up. Meanwhile, my dad hunched his shoulders over the table as if he wanted to hide, rubbing his bottom lip.

"Run this by me once more?" he asked. I explained it to him, though I could hear the nervousness in my voice. Word for word, he repeated back what I said, as if he were stalling for time, or maybe the project was so incomprehensible as to leave him speechless. He went back to rubbing his lip. It made me think of a genie's lamp. Back and forth went his thumb, as if he were trying to conjure assistance. I looked at my hands, nails chewed to the quick. My mother appeared in the doorway, arms crossed, pressing her slim body against the frame.

"I don't suppose you've come up with anything, have you?" she said to my dad.

He shook his head. "I'm thinking," he said.

"On something like this," she said, "shouldn't Meredith be asking her own parents?"

I felt completely stupid.

"They don't have to be living," I persisted, refusing to accept that my involvement was futile. "They can be dead. As long as they stayed a couple." Foley nuzzled my leg under the table like he was telling me to quit. The kettle began to howl. My dad read a lot of big hardcover biographies so I was sure he would come up with someone.

Whatever ideas he had, though, he didn't get much of a chance to suggest them after what my mother said next.

"Better dead than living, I suppose."

Meredith didn't show up for school Monday. She called the headmistress's office, though, and left me a message. She wanted me to come over after eighth. I walked to her building and the doorman buzzed me up. When I stepped off the elevator, the door to her apartment was wide open as if the place were a crime scene. I heard music being played in her room and Bogart came across the parquet floor to greet me. He barked twice, then turned back down the hall. I followed. My heart felt small with fright.

I recognized the music soon enough. It was from the *Nutcracker*. "The Dance of the Sugar Plum Fairy." I knew because my father took me to see it last Christmas. It only made me sad. He kept saying how he'd taken me when I was five, as if that were the only reason we went, so he could pretend that nothing had changed, that I was still his little girl and he wasn't getting old.

Inside Meredith's room, the furniture was all rearranged. The bed, the dresser, the chair—everything was pushed against the wall to make a clearing. It was like a stage. Meredith stood in the center in a white leotard and tutu, fingertips touching overhead.

"Look!" she cried out. "First! Second! Third! Fourth!—"

She raced through the five positions, her feet springing like coils nonstop in motion. It was a Morse code of flexes and points, only I didn't get the message. As soon as she finished one cycle, she raced without missing a beat through the positions again. Then she shouted, "What happened at school?"

Given the bizarre urgency of her dance, I couldn't believe the question; it was so banal. "Miss Dyson was sick. We had a substitute."

She was leaping back and forth before her bed, her tutu shaking feverishly.

"Did anyone ask after me?"

"You mean people or teachers?"

"I don't know. Anybody."

I should have thrown out a name just to be kind, only I couldn't think of one. My mind was blank. Something about her movements— the awkwardness, the speed—was terrifying. And mesmerizing, too. I was struck with that same sense of helplessness I felt when I heard my parents yell at each other. The music stopped and another piece began, the grande finale waltz. Pliés, coupés, arabesques, she raced through them all, breathless, flinging her limbs at perilous angles. She had scared me with the cuts on her arm, but this I thought was worse.

This was way over my head.

The tempo quickened.

"Look." She pointed to the window. She had pulled down the curtains, stripping the windows bare. Taped on the glass was a giant blank sheet of posterboard.

"That's the back. Lift it up and check out the other side," she ordered. Her arms fluttered like a swan, her body turning three hundred and sixty degrees in a single jump.

The poster was attached to the window on all sides with black electrical tape—leftover, I presumed, from her days as Anne Boleyn.

I approached the window.

The bottom tape came away with a yank, and I lifted up the posterboard.

It was another collage, the one about marriage. I guess she'd given up on getting any examples from me so she had decorated it instead with pictures of brides and grooms cut out from magazines. There were brides of every persuasion, dozens of them: princess brides with cathedral trains, miniskirt brides, suited brides, black brides, white brides, Japanese brides in kimonos, even a pair of nuptial twins.

"Did you read what it says?" she asked. Her voice was high. I wondered, *Was that a ballerina thing or was she cracking up?* She'd set her hands on her hips and started bending side to side at the waist. It seemed more like aerobics than ballet, as if she had run out of moves.

"Did you *read* it?"

My heart was thumping. Of course I'd read it. It was impossible not to. The words were stenciled with red ink in big block letters across the top of the sheet.

REMEMBER THE SACRED VOWS

The music changed and a march was on, the sound of occupying forces. It was strangely apt. For some time it had seemed that Meredith herself had been occupied, that she had been taken siege by forces beyond her control. Forces beyond mine.

"Did you see what she did?"

"What?"

"Look. *Look at her window.*"

I looked out the window and across to 11D. The shades over there were drawn. I had the feeling we were being watched. I wanted to leave. Meredith kept talking.

"She closed her shades. I saw her do it. She *knows*." She gave a wild smile, her cheeks glowing and flush.

"She knows what?"

"She knows we're *here*. Wait till she sees me do *this*," she said, launching into a pirouette. Halfway into the spin, she knocked over a brass standing lamp. It hit the floor. The bulb went out with an aspirated pop and the room was dimmed.

I said I had to go.

"No!" she cried. *"Don't!"*

"I have a math test."

"Can't you stay? *Please?*"

I shook my head. "I have to study." It was a lie.

"Okay," she said, suddenly despondent. "But promise me one thing." Her voice was pleading. "Call me tonight."

I found my way to the door. Behind me, the music blared. Not exactly the *Nutcracker* I remembered, the waltzes and gavottes, but the sounds of battle: drumbeats and trumpets, the sounds of war.

As it turned out, I didn't call Meredith that night. I didn't call anyone. But Meredith called *me*. She was sobbing. Her parents had yanked the phone from her room and banned her from making calls so she was talking on the portable outside her apartment behind the back door, whispering.

I didn't pick up the phone. I heard the whole thing on my answering machine.

What I got was this: Mrs. Weisgall had seen the collage taped to Meredith's window and sent her husband, later that night, to talk to Meredith's parents. Apparently, this was the last straw. According to Mr. Weisgall, Meredith had been calling them late at night and hanging up—they had caller ID. He said she'd been sending his wife what he called *offensive materials*. He said Meredith had stalked his wife fourteen blocks down Lexington Avenue and then waited outside on the street while Mrs. Weisgall went in for some doctor's appointment. He was ready to press charges. Meredith was a *junior mental case*, he said, and they would have a lawsuit at once if she didn't leave him and his wife alone.

Of course to her parents, Meredith denied everything. Even to me, or rather to my answering machine, she denied the part about following Mrs. Weisgall down the street. I listened to her voice, but I did not believe what she said.

She called back twice. Each time, she begged me to pick up, as if she knew I was there on my bed, buried under a mass of blankets. But my hands didn't touch the phone. Finally, I unplugged it, though it was barely nine.

I had my own calamity, and before I set out saving someone else, I decided, I'd better save myself.

That night, after dinner, my parents had come to my room and sat on my bed for a talk. My mother did most of it and the whole time that she did, her voice had this unprecedented calm. One of the things I kept on my bed was the blanket they had laid in my carriage as a baby. It was a Stewart plaid, with fringe along the length of the top and bottom edges, sized for a crib. They had bought that blanket as a souvenir on a trip to Scotland when they first were married. At the time, my mother thought that if they brought the blanket home, it might act as a charm, and she might soon be expecting. It must have worked, because not long after they had my brother. A few years later, they had me.

My mother talked, and I started braiding the fringe, working the ropey threads between my fingers. They felt pliant and soft. I remember thinking how each individual braid was the perfect amalgam of three.

"People change," my mother said ominously, "and sometimes circumstances change with them. Husbands and wives, they grow apart."

They were getting divorced, only she called it separating. My dad
stared at the floor and pulled at his bottom lip. He was moving out. I
could live half the time with each of them, back and forth to wherever
he moved, or I could live mostly with my mother.

"You don't have to decide now," he said, and I heard in his voice
the flat hollow of remorse.

My mother concurred. "It's not a popularity contest."

It was strange, hearing them agree.

I looked down at my hands. I'd braided every piece of fringe along
the entire edge of the blanket, only the strands didn't divide into three.
My father touched at the last remaining strand.

It dangled alone.

He asked if I had any questions.

I said no. Only the big one, which I didn't dare ask.

THE CLOSET

knew something was wrong when I heard the kitchen buzzer. It was too early in the morning for anything good. I wasn't dressed. Neither was my mother, though Abby was. She was always first to be dressed. She was first to hear the buzzer, and she answered it. I could tell it was something bad by the way she raced down the hall.

"Mom!"

My mother stood in her bathrobe before her bedroom closet, weight on one hip, sipping coffee.

"It's Daddy," Abby said. "He's here."

"Where?"

"Downstairs. In front of the building."

"How do you know? Did you see him?"

Abby shook her head.

"The doorman said. On the intercom." She started toward the window. My mother took her by the arm.

"You stay back. I'll look."

Next thing, my mother was down on all fours crawling toward the window. She was like a soldier in ambush. She got to the sill and braced her hands against the edge for support. Slowly she raised her head to peer down below.

"That's him. Definitely."

"Now what?"

"He has two cars." She paused. "One of them looks like a tank."

This was evidently too much for Abby; she made a dash for the window and copped a view.

She gasped.

"That's not a tank, Mom. That's a Hummer."

"Get away from there!"

"But Mom, it's a Hummer." Abby was a stickler for facts.

"I don't care what it is. I want you away from the window."

Abby withdrew. My mother crawled away from the window to the corner and straightened herself up. Then she pulled down the roller shades. The room darkened.

"We'll make like we're not home."

"What if the doorman already told him we're here?"

Mom glared at her.

Abby sat down on the bed, which was nearly covered with clothes. My mother hadn't decided what to wear. She was a size four.

"You're too visible there," my mother said. "He could see you. Get on the floor."

"But you already pulled down the shades. How can he possibly see?"

My mother didn't answer. Abby slid off the bed to the floor and sat, tucking her knees against her chest. As for me, I stood in the doorway, half-inside, half out of the room, far enough from the window so my mother could not object. The two of us stared at my mother's back as she leaned over, squinting her eyes at the sunlit crack between the window and shade.

I wanted to see, too. Otherwise it wouldn't seem real.

I slipped across the hall to my room, the room I shared with Abby. Like my mother's room, this one faced east and was flooded with brilliant morning light. For a moment I was blind.

I loved our room; it was like a fortress filled with everything familiar and safe. We slept with our beds flanked against the wall head to head.

At night when I had bad dreams I could reach out my hand to hers and she would hold it tight until I fell back to sleep.

I stood waiting in the door while my eyes adjusted. Slowly the room came into view. Only minutes had passed since I had left it, but in that interval the bedroom had changed, the playthings and furnishings somehow disheartened. I made my way to the window, leaned forward slightly, and looked down five stories below.

Parked in front of our building, double-parked really, was the thing that Abby had called a Hummer. My mother was right; it looked like a giant tank. At each corner of the hood a miniature American flag snapped in the wind. Behind it, like a kind of rear escort, was a regular black Towncar, similarly ornamented with stars and stripes.

Pacing alongside the Towncar was my dad.

I felt suddenly weak.

He was wearing a trench coat and a white skipper's hat. His hair was long and he was talking to someone inside the car, gesticulating in the air. Even from such distance, I could see he'd gained weight, maybe twenty pounds since the last time we saw him, only a month or so before. He was well then, and when he was well he was a regular dad, taking us skating in the Park or doing magic tricks. We saw him on weekends. When he was ill, he could be terrifying, and we were kept away.

Hanging by a strap from his wrist was a giant megaphone.

Beyond him everything looked normal. There was the usual morning traffic in the street: people going to work, children going to school. A few people stopped to gawk. Mostly, though, it seemed people didn't notice. Or they pretended not to. I wanted to pretend, too.

I had seen him ill before—the convoys and the crazy outfits, too—though I'd never seen a Hummer. Until then he'd hired only Towncars to squire him around on what he called his "missions." I had even ridden in one of them, once when we didn't know he was manic and my mother let him take us to the zoo. I was five. Later she said it had seemed a little unnecessary, hiring a car and driver just to go to the Bronx, but she let him take us anyway. Maybe she just needed a break. We got in the car, and he told us his plan. He had read a book about mind control, and he said he'd found a surefire way to make people follow his commands. He wanted to test the technique on the lower primates before practicing them on humans—it was that dangerous, he said. If it worked he said he would get us each a monkey who would do whatever we asked. It sounded good to me, but I could tell Abby was worried. As it turned out, the car ran out of gas on the Bronx River Parkway and we never got to the zoo. We were still in Manhattan when the driver kept suggesting we pull into a filling station, but my father wouldn't let him stop. Like a mantra, my dad kept telling him, "Time and tide. Time and tide." There was a fight. My dad pulled out a knife, which turned out later to be a letter opener. The police took us home.

He climbed to the roof of the Towncar and raised the megaphone to his lips.

He was barefoot.

His voice boomed from the street.

"Sound the alarm! All troops report to their stations! The mobilization has begun!"

I felt sick.

I thought of the aquarium. Back in the fall, he had taken us there to see the fin-tailed sharks. For the longest time I watched them cruising back and forth. Even in captivity they were menacing, and for weeks afterward I had dreams of them hunting me down in the deep. The strangest part was that though I could breathe underwater like a fish, I somehow couldn't swim. All I could do was paddle like a dog, treading water under the water, unable to escape.

Now I watched my dad. It seemed he was trapped inside one of those giant wall-to-wall fish tanks himself, and he was drowning. I watched through glass, powerless to save him.

I shuffled back to my mother's room.

She and my sister were gone.

The room was dark, shades drawn, the closet door ajar.

My mother had a huge stash of clothes: dresses, blouses, trousers, skirts. Items that had defied the usual descriptions. I was familiar with just about everything in there because she dragged us along when she went shopping. She could spend an entire Saturday trolling department stores, Saks or Bergdorfs, for clothes. Sometimes the salespeople would feed us gummies or pretzels, she took so long trying on stuff and they could tell we were bored. By the end of the day, she'd have so many bags, someone would have to help us to the door and put us in a cab. There was too much stuff for one person to carry.

Sometimes she'd buy clothes for us, too. We had a vast selection of party dresses, though we rarely had occasions to wear them. The salesperson would ring up the sale, and my mother would give us each a colossal hug. I didn't like those hugs: they lasted too long and they were delivered always in front of strangers. They felt a little desperate, too, as if her real reason for giving them was to get something in return.

After we got home from shopping, she'd lay all her loot on the bed, strip herself naked, and light up a smoke. She'd say she was exhausted, but she'd have an enormous smile. Then she'd ask us to help her pick which outfits she should wear to work that week.

That was our reward, when we knew she loved us, her asking us for help.

Suits and dresses, trousers and shirts. They hung before me lifeless and still, a haven of gabardines and silks. I crawled inside behind the suspended wall of garments and comforted myself against the shoe rack.

My mother loved her clothes. I thought that by tucking myself behind all those duds and finery, I could feel how much she loved me, too.

Footsteps sounded down the hall. I pulled the clothes in front of me to hide.

My mother's feet appeared at the door and padded toward the bed. My sister followed.

"Abby, I'm making a call. I need quiet."

I pushed aside some dresses to crack open a line of sight.

My mother pushed the telephone buttons. I guessed she was calling the police. If it played out like most of the times he showed up like this, the cops would come, two of them like Tweedledum and Dee, and he would have already left, eluding them. They almost never caught him.

And on those few times when they did, there was usually nothing to book him for. Or he'd tell them he was doing research for a new part in a film. He'd been the star of a TV series about UFO investigators in the early eighties and when he told them who he was, they usually recognized him, though he hadn't had any big leads since. But that was enough to impress them, and they'd let him go. It even worked one time when they came and found him in front of our door wearing only a tape recorder around his neck and a bathrobe. My mother said it only showed that being crazy was just another privilege of being famous. Or maybe that even battle-weary New York City cops couldn't let go of the fantasy of outer space.

My mother sat on the bed with her legs crossed, clutching the telephone, pivoting slightly to turn herself away. She became abruptly animated.

"Val, it's Diane. I'm late." She paused. "It's the girls. They're sick. Both of them, and I can't leave until I find someone to sit with them." She paused, glancing back at Abby, looking her up and down.

"No," she went on. "Just vomit. It's everywhere. I was up all night."

This struck me as unfair. It wasn't our fault she was going to be late. None of this was our fault. But hearing her blame us made me want to shrink farther back into the closet. Maybe she was right. Maybe it was our fault. Maybe if only we could love him more, my father wouldn't get sick. He would take the medicine, and he would stay well. If we loved him enough, we wouldn't have to be afraid, but it was fear that stopped us from loving him more and I don't know how we could have got around that. I don't know how my mother ever reasoned it herself. She had loved him, you could tell from photographs of the two of them together. They had dozens of them in as many romantic venues—the Grand Canal, the Cliffs of Moher—thanks to my dad's deft use of the self-timer.

I hated my mother for lying.

She told Val to cancel her first appointment. "But call me right back if they can reschedule in the afternoon." She said good-bye and hung up.

I saw my sister's loafers draw near.

She reached inside the closet and pushed aside a mass of clothes. The hangers screeched metal against metal as she dragged them along the crowded rack.

"What do you think you're doing in there?"

"Nothing."

"Get out!"

I crawled out and stood up, unbending my legs.

"Cece," said my mother. "What do *you* think?" Either she didn't notice that I had been hiding or she didn't care. "Should we call the police?"

A noise sounded from the kitchen, startling me. The buzzer. Abby rushed to answer.

"Mom!" she called from the kitchen. "The bus is here."

It was 8:15. The school bus was always on time. I was getting a little old for taking it, since I was already eleven, and Abby certainly was, but my mother didn't like us riding public transportation. She said it wasn't safe.

She went to the window to investigate, lifting the shade a crack, close to the wall for cover.

She groaned.

Abby appeared at the door.

"What did you tell him?" my mother asked.

"Who?"

"The bus driver."

"It was the doorman."

"What did you tell him about the bus? Did you tell him to say he could leave?"

Abby shook her head. "I didn't tell him anything."

"For Christ's sake, Abby, did you think you were going to school with your father downstairs like a lunatic?"

Abby was silent. My mother went on.

"I guess I'll talk to the doorman myself." She stalked off to the kitchen. I heard her shouting into the intercom. She returned to the bedroom and peered out the window.

"He's gone."

"Who? Daddy?" I asked. I was hoping. I had shifted positions, leaning into my mother's bed, bending at the waist, pressing my elbows into the mattress. I was in the room, but I could still quickly clear out.

"The driver. He left." She took a sip of her coffee. By now it had to be cold.

Sadness came over me. That was my bus, the bus that could take me away, and I wanted to be on it. I pictured my usual seat: third row on the left, against the window, Abby sitting beside me. I wanted to be wedged there now, going to school where everything was predictable. Where there were no surprises.

The phone rang.

"That's probably Val," said my mother. She put a smile on her face, brushed her hair behind her ears, picked up the handset, and said hello. There was a pause. Her chin stiffened in tension. She was taken aback.

Abby whispered, "Is it *him?*"

My mother nodded, frowning.

Abby went to the window.

I followed.

Downstairs, on the south corner of our block, we had perhaps the last old-fashioned phone booth in all of New York. In truth, it was only the remains of a phone booth, the glass panel walls long ago shattered and removed, all of it slated for imminent replacement. But there he was, standing inside the little half shelter, cradling the phone to his ear, an anachronism himself, his oversized body cramped and misshapen like some human forebear long extinct. He was wearing the hat, but I could see the fringe of hair underneath. He was growing it long. I was surprised he wasn't using his cell, since usually even when he was well, he kept one close at hand, and in his fevered mania he'd probably have three. But he had just as likely lost it. Or given it away.

He wasn't alone. Huddled beside him, curling her back around his, was a woman. She was extremely tall—nearly as tall as my dad—with a big poof of red hair and a skirt so short she seemed nothing but leg.

She pressed against him like a vine on a trellis, twining her limbs around his. She wasn't any of the girlfriends we'd met. She was new.

"I hope they're not married," Abby whispered. She gave me a worried look. The notion was not impossible. The last time he was ill he'd gotten married to a woman he'd met in a sex addicts chat room six days before.

Meanwhile my mother sat at the telephone, listening in silence, her smile leveled into grief. He was doing all the talking, no surprise. It didn't matter what about. Just hearing his pressured speech could make any of us sad. From my perch at the window, I could watch them both. It was like a split screen on TV, cut diagonally, my mother in one right triangle, my father in the other. Minus the sound.

She started laughing.

"I never said *that*." She was flirting. He was probably flirting, too. He could be charming and attentive even when he was nuts. But he wouldn't necessarily stay that way. He could be lovable one minute and cruel the next. I wasn't surprised she was flirting back. They did so when he was well sometimes and he was picking us up to take us somewhere or dropping us off. She'd had a lot of dates since they split, but none of them had stuck. There wasn't the chemistry with those men, she said, that there was with my dad. We didn't have to ask her why she'd insisted they get divorced. The episodes were lasting longer, sometimes for months, and they were coming more frequently. In the last year, he'd already had two.

She switched the handset to her other ear. She was silent again, her expression worried. She started toying with her cigarettes.

"You don't want to do that," she said coyly.

"Seriously, *don't*." She deepened her voice.

"*Don't you dare*." She stood up.

"*You do that, and you're likely to get me fired.*"

There was a long silence. Her face was pained. She was listening intently.

"Okay. Name your terms." Her lips pursed. She tapped out a cigarette.

Another long silence.

"How do I know you'll keep your promise?" She lit up and inhaled. Then she was nodding.

"Okay. Two minutes. You get two minutes. That's all."

She pressed the mouthpiece to her chest and called to Abby.

"Honey, here." She held out the receiver, smirking. "Your dad wants to talk to you."

Abby walked to the bed.

"Are you okay?" she asked my mom.

She nodded, smiling, though it seemed a little forced.

Abby took the phone and held it cautiously to her ear. I watched and waited. She said hello. Next she was giggling. I thought maybe it was only nerves, but soon she was laughing for real. And she was talking, telling him about her project for social studies—it was on Tibet—and about her friend Trina's new parakeet. They were having a regular conversation, as if there were nothing strange about the circumstances at all.

I would have been scared to talk to him myself, but her relationship with him was different. She had some small reserve of courage, or maybe it was love, I don't know, that made her feel connected. Maybe because she was born first, and she'd had those extra years with him all to herself.

She grew quiet, listening.

"I promise," she whispered.

She looked uncomfortable. A tear rolled down her cheek.

My mother stood at the window, still in her robe, smoking.

Abby pulled the handset from her mouth and called my name.

"He wants to talk to you."

My mother turned from the window. I felt my stomach buckle.

"Do I have to?" I said.

She nodded.

"Why?"

She didn't say anything. She only shrugged. Then she stubbed out her cigarette and cleared her throat.

"I'm sorry, honey."

She didn't have to say anything more. Somehow I knew. They had made a pact and we were part of the deal. Two minutes on the phone with each of us, and he would refrain from doing whatever it was she didn't want him to do. Call up her boss and bad-mouth her? Show up at the office and pick a fight?

I wanted to crawl back into the closet, but they'd only come after me. They'd haul me out in a heartbeat.

"Cece," my mother said, "do it for me."

Abby passed me the phone. The handle was warm where her hand had been. I put it a few inches from my ear but still I could hear him.

"Hello? Hello?"

It was my dad, only his voice was scratchy and hoarse, as if he had been talking nonstop, which in fact was probably true, and it was booming. Like he was miked.

I didn't say a word. I tried to swallow but it was like I had forgotten how.

"Fuck! Is anyone *there*?"

"Hi." My voice was pitched high and thin. It didn't sound like me.

"Who is this? Is this Celia?" He called me by my real name. Only my mother called me Cece.

"Uh-huh."

"What do you think of our little party here? I was thinking I'd take you to school."

I said nothing.

"I wanted to meet your friends on the bus but your Nazi doorman sent the driver away. Don't you have a friend called Lisa?"

I was afraid to answer.

"Don't you?"

"Uh-huh."

"We're friends now. I met her. She was in the front row. I gave her a big bag of M&M's. I gave them *all* M&M's. Males for the girls, females for the boys." He paused. I knew what he meant. The plain M&M's were females. Peanuts were boys. It was an old joke. "She's your friend, isn't she?"

"Not exactly."

"She is now. I gave her a big kiss on the cheek."

I was beginning to feel numb: my feet and then my knees. I was losing sensation from the bottom up. I was mortified. I had a friend called Lisa. I had probably even told him about her. But she wasn't the one on the bus. The one on the bus was older, and we weren't even bus friends.

"She's not my friend."

"Come on. You sound like your momma. You know, when I met your momma she didn't have a single friend to speak of. No *girlfriends*, that is. *Men* she had in spades. A great cock tease, your mother. Ask her about her technique sometime. I'm sure she'd tell you."

By now my entire body was numb. I could feel the weight of the telephone in my hand, but I had no sense of the fingers that were holding it. There was a voice emanating from the earpiece, and it was my father's voice, but at the same time it was not. Something had stolen him away. He was under a spell, possessed.

I set the handset down on the bed.

"Did he hang up?" asked my mother.

I backed away from the bed. Abby reached for the phone but my mother beat her to it. She cupped the receiver to her ear and listened.

"He hung up. Maybe he left."

Abby went to look.

"He's gone. But the cars are still there."

We were stuck. All we could do was hope that he'd leave. And hope he didn't come upstairs.

There was a lull.

"I could still call the police," my mother offered.

"Don't, Mom. Please." I knew why Abby objected. There was always the possibility that my father would do something stupid and give the police an excuse to use their guns. I was afraid of that, too.

I decided I would get dressed, whether we were going to school or not. I went to my room. The light had become subdued. I looked out the window. The Hummer was there, and the Towncar, too, but my dad was nowhere in sight. I got changed.

I came back wearing my uniform. My mother eyed me suspiciously.

"Where do you think you're going?" she asked. She went over to her closet and began poking at the contents. I could tell she wanted to get out of there, too.

Meanwhile Abby had kicked off her loafers, settling in as if we were home for good. I wandered into the kitchen, found a pack of instant oatmeal, and poured it in a bowl, adding hot water from the tap. I put two spoonfuls in my mouth and gagged.

I dropped the oatmeal into the garbage, bowl and all.

My thoughts turned to Lisa. The one on the bus. She was one grade above me. She got on the bus first, and sometimes she smiled when I came up the steps. Everywhere else, though—at lunch, on the playground—she never looked at me. I thought of my dad giving her a kiss. I didn't think I could ever look her in the face again.

I pictured my classroom at school. I pictured Mrs. Lassert, my homeroom teacher. Sometimes she smiled at me for no reason at all.

The buzzer rang. Abby came to answer. I wasn't touching it.

She unhooked the earpiece, held it to her ear, and listened. Her face turned ashen. She replaced the device.

"It was the doorman. He called the police."

Now I was really scared. I felt the pulse in my neck, something pushing at the back of my throat. I followed Abby down the hall. She gave the news to my mother, who by now was dressed.

"He did?" she said, surprised, though of course she had considered calling them herself.

"He said he had no choice."

My mother looked suddenly relieved.

"Maybe it's for the best."

"He said to tell you he was sorry."

"Who?"

"The doorman."

"Sorry for what?"

Abby shrugged. My mother looked confused, then suspicious. She turned to the window and skulked over. She was wearing a beige tweedy skirt with a sweater I happened to like. Perhaps from instinct, or perhaps from fear, Abby didn't follow. My mother lifted the edge of the shade and leaned into the crack.

There was a silence.

"Oh my God."

"What is it?" asked Abby.

My mother turned her back to the window.

"You can't see."

"Why? What is it?"

I ran to our room, compelled to look. I got to the window. The shades in our room were up, so I pressed my back against the wall and leaned over. My stomach cramped and I tasted vomit.

Down on the street was my father. He was standing in the small space between the Hummer and the Towncar, facing the latter. Wrapped in his arms, in an embrace, was the redhead. He was leaning into her, face-to-face, her back against the car, one foot on the fender, her hair spilling behind her, my father's coat cloaking her legs. Behind her, upside down on the hood, was the skipper's hat. My father's body moved in quick short thrusts, pressing into her, lifting her up onto the car, making it shake.

A siren sounded from down the street.

From across the hall I heard a sound, something like a wail.

I went into my mother's room. She was sitting hunched on the bed, her face buried in a white crepe blouse she had thought about wearing, and she was crying, rubbing her eyes. She would stain that shirt with her makeup, I thought, but she didn't seem to care. She said something about Val and something about work, but most of it I couldn't make out.

Abby had her arm around her, sitting beside her, speaking softly, but it was as if my mother couldn't hear.

She looked so small, my mother, smaller than Abby, but Abby seemed to have expanded, swelling to uncertain proportions like a balloon ready to pop. By comforting my mother, my sister had grown large, as if she could feed on my mother's frailties, as if that were love.

It wasn't the kind of love I wanted.

No one in my family was living their right size. They were all either too big or too small, or they were both, oscillating wildly. But I was one of them, and if I had to make a choice, I would make myself small.

I crawled into the closet.

I would hear them in there, but I wouldn't have to watch. All those clothes, they were costumes, decorative exteriors to hide the ugliness beneath. I had a lot to hide already, and already I was learning how. Just my uniform was a start, a kind of camouflage, making me one of many rather than someone separate and alone. Though of course I was alone.

I stroked the hem of my mother's favorite dress, the silk so finely interwoven, like gossamer threads.

HELEN OF ALEXANDRIA

They were deep in Book Nine of the *Iliad*. Panic had routed the Greeks. The firm, oiled bodies of their finest young men lay bloody in the dust, stripped of armor, dogs and birds circling for the feast. Dorothy Hendl felt invigorated. This was one of her favorite parts to teach, and she made no secret of her enthusiasm, shaking her fist in the air for joy whenever a Trojan fell, thrusting her hand as if driving in the spear herself.

Neelie, meanwhile, had not once looked up from her back-row desk. (Her name was Cornelia, but like most of the tenth grade—and all the lifers in the class—she had a nickname.) Solemn as the oracle at Delphi, she concentrated on the words she wrote on the white loose-leaf pages before her. It wasn't so much the doodling that sparked Miss Hendl's fury; it was the markers, one silver, one gold, and fat, like sticks of dynamite, only they rattled. She considered the noise not just an outrage but an insult, and each time Neelie gave the pens a shake, she doubled the offense. The girl didn't actually write much—merely the same three words on every sheet, but in her round expansive script, she filled the page. Then she'd turn to the next page and write the words again with the other pen, first shaking it to make the ink flow. The sound was like someone shaking a bottle of nail polish, the unseen pellets whacking the glass.

Clack!

After only six months of teaching, Miss Hendl had become skilled at reading upside down and from considerable distance. Standing behind her desk, she leaned forward, craning her neck to spy Neelie's opus. It was a name, a *boy's* name, in oversized boxy girls' school script, *Thomas Baylor Cabell.* Miss Hendl studied the technique. Neelie took her time with the B, looping and curling the ends like the letters on a fancy wedding invitation, the pen cap lodged between her teeth. To Miss Hendl, this was abuse. She took it personally that her lesson was not engaging enough to capture Neelie's attention. She was raging, and she was envious. There was so much, it seemed, that Neelie had over her: her youth and her looks but also her friendships, not only with the other girls in the class but with boys. Who they were and however many, Miss Hendl had no idea—Brenner was a girls' school, after all—but she imagined them legion.

She tried rising above it.

Braced against the desk, she kept talking, a carefree maestro before an orchestra in mime, pressing upon the girls the epic poem's epic tragedy: Agamemnon's stony heart, Achilles' refusal to fight, and the woman who started it all, Helen. Hoping the timeless words of the bard would drown out the offending din, Miss Hendl recited from her book, which she held perched in her hand like a hymnal.

> *Control your passion, though, and your proud heart,*
> *for gentle courtesy is a better thing.*

As if entranced, she paced before her desk, hoping that Odysseus' wise counsel in the embassy to Achilles would somehow reform her charges. She had taught the girls, as she herself believed, that the Greeks of Homer's time were a higher form of men, nobler and more purely virile. She so much wanted the girls to like her.

From the back row: the snap of a page turning, the crack of the pen.

Miss Hendl winced; the sound was like a hundred twirling cheer-leaders snapping gum in unison.

That was it.

Slowly she started walking to the back of the class, the pages of her book fluttering like wings. Odysseus was all but begging Achilles back to the front and Miss Hendl kept reading, droning through the catalogue of gifts—tripods and horses and women—though if she had inserted a Buick or a VCR the girls would not have noticed.

Clack!

Miss Hendl neared the back of the room—the noise growing louder, filling her head. She felt a prickling at the back of her neck. Each *clack!* sent a tiny electric shock through her body, throwing her off course. She half tripped over the wire from Ashley Hawkins's boom box but soon recovered, carrying on unnoticed. She knew this part of the poem well enough to fudge some of the words. Her mouth was dry with fear.

Clack!

She was nearly at the back of the room. She had no idea what she would do when she arrived at Neelie's desk, and she was aware that that in itself was a problem. Still, she knew to be stealthy. She wanted to ambush the girl. Dorothy Hendl had lost face to Cornelia Wakefield Watson too many times to settle for less—like being tricked in the middle of class into mispronouncing the name of the band INXS. And the time Neelie got her to admit in front of everyone that she didn't know how to keep score in tennis. She knew "love." That was all.

As if Athena herself were favoring her, Miss Hendl knew her advantage: Neelie was nearsighted. She was also careless. The week before, she had lost another pair of contact lenses, her fourth that year. Too vain for glasses, she hunched over her desk, her nose only an inch or two from the page, her ash-blond hair hanging before her face like curtain sheers. She hadn't noticed Miss Hendl's approach, though by then everyone else in the class had. Some of them were watching, heads turned one hundred and eighty degrees, mouths wide open. Even Beatrice Ahn, who didn't like seeing anyone shamed in public, had turned to stare.

Clack!

Never before had Miss Hendl confiscated Neelie's playthings—not the Victoria's Secret catalogue she smuggled inside her vocab workbook, not even the blue-haired plastic trolls—but the teacher was sick of being humiliated. In one swift, arresting arc, her hand swept down and snatched the offending implements.

Neelie looked up at her, glaring, the gold pen cap still poking from her mouth. She let it drop. It hit the floor and rolled next to Boomie Simcox's blucher moccasin, though she didn't dare touch it. The room was silent. Slowly, Neelie stood up. She had changed after lunch into her kilt for lacrosse, and she didn't seem to notice the side was wide open, exposing her underpants, tomato red with pistachio green lace trim. Some of the girls said later she was shaking. She grabbed the edge of her desk, special for lefties, and pushed it sideways to the floor. Everything crashed to the carpet: her three-ring binder with its MTV and Save the Whales stickers, her Louis Vuitton key case, and her Warriner's *Grammar,* the spine barely split. As usual, she hadn't brought her *Iliad* to class.

Miss Hendl held the markers raised in her fist like a firebrand. She had half an impulse to slap the girl on the cheek, but the pens in her hand, she knew with some relief, prevented her. She wanted to speak, but her thoughts were as scrambled as the Achaeans in retreat, and Neelie beat her to it.

"If you don't give me back my markers, I'll have my parents *sue.*" She parked her hands on her hips and narrowed her eyes so only her lashes were visible, though Alice Mayley later said she saw tears.

Miss Hendl stared back, silent, her lower lip visibly stiffened. The pulse on her neck was chugging like a piston, her mind blank with fear. She had come so far, yet she had no idea what to do next.

"Out," she said, amazed that the words were actually hers. "I want you out of this classroom."

Neelie gathered up her loot and stormed out, turning at the door for a defiant backward look.

Three days later, Neelie hadn't stepped foot in the classroom since.

She hadn't shown up for school. Her mother, Mrs. Klostermann (divorced, remarried, and divorced), called her in sick. She spoke by telephone to each of Neelie's teachers and catalogued the symptoms: high fever, cramps, her stomach unable to keep down anything solid. But fevers were easily faked, and every self-respecting Brenner girl could make herself vomit. All the teachers, including Miss Hendl, who was the youngest and least experienced, suspected Mrs. Klostermann had been snookered. She had been snookered before. The girl was a kaleidoscopic liar.

It was written in the school's mission statement that every Brenner girl was exceptional, but Neelie was exceptionally so. Already she'd had one suspension that month after Dr. Derrigan, the biology teacher, discovered the lending library operating from her third-floor locker. Every book and video was pornographic, the library cards stamped "XXX" in red. She even drafted membership laws and charged late fines—69 cents a day. She was also a bully, arm-twisting Ninky Morrison every day since ninth grade to copy her French homework.

Miss Palatino, the drama teacher, said Neelie had stage presence, if only she would learn her lines. But she applied herself to nothing except lacrosse, where she was goalie, the first tenth grader to make varsity in seven years. In everything else she was delinquent, rarely if ever doing homework or taking notes in class, unless it was one to pass to a friend. She would have flunked out ages ago, if she hadn't been smart enough to get by, earning C's by default. She saved her worst behavior for Miss Hendl's sixth period English, as if she knew how little the teacher could take.

Sometimes it seemed even Neelie's own mother had given up on her. Neelie no longer had a nighttime curfew, for example, and whatever new gadget or clothes she coveted, her mother simply forked over the cash. The last time Mrs. Klostermann was called in to see the headmistress, she talked nonstop for more than an hour about her recently estranged husband, *the congressman*, and his latest airport-lounge tryst which, thanks to the Style section of the *Post*, had become public information. It was Mrs. Russell's last appointment that day, so she had no excuse to cut the meeting short. Fifty-seven minutes later, Mrs. Kloster-mann left, shuffling her pink Tod's across the faded Bukhara rug, past the William Morris curtains and the period furniture from the original Virginia plantation house that was the school's main building. Her eyes were swollen from tears.

"If Neelie is absent," said Miss Scheinker one afternoon from deep in her dilapidated club chair in the faculty lounge, eyes blinking as if in dream sleep, "that is because she is ashamed to have been defeated in front of her peers." More than twice Miss Hendl's age, Miss Scheinker was the department head, as well as the younger woman's mentor. She had taught at the school for thirty-two years and had spent a good part of that time, when she wasn't teaching, in that same leather chair. Like the Brenner girls, Miss Scheinker was native to Alexandria, but she had attended the public school, which, as far as they were concerned, meant she might as well be from Omaha. Back in September, when she gave Miss Hendl her class lists, she had ticked with a fine-point automatic pencil the names of students who were *First Families of Virginia*. The students called her "the Wanker."

"You did well," she told Miss Hendl, who was likewise a product of public schooling, "though I always say the girls should be taught to put away their toys on their own."

Miss Hendl had an urge to hug the woman, but as Miss Sheinker was holding court on her throne, Miss Hendl couldn't figure out how to get low enough to do the deed without falling forward. Nevertheless, she felt vindicated—victorious. She pictured herself marching like some ancient Greek hero through her own triumphal arch in glory. Neelie, she thought, was squashed for good.

In Neelie's absence, the thirteen students remaining in the class were pacified, sitting stiffly forward in their molded plastic seats, respectfully taking notes or at least seeming to, their faces flaccid and blank. Ninky even asked a question, her first since January. She raised her hand and asked Miss Hendl to spell the word *hubris*, which she did, though be-grudgingly, as she had introduced that word in the semester previous and *hadn't she used it every day since?* Yet for three days, the girls were on best behavior—no laughing fits, no protracted trips to the bathroom, no whining. They were absolutely hushed.

Miss Hendl was delighted each day to complete her lesson plan, and she realized now how much time had been lost from having to ask Neelie would she *please* not hum or could she *please* put away her Smashing Pumpkins tape until after class. Friday, with a heady mingling of relief and joy, she finished the lesson with six minutes to spare. She closed her book and touched the corner hinge of her eyeglasses, checking that the screws were in place.

"You girls have been so good, I'm giving you no homework this weekend."

At once, the girls all screamed. This was the last class of the day. Fridays were shortened to six periods instead of eight, mostly to speed the girls to their Piedmont horse farms or cottages on the Eastern Shore. The weekend had begun. A roar came over the room as the girls gathered their loot for departure: book bags, binders, boom boxes, and (for the lucky few who had made JV) lacrosse sticks. In seconds, they were gone, all but Beatrice. She was Vietnamese, the only nonwhite girl in the class, and one of only three tenth graders whose hair was not blond. Even the one Jewish girl in the grade was towheaded. By February of that year, Bea had read every novel in the upper school library. She was often the last to go, sidling up to Miss Hendl to ask her to recommend some new author or book. She used the city library now.

Miss Hendl stacked her books on the desk and scooped them up, holding them against her chest in a fashion not unlike the Brenner girls themselves.

"Turn off the lights when you leave, Bea," she said, making her way to the door. Bea followed her out. Miss Hendl got the feeling that the girl was aiming to chat her up about some new novel she had just read. She was not in the mood; she found Bea humorless. She quickened her step, adjusting her emerald grosgrain headband. It was sliding forward on her head, threatening to pop off, so she removed it and put one end in her mouth. She held it there between her teeth like a racehorse chomping a bit. She had two dates ahead of her, one that night and one on Sunday. Like the Brenner girls, she was ready for the weekend, and she didn't want to get mired in conversation.

She turned into the empty hall, then sprinted down to her office.

"Miss Hendl!" Bea's voice rebounded against the white cinder-block walls. She stood on the landing, leaning over the central rail, wide-eyed at her teacher one flight below. "Your pocketbook!" She held the bag at a distance, respectful of its contents. The chestnut brown satchel was nearly new; Miss Hendl had just purchased it from the Coach store in Georgetown after having equivocated for two months: Should she splurge or should she not? Only afterward did she realize that five of her students had the exact same style, but in colors more daring, oxblood or black.

This was the second time in a month that Bea had saved Miss Hendl from losing her pocketbook. Plus there was the time she found her gloves in the parking lot. Sometimes Miss Hendl thought Bea lingered in the classroom deliberately, just to see if she could make herself useful. She took the pocketbook and thanked her, turning away to conceal the embarrassed blush racing across her cheek.

They had planned to meet in the lobby of the Radisson. It was a public space, poised at the north end of Pentagon City next to Macy's, and she figured if any of these strangers tried something untoward, all she need do was flag a hotel detective. Having sat through several of these dates already, she knew by face, if not by name, the lumbering plainclothes policemen who guarded the lobby.

Her prospect tonight was Calvin Nadler: tall, black-haired, wire-rimmed glasses, or so she had been told. The dating service, which had cost five hundred dollars to join, was called Off Campus Connections, catering only to graduates of what they termed the "elite colleges." That meant graduates of the Ivy League and Seven Sisters plus a few extras thrown in for diversity, Stanford and MIT. Miss Hendl did not exactly qualify, having taken her degree from UMass, but she had been allowed into the fold by virtue (thank goodness) of an upper-level seminar she took one semester at Mount Holyoke. The class, which she considered one of the high points of her education, was entitled "Latin Lyric and the Latin Lover."

It had been her mother's idea to try the dating service. Her mother even paid the fee. No one in her family had attended any of the qualifying institutions, and she wanted her daughter to "marry in." She heard about the service from someone in her garden club—she had just joined a garden club—and since she never heard her daughter mention any dates with men, she wrote out the check. Of course, Mrs. Fastowe never heard much of anything from her daughter, as Miss Hendl rarely called her. It was she who always initiated contact, each time posing the same probing questions, such as, *Are you seeing anybody?* Or, *Did you have your hair cut yet?* She was convinced that if Dorothy wore it short in a bob she would attract a man who was ready to commit.

Miss Hendl had never thought of joining a dating service herself. But she went along with the idea. Not so much because she wanted to please her mother, but because she was afraid of the consequences of not pleasing her.

So far, Miss Hendl had met six men from the dating service. They were graduates of places like Harvard, Yale, or Penn, but they had all been different, a breakfast cereal variety pack. She hadn't clicked with any of them, but then she didn't necessarily believe in chemistry. Of the six, only two had asked to meet her again.

She waited in the velvet hotel lobby chair, ankles crossed. The chair swiveled at the base, designed for conversation. She turned hers away from the hotel doors so as not to appear eager, and faced instead the front desk. She glanced at her watch, then raised it to her ear to check that it was ticking. Four minutes late. Calvin. When they spoke by telephone, he said he liked to be called Cal. Or was it Alvin who liked to be called Al? She felt a surge of heat rising from her breastbone up through her neck and into her head. Anxiety. She was flooded. Was this the right place? Maybe she had the wrong time. Maybe it wasn't Calvin-Alvin Nadler at all but some other man she was supposed to meet,

another stranger whose hand she would clasp once to meet, and once
again to part. She took a deep breath and released the deoxygenated air
through pursed lips, one hand covering her mouth so no one would see
her expression and think she were practicing a kiss.

She fetched the date book in her bag and turned to the page for
January 1. The month was April. She had bought the diary on Valen-
tine's Day, half-price because that much of the year had passed. She
used the January pages to record her impressions after every date, one
page for each man.

She found him on January 7. *Yes.* Calvin it was. Cal for short, but
the last name was *Nagler.* Government lawyer, SEC or something like.
She had eight names and phone numbers in all, counting the brunch
scheduled that Sunday, the former navy pilot.

First in her book was Fred Tansor (Cornell '75); he was January 1.
He had lied to Connections about smoking; his breath gave him away
before he even lit up. Twice during their meeting he touched her knee-
cap. The first time she wasn't sure it happened, but the second time she
knew, because his nail pulled a snag in her stocking. After Fred came
Mitch, then Bob. It was all in her notes. After each date, she logged her
impressions on the page under his name. The notes read like the comments she wrote on student essays, only the sentences were fragments
and the subject matter different.

> Necktie stains (probably from lunch?) (MIT '81).
> Breathes through his mouth (Princeton '77).
> Big ears, could be cute (Harvard Business '82).

Miss Hendl closed the book.

"Dory? Dory Hendl?" She swiveled to the right and smiled, flustered
slightly, despite her waiting.

"It's Cal, right?"

He nodded. She stood up and extended her hand.

"I go by Dorothy, actually." She had been Dory in college, but these
days nicknames reminded her too much of Brenner girls.

"No problem. *Dorothy.*" He nodded his head as if swilling the name in his mouth, tapping his foot on the floor perhaps for emphasis, reminding her of a horse. "Shall we have a drink here?" She nodded. She could see the bones in his face. He was handsome, sort of. His hair was thinning on top. He draped his jacket across the back of his chair with a breezy confidence and turned to signal the waiter. His face was cast in a different light, making his complexion appear gray as if he stayed too much indoors. *He's no athlete*, she said to herself, *but then neither am I.* They ordered drinks, a Chardonnay spritzer for her, a Molson for him. This was his first time out with the dating service.

"I didn't expect it to be so easy."

She blushed, taking that as a compliment. He went on.

"What I mean is, walking into a hotel and finding someone you've never met before. I thought that would be hard." She laughed.

"I've only just started doing it myself," she said. "Twice, maybe, that's all." She smiled, squinting slightly. The waiter set the drinks on the table. "You're an attorney?" She thought that was a good tactic, asking about work. He was at the IRS. He had gone to Brown. She leaned closer, hair spilling across her face. She wore it loose, no headband, no barrettes. His voice was hushed and low. Most of his work, he said, involved investigating large corporations for tax fraud. He mentioned some big cases in the news. She didn't recognize them, perhaps because she hadn't read the paper in weeks, but she was impressed.

"Really?"

"We keep making the laws tighter, but that only means these guys find new ways to wriggle out of them," he said smiling, as if that was what he liked about it, the chase.

"And you enjoy it?"

"It's fun. It's great when we bust 'em."

Miss Hendl could see how that was exciting.

"Unfortunately, the government doesn't give us commissions," he said laughing.

He had poured his beer into a glass but hadn't taken a sip. She recalled her own tax debacle ten days past. She had left everything to the last minute and filed for an extension. She wondered if he would consider that cheating. Often she suspected her students of cheating; she knew Neelie did, but she hadn't confronted her. It was easier to look the other way than go head-to-head with a Brenner parent on the Honor Code. She looked at him now. The bone across his brow was like a steep promontory, shading his eyes. He was talking about his boat, an eighteen-foot cabin cruiser he kept on the Chesapeake, but her concentration had shifted to her left instep. She had a muscle spasm. The pain was excruciating. She had to rub.

"What about you?" he asked. She had two fingers wedged inside her shoe, working it.

"I teach high school."

"That's right. I remember. Where do you teach?"

"At a girls' school. A private school."

"Which one?"

"Brenner."

"I've heard of it, of course." Miss Hendl wasn't so sure.

"What do you teach?" he asked.

"English."

"I'd better mind my grammar!" He laughed. She gave a weak smile. She had got that reaction before. She would tell some man she was a teacher and he would become withdrawn, as if he thought she might grade his elocution. Or he would wax sentimental about his third grade teacher, how much he lusted after her. Next he'd be giving her lewd glances, hoping to flesh out those schoolboy fantasies with her. Some men found her work plain boring. Cal Nagler, it seemed, landed in this camp. She wondered, *Maybe I've lost him already.*

"That's the life," he went on. "I bet you go home every day at three." She resented that assumption.

"Sometimes. When I'm not running one of the clubs. And I take a lot of work home."

The spasm subsided. She took a look at him, his short-sleeved shirt, the unremarkable necktie. He needed a haircut. He was from Missouri and his speech was slow. He would make the kind of Dad her students would snicker at, standing behind the white chalk lines at lacrosse games, if he was lucky enough to have a daughter who could cradle. She couldn't see herself asking him to the Junior-Senior Soiree in May, to which she had been assigned for chaperone duty. Maybe there was room for improvement.

"Do you have any hobbies?" he asked.

"Hobbies?"

"You know, sports or something. I used to play a lot of chess. It's like tax law. You always have to be thinking a few moves ahead." She nodded, stalling. Her mind was blank.

"I like movies."

"Me, too. I just renewed my subscription at the AFI. They had a great Lubitsch festival last month."

Miss Hendl searched her mind for a film she had recently seen. All she could think of were the films she saw on AMC. They were the only films she ever saw and she never remembered the titles. She needed a different tack.

"Actually, I read a lot."

"Any recommendations?"

"What do you mean?"

"Books. Can you recommend any books?"

She reached for her drink. It was down to the last sip. She had read a great biography during the Easter break, but what was it? That aviator woman? Or was it something on the Windsors? She let that go.

"Mostly I read what I'm teaching. Right now we're doing the *Iliad*." She paused for his reaction.

"Ah! The Greeks and the Trojans!" he said enthusiastically.

"Yes, Greeks and Trojans," she echoed nervously, unsure whether he was really impressed or whether he was making a joke of the double entendre. She was used to that with the Brenner girls. They made those jokes all the time, about condoms and penises. With Cal, she couldn't be sure. She decided to shift to another subject.

"I read magazines."

"Oh? Which ones?"

"*National Geographic. Barron's. Southern Living.*"

These were the magazines on display on the butler's-style table outside the headmistress's office at school. They were spread in a perfect fan for nervous parents to browse, waiting for their dreaded appointment. Miss Hendl had sat there nervously, too, once when Mrs. Russell called her in to say that some of the parents had not been pleased about her telling their daughters the explicit nature of the ancient Bacchanalia.

As for the magazines, Miss Hendl never touched any of them.

"And I grade a lot of papers," she added, in case what she had said was not enough.

He nodded. They were quiet. She checked under her chair for her pocketbook. His smile was gone and he reached for his beer. The dinner hour was approaching. Couples and men in business suits streamed into the hotel restaurant. She watched the small crowd collecting at the restaurant door, waiting to be seated. The corners of her mouth fell.

"I carve," Cal said.

"Sorry?"

"I said, I'm a woodcarver. Balsa. I'll show you." He unsnapped the locks of his briefcase and searched inside, a playful frown on his face. He was odd, perhaps, though no more so than the six men before him, she thought. She liked his ears, small and unassuming, like whelks.

At last he found it, an owl, small enough to sit in his palm, perched on the branch of a tree, carved from a single piece of wood. The hatch marks gave the appearance of feathers, textured and luminous, the eyes set deep and searching. The branch was very like a tree, with bulges and knots here and there on the fluted bark. It was also hollow. Watching her face, Cal raised one end to his mouth, pursed his lips, and blew. The sound was like a cello, the bow drawn on an open string. He took another breath and blew again, this time through a hole underneath. The sound emerged from under the wings, the wind lifting them slightly in the air as if they could flap and take flight. He held it out as an offering.

"It's for you."

"No. Really. I couldn't."

"I've got another just like it."

She felt profoundly touched, though she wanted not to show it. Her eyes and mouth, however, gave her away. Her features sometimes did that, betrayed her, sometimes even to students, who saw through her posturing authority to the uncertainty beneath. She felt a sadness, too, knowing that so few people in her life had ever made even so small a gesture of generosity.

She accepted the gift.

Soon they were standing up to part.

They had parked on different levels of the garage, so they said their good-byes in the lobby. He put out his hand, she offered him hers, and she felt in her knees a little quake. Her mind flashed on the possibility of a kiss, one in a very small denomination, of course, perhaps a peck on the cheek, but at that moment when the kiss might have occurred Cal's cell went off in his jacket pocket. He checked the number on the screen, looked at her apologetically, and took the call.

The kiss did not happen.

Still, in some immeasurable way, after they separated Miss Hendl felt light-headed and limber, the top flap of her shoulder bag flung open, precious contents exposed. As far as she was concerned, they might as well have shared a full-course meal, perhaps uncorked a wine, though in fact they'd had only one drink each. She walked to her car, brandishing the key in her hand, thinking, *Maybe he'll be the one.* An owl, she knew, was an omen, a symbol of wisdom to the ancient Greeks and the loyal familiar to Athena. He said he would call next week.

Inside her small apartment, she set the owl on her bedside table. Seven was a lucky number, and Cal was the seventh man she had met. She planned to spend the rest of the evening in peace and quiet on the bed. She wanted to contemplate their future together: where they would live, what kind of vacations they would take. They would lose the boat; she was prone to seasickness. The girls they would send to Brenner, if they had boys, St. Mark's. But just as she got settled in her pajamas, the phone rang.

"So what happened?" asked the voice.

"Oh. Hi, Mom."

"Don't you have anything to tell?"

"About what?"

"You know."

"No, Mother, I don't know."

"About the date. The lawyer. How was it?"

"Oh." Miss Hendl had made the mistake of mentioning the date to her mother.

"They make good husbands—lawyers. Terrible lovers, but good husbands."

"Mother."

"I'm just speaking from experience." Her last—and third—husband, Mr. Fastowe, had been a retired lawyer for a cattle growers association in the Midwest. Marrying him had been her first solid footing in what she called the "professional class." Miss Hendl was not interested in their sex life. She hardly knew Mr. Fastowe, having met him only three times. When he died ten months ago, Miss Hendl expected her mother, who lived conveniently in Chicago, to bounce back and acquire a fourth, but she instead picked up a whole new course of study, which was her daughter, though in one respect only—her prospects for marriage. No other area of her daughter's life attracted her interest.

"So how was it?"

"It was okay."

"Just okay?"

"Well, maybe a little more than okay."

"Did you make a plan to meet again?"

"Not exactly."

"What do you mean, *not exactly*?"

"Well, he didn't say anything specific, but I got the feeling—" She reached for the owl on the table beside her, clasped it in her hand.

"What kind of feeling?"

"Well, I have a bit of a hunch he'll be calling me."

"Why wait? Call him yourself. Part of attracting men is letting them know you're interested. I can't believe you never learned that."

"Thanks."

"When's the next one?"

"The next what?"

"The next date. Don't you have another coming up?"

Miss Hendl knew better this time than to tell.

"I don't know. I don't have my book."

"You should always have another man waiting in the wings."

"Yes, Mother."

There was a pause. Miss Hendl felt she had revealed enough.

"Well, then." Another pause. "I'll call you next week."

They hung up. Miss Hendl was relieved.

But the next date did not come to pass. On Sunday the ex-navy pilot called to cancel. Miss Hendl hadn't the nerve to suggest rescheduling.

Monday, Neelie was still absent. Miss Hendl waited two minutes past the bell before starting class in case she came late, but she didn't show. Tuesday she appeared, and Miss Hendl had been at Brenner long enough to know why. Thursday's lacrosse match was against Feld, Brenner's arch rival, and players had to be in school for three consecutive days to be allowed on the field. As varsity goalie, Neelie's attendance was crucial.

Class that day was quieter than it had been all the days preceding, as if the girls were expecting an explosion. They finished Book Twelve. Hektor breached the Greek wall, and the ruin of the Greek camp seemed imminent. Neelie brought none of her playthings to class, only her book and binder, and she took notes. Sometimes she would stop, put down her pen, and gaze at Miss Hendl, as if engrossed in the lesson. Miss Hendl felt she had at last won the girl's respect.

Wednesday she gave the test on Books One through Twelve. In an unaccountable wave of munificence, Miss Hendl told Neelie she could take the test another day, as she had been absent for much of the discussion, but the girl declined the privilege and took it with the group.

Miss Hendl sat back in her chair and watched the tapping of pencils on particle board desks. Neelie was genuinely reformed.

After the test, Miss Hendl stopped her on her way out.

"Here," she said, extending her hand. Inside were the markers. The gold one was missing its cap—she never found it after it rolled across the floor—so she had covered the tip in aluminum foil. It had dried up anyway, but the gesture, she thought, had meaning. She didn't want to be despised. Neelie looked at the pens as if they were untouchable, like somebody else's retainer left stranded on the lunch table. She took them.

"Thanks, I guess. *Whatever*." Neelie disappeared down the hall and into the stairwell.

That night at home she sat at her kitchen table, which doubled as her desk, grading the tests. She set the owl in front of her to keep her company as she worked, hoping Cal would call before she marked the last test, writing extralong comments to increase the odds. The grades averaged higher than usual, though Miss Hendl wondered if that was thanks to her own buoyant expectancy. She graded Neelie's last, her score a towering 91. Miss Hendl felt personally responsible, almost as if she had written the answers herself, though Neelie had learned most of the material on her own, having been absent. Miss Hendl closed her roll book. The telephone had not rung once.

The next day, during her free period, she called the dating service. Kerry, her Connections counselor, gave her two new prospects, one a Fannie Mae executive, and the other a research doctor at NIH. She penned their names in her book on January 9 and 10, leaving the navy pilot on January 8 in case he rescheduled. She wrote in the hand of her students, half-script, half-print, the letters angular and wide, unerringly feminine. She looked at the names, mannish and undiscovered, like towns on a map she had yet to visit. She felt proud of her organizing skills, lifted in a swell of possibility.

In class that day she returned the tests. They had done so well, she had brought them a treat.

" 'Ode on a Grecian Urn,' " she said and she distributed copies. She had considered giving a lesson on women in mythology—Antigone, Eurydice, Medea—but their lives were too full of suffering, their ends all tragic. Miss Hendl cleared her throat.

> *Thou still unravish'd bride of quietness,*
> *Thou foster child of silence and slow time . . .*

She was nearly whispering. After so many years, those lines still gave her shivers. Stanza two was her favorite. She got to the part about the lovers.

> *. . . never, never canst thou kiss,*
> *Though winning near the goal—yet, do not grieve;*
> *She cannot fade, though thou hast not thy bliss,*
> *For ever wilt thou love, and she be fair!*

She lingered on the word *kiss*. She sighed. She read the rest of the poem. Then she read it through again. She looked at her students. They were staring, mute. She let the silence hang in the air, hoping to make a statement. Then she turned to the books stacked on her desk and extracted one on the bottom. It was an art book, oversized with thick glossy paper, bought on remainder at the Super Crown in McLean.

"By now you can probably recognize some of the gods and heroes," she said. She sat herself on the desk and held the book up for show. It was a book of Attic vases. Lisbet Jenner, who'd been tested three times to get an LD diagnosis just to take her PSATs untimed, called out first, pointing to a figure bending at the waist, lacing his shoes, wings spread across his back.

"Hermes."

"Yes, that's right," said Miss Hendl. Alice spoke up next.

"Is that Helen?" She pointed to the figure of a woman gazing into a mirror, her gown diaphanous.

"Good call, Alice." Miss Hendl smiled affectionately at her charges. She turned the next page.

"That's *disgusting!*" a voice cried out. The class erupted in groans and laughter. Flustered, Miss Hendl looked down at the scene in the picture. It was a symposium, the figures all men, some of them reclining, others on their feet. Two men stood face-to-face in an embrace, naked above the waist.

"My stepdad says the Greeks were a bunch of queers and it's morally delinquent that we have to read about them."

The room fell silent.

Neelie had spoken.

Lisbet let out a giggle but she squelched it when Boomie gave her the look. Miss Hendl closed the book and set it on the desk. Her heart began to race.

"Do you wish to explain that remark?" she said, looking straight at Neelie. The girl's mouth went slack. The question hovered in the air like hair spray, stinging and rank. "Because if you don't plan to explain it, we'll move on to something else." She paused, having noticed the surge of her voice. "Like homework."

Alice, who fancied herself a writer, made a request.

"Can we please have a creative writing assignment? *Please?*" Other girls seconded her, their voices just this side of whining. Everyone knew creative assignments were graded more leniently than any other kind of work. Miss Hendl gestured for quiet. Her hand was shaking. Her wall had been breached, but she still felt control.

"Please, Miss Hendl, can we?" cried Lisbet.

Miss Hendl felt a shifting inside, like something changing shape, the way a sandbar reforms itself from tide to tide. Until then everything had been going so well.

"Since you've mostly been good—" The voices roared. She waited for their attention before starting again. "You've been so good, I'll say okay." They cheered. In moments like this they seemed to love her, and she could almost love them. "How about writing a story for homework?

But you have to base it on one of the myths we've studied. The Greek myths."

Just then the fire alarm sounded. They filed out in practiced twos, leaving their books and boom boxes in the phantom blaze.

Outside, Miss Hendl watched as the girls lined up silently on the playing field. They formed four columns, one for each grade of the high school (grades one through eight occupied a separate building across campus), arranging themselves alphabetically, A's in front. The wind was blustery, and the girls had to hold down their skirts or the gusts would lift them, flinging them up and inside out, like upside-down lamp shades. The first girl in every row turned and counted the heads behind her, chin raised, pointing magisterially at the string of bored faces. For the tenth grade, that girl was Bea.

To Miss Hendl, there was something ghostly about this procedure, as if the girls were rehearsing themselves for death. The numbers were never right anyway, what with absences and orthodontist appointments and early dismissal for games away. A moment's glance at the slouching row of tenth graders showed several girls missing. Neelie, for one. Miss Hendl thought of reporting her absence but decided not to. She'd had enough scrapes with that girl.

The fire marshal blew the horn to signal the end of the drill, and the girls broke from their chaste rows into their usual dawdling chaos. Miss Hendl took a detour downstairs to the faculty lounge bathroom. She never used the regular stall toilets if there was any chance a student would walk in. The wind had made a mess of her hair, but her brush was in her pocketbook, which in the hubbub of the drill she had left in the classroom. At least the day was done.

When she returned to the classroom it was empty. The girls had raced back before her, grabbed their stash, and left. The pocketbook was on her desk. Hadn't she left it hanging from the chair? She wondered.

The art book, at least, was where she left it on the table. She looked closely at the back cover. It showed a black-figure vase with three women running and brandishing scourges. Alecto, Tisiphone, and Megaera, the swift, avenging Furies. Or were they flying? Their heads were wreathed with serpents, their prey before them—a beautiful woman. Young and lithe.

Brenner beat Feld, 5 to 4. Neelie was the star without having to score. Three times she blocked the Feld ball from the goal, spreading her body across the mouth of netting like a human spider, darting back and forth across the scoring pen with an uncanny combination of speed and bulk to stop the tiny hurtling globe. Dressed as for combat, she could absorb astounding impact, her stick a fearless extension of herself. Miss Hendl watched the game until the half and went home. It depressed her, how her students cared more about sports than schoolwork.

She stepped into the kitchen. The message light on her phone machine blinked. One message. She crouched by the machine to listen. It was from her mother, asking if she had called anyone special, by which she meant *Cal*. Miss Hendl erased her message before the end. She sat down at the table. The pale wood owl looked at her forlornly.

She waited, but Cal did not call. Nor did she call him. She reviewed her lessons for tomorrow, though she knew them well already. Before turning to bed, she heated a cup of milk on the stove to help her sleep. She set the cup on the table and removed the owl. She opened the cabinet above the stove and tucked it there among the spices. That way she would see it sometimes, searching for chervil or oregano. Sitting at her table, she took out her date book and turned to the pages with the names of her next prospects. She doodled around the edges of the paper as if making a frame. She would call them tomorrow.

At school the next day, the girls were irrepressible. It was Friday, and Mrs. Russell had ordered all classes shortened three minutes for a morning victory rally on the field. The giddiness bubbled over the rest of the day, and by the time her sixth period class came tumbling into the room, Miss Hendl had given up starting Book Thirteen. Instead, she let them read their stories aloud.

Alice volunteered first. Her story was based on the myth of Persephone and the pomegranate, which made everyone snicker, since she had written practically the same story in seventh grade. Boomie's story was about Medea, except the Jason in her version came back driving a red Miata. Bea wrote about a Penelope who spends her life in Saigon waiting for her husband to return from America. He never did. Her story was longer than everyone else's, and when she finished reading, there were amplified yawns from the back row. Miss Hendl didn't look to catch the offenders. She glanced at her watch.

"I guess we have time for one more," she said. For the first time in weeks, Neelie's hand slid upward, cupped like a snake. She was the last volunteer.

"Do you have a story?" asked Miss Hendl.

"I do, and it's awesome. I based it on Helen of Troy." The class cooed, impressed. Miss Hendl felt she had no alternative.

"Go ahead, then," she said. Retreating to her desk, she sat, arms folded across her chest.

" 'Once upon a time was a princess, and her name was Helen. She lived in the great walled city of Alexandria with her husband *Manny Laius.*' " She paused at the name, which she overenunciated to drive home the pun. " 'But he was homely and dull.' "

Alice and Lisbet giggled, covering their mouths with ink-stained hands. Neelie's face stiffened in restraint.

" 'One night, Manny's business colleague came to their house for dinner. He was handsome and tall, and that night, after dessert, Helen decided to run away with him. His name was *Fred.*' "

More giggles. Miss Hendl looked around the room. The girls were all staring at the ceiling or into their laps, avoiding eye contact. Miss Hendl glanced at the wall clock. In less than two minutes, the bell would sound.

"Are you sure you have time to finish?" she asked Neelie. The girl looked up from her desk stunned, as if she had forgotten where she was. She nodded and returned to her tale.

" 'So she ran off with Fred to his McMansion in Potomac. But Fred, she discovered, had a problem. He drooled. He drooled so much that all his neckties were stained with spit, so she dumped Fred and ran off with his neighbor, who kept a cruiser on the Chesapeake. Helen found him much more exciting, and no drool. His name was *Mitch.*' "

Boomie and Ashley eyed Miss Hendl for her reaction; she registered nothing.

" 'But soon Mitch made her sick with the way he breathed through his mouth, panting like a dog. So Helen left Mitch for *Cal.*' "

Neelie sneaked a glance at Miss Hendl.

" 'For a while, Helen was happy. Cal was not athletic, and his skin was sort of gray, but he was handy around the house—' "

All the girls were laughing, except Bea. Her head was down, her hands folded in her lap. Miss Hendl uncrossed her arms and clasped her hands, rubbing them together. Then she crossed her arms against her chest again the other way. Beneath her clothes, she was burning, flashes of heat and panic pulsing through her body. The names in Neelie's story were the names in her date book. Miss Hendl knew it, and the students knew it, and that was why they laughed.

For a moment she considered marching up to Neelie and snatching the story from her hands, but the battle, she knew, was already lost. Any retaliation now would be only a Pyrrhic victory, and that wasn't what she wanted.

She had no choice but to let the girl finish the tale and pretend she felt nothing. She thought of all the humiliation standing in bars and hotel lobbies waiting for strangers. The way she had practiced small talk, the hours spent choosing this dress or that blouse, the phone calls that were only promises, undelivered. Things no Brenner girl could ever imagine, things they would never endure. She might never get past this juncture in life, as if trapped inside a stockade she could neither see nor breach. She had looked on characters in stories and books as a way of denying herself, but even her students had seen through that. Nothing could protect her, not hotel detectives, not Kerry from Connections nor her mother, not the owl, and certainly not herself. She was moving through life as through a crowd of strangers, connecting to no one. All these bodies in the room with her now, these half girls, half women, they were strangers, too, people she might meet again, as indeed she would on Monday and innumerable days after that until the school year ended in June. The Brenner girls would remain forever alien, no matter how many frailties or family secrets they revealed. She would never be like them; try as she might, she could never have their ease or assumptions, whatever she did.

Perhaps when they were older they would look back on this differently. They had acted with the cruelty of youth. They knew nothing of life as a woman for whom wealth or beauty was not an assumption. They saw themselves as wondrous as Helen; perhaps one day they would see themselves betrayed, as Medea.

WIVES

THE MAGINOT LINE

They stood on the pavement seven inches apart, face-to-face, so close the breath from Rick's lips tickled her nose. For Kim, standing beside him in the full blast of midwinter sun was infinitely more difficult than walking the twelve blocks down Broadway. She didn't have to face him, just look ahead as they walked south. She didn't mind that it blinded her. Four times he had made her laugh so hard she buckled over, clasping at her waist. And he flattered her, serving tributes like a waiter in a four-star restaurant, saying she looked *very* Montana Boulevard (no matter she'd never been there). As long as her feet kept moving she felt safe.

But there was no walking farther. Here was where she lived. She couldn't pretend otherwise; he knew the address. Two weeks before, he had sent a postcard announcing his visit, a still from the war dance scene in *Duck Soup*: the cabinet and citizens of Freedonia on all fours, kicking their feet in the air behind them. It was a loaded gesture; their first date, thirteen years before, had been a double feature of *Duck Soup* and *Co-conuts*. She had no idea why he had chosen to resurface in her life right now. Her first thought was that he must be in trouble—he needed money or maybe he was ill. But that, it seemed, was not the case. She had long ago accepted the possibility that they would never meet again, and that had come, in the end, as a relief, as it meant one less fantasy floating in her head, one less distraction. To see him now was especially peculiar. She was five weeks pregnant and she had not told even her husband. She felt herself in a kind of wilderness, without a map. Until two months ago, she had no idea where Rick was living—or *if* he was living. She never would have guessed to find him in some small town north of San Francisco, working in a casino. But he had found her e-mail address through some search engine, and they had reconnected in that way that was both real and so synthetic. Once they got started, it seemed they had hardly been apart.

Of course communicating was easy when she had only to look at a computer. For weeks he sent her messages that bordered on confession, however fleeting and illusory. Talking live and in person was a challenge. Words that would have been flat or one-dimensional onscreen became subtle and ambiguous—if not fraught with innuendo—when delivered with gestures and glances. It would have been easier if he didn't look so good, but he did, the lines around his eyes and mouth softening him in a way that made him seem especially vulnerable. So vulnerable, in fact, that soon after he walked into the diner where they met that morning for breakfast, she found herself listing in her head the reasons that seven years before, they had parted.

1. He's cheap;
2. he's dishonest;
3. he's sarcastic.
4. He still owes me two thousand dollars.

She stepped into the shade of the awning.

"This is it?"

She nodded.

"I thought a little elf would come out with a dolly and whisk you away."

She laughed.

"He's on his lunch break," she quipped. "At the toadstool." She wished she could be quick-witted, too. He looked down—at her shoes? Had she stepped in something? All that caffeine, she was paying for it now.

"It's been great."

"What?" She knew what he meant but she wanted to extend the conversation. She wanted to keep glancing into his eyes, those blue crystalline circlets, bluer than hers, which had led her once to reason that they should fuse. Andy's eyes were brown, and she loved him—she loved his innate gentleness and his knack for solutions—though she loved the totality of his face more than any one feature. To look in Rick's eyes was like stepping into the quiet of a church, the whir of sirens and the jangled street noise falling away. Her mind became hushed. She found it sublimely seductive. She wished they were still in the restaurant, where they had lingered so long people were tucking into lunch.

"Seeing you is great. We should do it again in another seven years."

She laughed nervously.

"Seriously, I enjoyed it."

"I did, too."

There was a pause. She noticed his coat, how wrinkled it was. She wondered if it got that way in the restaurant, or if it was already. She suspected the latter.

"I have a meeting today, but not until later."

"Oh?" She fingered the buttons on her coat.

"Not until four, actually."

There was a pause. He was in town to settle some business regarding his mother's estate. She had died recently. Kim's mother had died three years before, and the loss became a spur to marry. Andy was willing, and he was sympathetic. He was older, and he had lost both of his parents already.

"I need something to do in the meantime."

"Like what, a museum?" This was a feint; in all their years together, Rick never once stepped foot in a museum.

He pushed out his bottom lip in a manner she took as provocative. There was another pause. For twelve blocks they had talked and all the while she had longed for an interval of silence. Now there were gaps in the conversation and she felt wary. The thought of inviting him upstairs was fogging her mind. He was so unlike the man she had married. The interior of her apartment was the embodiment of Andy's taste: the tight-back velvet sofa, the matching club chairs, the table in oak, not unlike a bordello in a Western. She didn't care for it, but she had agreed to it in much the same spirit as she had entered her marriage, like a visitor to a foreign country whose unfamiliar customs nourished her detachment. She could not picture Rick there, and she assumed his own place the antithesis: white canvas director's chairs; a sisal rug; a bare couch; each piece chosen purely for function. Or hardly any furniture at all.

"Do you still have those crystals?"

"You mean the prisms?"

"Right—prisms."

She nodded. She had three of them, each one a different geometric configuration: one with sixteen sides, one with twelve, and one a pointed obelisk like Cleopatra's Needle. She had bought them years ago at a flea market. Back when they were a couple, she kept them on the windowsill of her apartment and Rick would play with them mornings in bed, after he stayed over. He would hold them at different angles to the sun and challenge her to find the rainbow cast on the wall. It was a game she remembered well. He was turning up the heat.

"I loved those things."

"I know. I should have given you one."

"It's not too late." He nudged gently at her elbow. *"Give and let give."*

"I remember the time you dropped one on my foot."

"Oh." He looked regretful for a moment. "A small price for being worshiped."

"You call that worship?"

"A *form* of worship." He paused. "Does Andy like those prisms?"

He was pushing it now. She didn't like it, though that was probably his intention. She didn't answer.

"Enough about him." He touched her cheek. "What about us?"

He was being ironic, speaking in cliché to protect himself, but the touch was sincere. It worked with her because, like him, she was guarded, too. She felt herself regressing. It was the ancient reptilian brain; she was taking cues that were based not in the present but in the distant past. She loved the way he touched her. No one else touched her like that, not even Andy, though he was affectionate in his own way. He'd put his arm around her shoulders or around her waist or take her by the hand, and always on occasions that would warrant such gestures. But he never touched her in that way that was gratuitous, without purpose or function, merely to touch. Rick was both solicitous and impromptu, and Kim had forgotten how much she liked that.

"I've played this out a bunch of times in my head," he said.

"Played out what?"

He looked beyond her to the lonely park. They were nearly the same height, which delighted her, as if that made them equal. Andy was tall; she always felt she was stretching herself to be with him.

"Usually it's night—"

"It's almost noon—"

"—you rub up against my chest and give me a big open-mouth kiss."

Her face suddenly felt hot. He was teasing, but she liked it. She turned away. She wanted to defend herself with a clever retort, but she didn't have one. She stared at the glass doors of her building, scuffed and dirty. She should just let herself in, but that required extreme volition: finding the key, inserting it into the lock, opening the door, and shutting it behind her. She had only a faint desire to say good-bye.

She had thought this would be simple: bacon and eggs, a quick kiss good-bye on the cheek. Instead she met with the uncomfortable truth that she was still attracted to him. This was not what she wanted. She couldn't live with division in her life: to be married to one man, yet have feelings for another. Her first anniversary was five months past, yet she was still trying to figure out which parts of her life should be different now that she was a wife.

Maybe this was a trap, but she felt illimitable and buoyant, her five senses on red alert, as if the air were charged with the latest psycho-pharmacological miracle.

The smell of river stung the air.

She wasn't telling him she was pregnant.

"Your glasses are crooked," she said. She stepped closer, then lifted both hooks of his frames with her fingers and tucked them behind his ears. Her hands lingered a moment, grazing his neck. She wished she could do it again. She wanted to touch him, to care for him. He seemed so much to need her, and that made her feel worthwhile, more capable of love, as if with him she had more love to give. Andy had needs, too, but he had a habit of camouflaging them. Or he had them encrypted in a code she couldn't break, and he never laid them bare.

"That's nice," he said.

He took her hands. She felt the heat travel through her body like a double bourbon. How soft his hands and how warm.

"Show me your apartment."

"Are you serious?" She shoved her hands in her coat pockets.

"Of course. Why not?"

"It feels like you're testing me." She was telling the truth. She pictured him in her apartment and she pictured them lying in bed. Had she known she would arrive at this situation, she would have stopped responding to his e-mail. Maybe it was just their bodies that craved each other, some genetically determined compulsion for one another, fooling her to think there was anything personal.

"Come on. I want to see more of your life."

She let out a loud, obstreperous laugh. Life for her was becoming intricately more complex with every split second, the thousands of invisible cells dividing within her at an unstoppable rate. Cells that cared less about loyalty or love. Cells with already a destiny. They weren't even alone.

"Kiss me," she said.

Rick looked perplexed.

"*Kiss* me."

She pulled him close and, pressing her mouth onto his, she entered her tongue. There was so much space, like an unimpeded sky. She roamed the hollow of his cheeks, his teeth, the roof of his mouth, her tongue a searchlight. He let out a soft moan. He enjoyed this, she could tell. She had forced this junction, and she hoped that would be the end of it. This was an experiment, mingling their bodies in an exchange of fluid, though *fluid* reminded her of what else was happening in her body. She wanted control. This could be the last time in her life she might have that option, so she had kissed him. Yet having done so, she had no idea where to stop. What kind of control was that?

He stroked her head, then pulled slightly away.

"Let's go upstairs," he whispered. He kissed her back. He was taking charge. She felt suddenly comfortable following. She had constructed in her mind a kind of Maginot Line, a faltering barrier, her body already surrendered. She was giving in. Andy would be gone all day. If nothing else, she at least knew this: She was sure she could not get pregnant.

"Okay."

She shook her bag and groped for the keys. Her mind had become a shallow reflecting pool. She had no faculty for speech. She felt completely aroused. Her bag was oversized and black and she could find the keys only by feeling, her gaze fixed on Rick. She didn't remember him being so serious nor so focused. She touched on her wallet, a gift from her husband, and she thought, *I married a man who gives me wallets.* But it was a beautiful wallet. And inside one of the pockets he had slipped one of their wedding photos, reduced to size. At first she thought the gesture was purely romantic, but by and by, as she came upon the snapshot so many times a day *every day*, she realized he meant it as a reminder. As if to say to her this:

You're married now. Don't forget.

The message was not without cause, as her track record had not always been perfect.

She shook the bag again and heard the muted clatter of keys. Her hand landed on them. Six on one ring, half of which opened doors that were no longer part of her life: the apartment of a friend who had moved to Vermont, an office where she no longer worked, the key to her mother's loft, though they sold it after she died. She was gadding about the streets of Manhattan with keys to nowhere feigning a sense of community and power. She lifted them out.

"Open the door," he said.

She fumbled for the key to her building. A woman appeared in the lobby. Kim recognized her as one of the people who saw the man in 3B for hypnotherapy. Dr. Kane. Once, Kim ventured to ask her what that treatment was like. She was curious, though she didn't dare tell Andy. The woman responded with a gush of words mostly about herself, except to say that Dr. Kane was brilliant. As for the actual treatment, she had only just started, so she had little to report.

The woman opened the door from the other side and stepped through, holding it ajar.

"Hey!" she said. She wore a fluffy red fur jacket and a hat like a cloche. She was older than Kim, but she dressed with a youthful flamboyance.

"I just had the most amazing experience!"

"Oh?" Kim's head was reeling.

"It was my first day of dream work! He put me in a trance, but it was just like real life. A total three-dimensional experience! I had this vision—I was flying over the Himalayas, and I got in touch with my kindred animal spirit!"

Kim glanced at Rick. He had that half smile.

"And that is—?" he asked with great deference.

"A kind of bird, but a really big one," she said, beaming.

"Like a hawk?" He loved this; Kim could tell. As for herself, she felt unmoored. She had made a decision, and the conversation was proving a distraction. She was beginning to resent it.

The woman shook her head, delighted by the attention. "No. A crane. A *sarus* crane."

"No kidding!" exclaimed Rick, seeming thoroughly intrigued.

Kim was skeptical. He could fake it, she knew. *No doubt he's a superb croupier,* she thought. *He can chat up anything on legs.*

"He looked them up in his book—Dr. Kane did—and read me the description. They have special mating dances, and they pair for life!"

She turned to Kim. "He's a doll, Dr. Kane. Are you still thinking of doing it?"

Kim was mortified. She didn't want Rick to know she was interested in hypnotherapy. He would only make fun of her—affectionate fun, but still it would hurt. Despite his curiosity he wasn't genuinely interested in this stuff; he was entertained.

Years ago, when finally they broke up, that was how she reasoned it, that to Rick, human attachments were merely entertainment. Or worse— they were sport.

Maybe that was how he regarded their reunion today, as a form of sport. For all she knew she was just another card player at the table, and he was counting the deck, manipulating the game.

"Is this your husband?" asked the bird woman.

Kim's keys slipped from her hand and crashed on the pavement. Rick picked them up and dangled them from his fingers.

"Brother," said Rick.

Kim was awestruck. He gave the lie with such poise.

"Funny—you don't look alike," said the woman. Still holding the door, she peered at them more closely. "It's the eyes, I guess." She hopped down onto the pavement, said good-bye, and vanished.

The door softly closed.

Rick handed her the keys.

"Where were we?" he asked waggishly.

Kim looked at the keys in her hand. Then she looked at him. "I don't think I can do this."

"Whoa—did I miss something?" His voice was cavalier, but she noticed something change across his cheek. A tension that wasn't there before. Around the lips. He looked dismayed.

"Don't ask why. I just can't."

There was nothing more she could tell. She had wanted him. She would probably continue to want him, but she could no longer privilege one desire against others. There was Andy, and if that was not enough, soon there would be someone else, a population uptick of fifty percent.

She was trapped by the limits of her own self-knowledge. She had only the next eight months to catch up.

She could bring him upstairs or go to his hotel, but there would forever be a witness.

She inserted her key in the lock and pulled open the door. It took unfamiliar effort. He cleared his throat.

"Come to think of it, I have to make some calls before this meeting." He was saving face. Like her, he didn't want to be the loser.

"I'm sorry," she said.

"Sorry for what?"

"You know."

He smiled, and she could tell from his smile that he was still a person who would go to any length to avoid pain. She shrugged. They were dissembling, both. It was the best she could do. She felt like a cheat. He would know the rest soon enough.

She pressed a finger to his lips and kissed his brow.

She turned and passed through the door. It closed behind her, brushing her shoulder with a soft thud.

Upstairs, she threw her bag on the floor and collapsed into the big club chair.

She saw her kindred animal spirit as a puma. Solitary, furtive, swift in flight.

PINK IS FOR PUNKS

The bed was never big enough for three. It was king-sized, but the two girls, Mia and Sam, could never be still, their limbs and arms reaching at angles, and they were growing, their faces changing daily, imperceptibly. Already, Samantha was talking about clothes and makeup, though she was only nine. Under her shirt rose two small points of breasts.

They came to the bed clutching their possessions like refugees boarding a ship. Mia brought a coloring book, a box of crayons, and her Winnie the Pooh. Sam carted a hairbrush and the white plastic lanyard she had found that day at school. The tiddlywinks would never snap and fly pressed against the blankets, but they brought them, too, the game a gift from their father. They made the bed their playroom and sparred for their mother's attention.

Sometimes Clare thought of getting rid of this bed—it seemed bad luck to keep it—and buying a smaller one, as if that could check the invasion. But they would probably prefer the crowded intimacy of a smaller mattress, a queen or a full. It would bring them closer together, and they would find only more cause to loiter. She could move the television into the living room, but she knew that was not the attraction, either. So she kept the television in her room as her only diversion when they clambered on top of the throws and pillows, four-legged and wild-eyed like the lemurs on the TV nature programs sometimes flickering behind them on the grainy screen.

"Do you have any gum?" asked Sam. Her face was round and large, her domed, tapered eyebrows vaguely wistful. She had painted her fingernails white the day before, but the enamel already was chipped.

"Gum?"

Clare was stalling. She was so tired that to reach for her pocketbook was a strain. She could swear she felt a stinging down there, though the test results that day again were negative. Three times she had given blood samples, though Dr. Meier reassured her false negatives were impossible. He told her today he would not write slips for any more tests.

Four months earlier, at her insistence, Daniel had moved out. He had left this bed, and Clare was convinced he had left her some disease. But the doctor said her symptoms were emotionally induced. Like a phantom pregnancy, she had a phantom STD.

"I don't know about gum," she answered, tucking Sam's hair behind her ear. "Did I promise you some? Look in my bag."

"Where is it?"

"On the floor."

Sam leaned over the side of the bed and pulled the bag by the strap, the crease in her brow a clue to her determination. What was it—mother's intuition or some innate female cattiness? Somehow Clare knew Sam would never end up like her. The girl had more sophistication at nine than Clare had when she graduated from high school.

Good luck, she thought resentfully, *to the man who tries deceiving her.*

"I want gum, too," said Mia.

"I called it first," Sam snarled, elbows deep in the oversized bag.

"Wait a minute. Who said you could have gum? It's practically bedtime."

"Can I have some?" asked Mia, the encroaching shrillness in her voice a prelude to whining. Clare could see the tangles in her hair. Clare had no gum. Sam pulled out a lipstick and toyed with it, turning the bottom of the gilded case so that the sleek coral tube rose and fell, a waxy cylindrical jack-in-the-box.

"Did your father call?" She had come home after the girls' dinner. They ate at six. The baby-sitter cooked. Three times a week it was chicken, fried, baked, or broiled. Sometimes she came home late just to avoid the smell.

"Sam?"

Sam pursed her lips, tinted like marigolds. Next she fished out a compact and examined herself in the mirror. She was enthralled.

"Did he call today or not?"

"No."

"He should have. You said he wanted to take you Saturday."

"So?" Sam said absently, fluffing up her hair for an imaginary camera.

"Today's Thursday."

"Oh." Sam looked suddenly deflated.

"Do you know what he has in mind?"

Sam applied another layer of lipstick, studying herself in the mirror.

"Sam! Answer me!" Clare was annoyed having to extract information from her own child, but she had no choice. Things had settled into a routine where Daniel made weekend plans with Sam before telling them to Clare, and thus the power between them, Clare and Sam, mother to daughter, had become inverted. This was for Clare no small cause of distress, and she wondered if she hadn't created with Sam a kind of bastard replica of her relationship with Daniel, where she had been so submissive. She felt that way now, inert and submissive, as if she were gliding headlong flat on her back downstream. She had come even to dislike the name Sam. It had been Daniel's idea to give their daughter a tomboy moniker, as if all along that was what he'd secretly wanted, a boy. It was a funny irony: A guy's guy, he was cursed with daughters.

Usually Daniel took the girls on Sundays, but last weekend he had told Clare, through Sam, that he wanted them Saturday instead. Just this once. She didn't ask why; she had quit keeping track of his social life.

"Sam—don't you have plans for Saturday?"

"*Mom*," said Sam, exasperated. "Don't ask *me*." The look on her face was manufactured, like the faces of child actors on television sitcoms, exaggerated and insincere. She was feigning indifference. It made Clare bristle. Behind all that, Sam was hurt by her father's omission, though her face said otherwise.

As the first child, Sam had become the confidante to her mother's distress. Whether in anger or despair, Clare had told Sam that Daniel was selfish, that he couldn't be trusted, that for all she knew he had given her a disease. Now she wished she could take it all back. She had wanted to punish Daniel, but the mistake had been punishing Sam. Even as she vilified him, she knew that not all of what she said was true. Still, she couldn't stop.

She touched her tongue to the roof of her mouth. Dry. She wondered if that was perhaps another symptom.

Wasn't it?

Clare was counting on this Saturday and she was irked that nothing was settled. Irked but not surprised; sometimes Daniel didn't call until Sunday morning. She needed a reprieve from mothering. She wanted to go shopping. She had Christmas presents to buy, and she wanted something for herself, something small, a chenille neck scarf or a perfume.

She didn't wear perfume, but she thought she'd give it a try.

"Did you call him?" she asked.

Sam nodded, her bottom lip pushed forward, fleshy and wet. It looked almost sexual, though she could hardly know it.

"Was there any answer?"

The child shook her head.

"Did you leave a message?"

Sam nodded.

"He'll call tonight, I guess."

"I guess," Sam echoed in a show of solidarity. She had been coached in it. But the instant Daniel walked in the door, her loyalty would flip. He gave them something Clare could not. She saw it in the way Sam leapt into his arms, wrapping her legs around him; in the way she treasured his gifts. After he left, Sam became once more Clare's child, re-orienting herself from west to east, like a young window plant shifting direction to follow the sun. Each time she watched this, Clare felt both jealousy and guilt. Jealous of the love Sam felt for her dad, and guilty, as if Clare herself were the sole cause of the child's unhappiness.

"Got any Ricolas?" asked Mia.

"Why? Do you have a sore throat?" Clare set her hand on Mia's brow, checking her temperature.

"I don't want Ricolas. I want gum," said Sam.

"I want Ricolas," said Mia. "The orange ones." Her eyes were like Sam's, green marbled with gray, but there the resemblance ended. Bony-faced and sallow, Mia seemed to lack her sister's hardiness; she was the second child, born as the marriage unraveled, a sign of its weakness rather than strength. They hadn't planned a second child; Clare had let it happen, nursing the hope that a second child would save the relation-ship. But after Mia was born, Daniel's absences became longer, his whereabouts elusive not only on weekdays but sometimes also at night.

Mia's birth, on a July afternoon, during a six-day heat wave when the rubber gloves doctors used in the hospital were self-combusting, only hastened the marriage's end.

Sam struck Mia's shoulder with the lanyard. "There aren't any Ri-colas."

"Mommy!" cried Mia. "She hit me!"

"Sam," said Clare, frowning.

"Don't you have *anything* in your bag?" Mia whined, hoping perhaps to capitalize on her status in that moment as victim. Clare found her hard to resist. She had been a younger sister herself, and too often she heard her own small plangent voice in Mia's. She rummaged through the bag and found a packet of breath mints, three identical pellets, oval and white. She bought them as a substitute for conversation, offering them to people when she had nothing to say. She would open the pert, decorated tin and display the powdered, white pastilles, extolling the taste. She'd gone through several brands in succession, though this particular brand she had kept to herself. It was imported from Italy, and though she liked the taste, the name, given her circumstances, was a little indiscreet: *Mental.*

"How's this?" said Clare. Mia put out her hand. "There's one for each of us," she added, knowing she needed to appear fair to avoid a fight.

"One of the eggs started hatching today," said Mia. She was in nursery school, and her teacher had furnished the classroom with an incubator and six fertilized eggs. Two of them had hatched last week but the chicks had died. "I saw the crack. I saw *inside.*"

"You did *not,*" countered Sam.

"I did so."

"No, you didn't!"

"Yes, I did. Mommy, tell her. I saw inside the crack."

Clare brushed the hair from Mia's eyes and smiled. She hated that tone in her voice.

"Stop it," Sam shouted to her sister, waving the lanyard as if to dismiss her. Mia's jaw was working the mint.

Mia's face was blank. "Stop what?"

"*Crunching.* Mommy said."

Clare stirred. "What did I say?"

"She's making that noise," said Sam, her insistence excruciating. "Like chewing ice. You said no chewing ice. You said it was vulgar."

"When did I say that?"

"Yesterday."

"Oh. Well, it's definitely a sound that doesn't make people want to be around you," she said pointedly. Certainly *she* didn't want to be around right now, not around *them.* She'd give anything to be somewhere else. In a movie theater, perhaps, a bucket of popcorn on her lap. Or at the beach, flat on her back in the sun.

What other assertions had she made that she couldn't now remember? And what form had they taken? Were they quick aphorisms or whole histories, the entire story of her life, before Daniel and after? He had taught her so many things: how to snorkel off a boat, how to track the bond market, how to fuck. She slid her hand up her trouser legs and peeled off her socks, dropping them to the floor. *This house is a sty*, she thought. If she had a day alone maybe she could do something about it. She hadn't vacuumed in weeks. Exposed to air, her feet felt tingly and elastic. She clasped her hands around her right foot and massaged the hardened flesh, the balls of her feet, the heel.

"Can I do that?" Sam asked, pointing to Clare's foot.

"Can I?" Mia was desperate.

Clare knew better than to decide between them. She sat on her heels and extended her hands faceup.

"All done."

Sam nestled against her, using her head to pry a passageway between Clare's rib cage and elbow. She stretched her legs parallel to her mother's, though her toes reached only half as far. She had painted her toenails, as well.

"I got my lines for the pageant."

"Oh?"

"A whole page. I have to learn a whole page of lines."

"Gee."

"And I tried on the wings." She was playing the angel Gabriel. Clare considered that one of her small victories over Daniel; that the girls attended a school with nuns. Not that she cared for religion herself.

Clare reached for the remote control. The slim wand lay on the red-and-gray tiled bedside table. She could only play, tape, and rewind, but holding the black panel in her outstretched hand she felt briefly omnipotent.

Retrieving the device, she knocked Mia's Pooh to the floor.

"Shoot!" Clare had made a habit of not cursing in front of her daughters, though nothing had stopped her from telling Sam the names of Daniel's girlfriends or explaining venereal disease. There was one strain of gonorrhea, she had said, that in women was asymptomatic. The one thing she had not told Sam was what she had known for sure, that Daniel had once given her crabs. She heard the returns of the last presidential election through the locked bathroom door, picking the tiny dead vermin off her body, the final, incontrovertible proof of his transgressions. But it took her another twelve months, and his own bout with syphilis, to get her to force him to leave.

Not that he'd told her he'd been infected. She found the doxycycline in his jacket pocket.

"I'll get it," Sam volunteered.

"It's mine," Mia shrieked, half under a blanket. "Pooh Bear is mine."

"I'm just *getting* it." Sam rescued the scrappy stuffed animal from the floor. She was becoming more and more like that, taking charge of even the smallest mishap, as if she sensed the need for someone to be in control. In her grip the bear seemed larger, its significance increased. Meanwhile Mia shoved three fingers into her mouth, sucking furiously in what looked like agony. The value of anything, thought Clare, is relative to whomever has his hands on it, and suffering is relative, too. She was suffering now, though she told herself things could be worse. She clicked on the television, zapped the sound to zero, and turned to the news. Sam set the bear at Mia's feet on the bed and assumed her place beside her mother.

"Want to play tent?" proposed Mia. She had drawn the edge of the blanket over her head, casting her face in shadow. Clare had to laugh.

"You look like a fallen woman," she said.

"What's a *fallen woman*?" asked Sam.

Clare touched at a lock of Sam's hair, stalling.

"Just someone," she stammered, "down on her luck."

"Sam," injected Mia, "will you *please* play tent with me?"

"Sam, your sister is asking you something."

Often Sam would join her under the covers and they'd drink tea from invisible cups. Clare would hear the exaggerated slurps and the abundant good manners, nothing like their real behavior. But Sam ignored the entreaty and Mia withdrew under the covers alone, one hand darting out from the darkness to snatch her bear. Clare heard her humming inside the tent. The sound made her want to weep. She turned to the television. A man with symmetrically gray temples was enunciating in silence and nodding, behind him a ragged map of Europe. She was thirsty. She had lingered at a bar after work with an officemate and eaten too many salted confections. They had looked like peas and twigs but were wholly man-made. Sam's elbow pressed uncomfortably into Clare's waist.

"I'm getting up," said Clare. "I need a drink of water."

Sam sprang to her feet. "I'll get it!" At the far corner of the bed, the blankets flew upward. Mia emerged from her den.

"No, let me!" But Mia couldn't extract herself fast enough from the layers of wool, and by the time she was free, Sam was nearly at the bathroom sink. Mia didn't stand a chance. Clare saw the disappointment on her face. Always when Mia looked like that, Daniel would scoop her in his arms, hold her tight, and say he could *squeeze* the sadness out of her, and every time it worked. But Clare could not gather the strength to comfort her. She felt disenfranchised herself.

"You can get it next time."

"Next time when?"

"Next time I'm thirsty."

Mia clutched her bear and sat down. Clare heard the water running from the tap. She had taught them to count to ten, running the faucet to flush out the lead. Daniel said that was ridiculous. She had taught them so many things to fear, he said. But what lessons had he taught them? Inconstancy and deceit. He hadn't wanted to leave; he begged to make amends, and for a while she let him. But when she found the antibiotics, that was it. Even now, she couldn't believe she was not infected.

In the weeks before he left, Clare weighed the pros and cons of separation so often that when he finally moved out, her biggest relief was not having to think about it. She hadn't known, however, that being alone would be so difficult. Sam and Mia were more needy with only Clare in the house. Daniel had provided for them in ways she hadn't known, and she was scrambling to make up the difference.

The water was still running. Sam was up to seven, counting louder and more slowly than necessary. That way she could keep the attention on her, though all the time she was out of sight.

"Are you thirsty again yet?" asked Mia.

"Not yet. I'm waiting for Sam, remember? How was school?"

"I *told* you. One of the eggs is hatching."

Clare made a sound denoting approval and reached for the magazine she had bought on her way home. *Vogue*. It lay on the floor beside the bed table. Sam shouted from the bathroom.

"I'm coming!"

"One of the eggs is hatching, and Mrs. Pressman says a chick will come out." Mia was shouting.

Sam emerged from the hallway holding in two hands the green plastic tumbler. It was filled nearly to the brim, as if quantity were a testament to love. Left and right the water rose against the edge, blessing the carpet. Clare met her halfway to avoid bigger spills and downed the glass in one gulp.

"Are you thirsty now?" Mia asked. She was shouting again.

Clare handed her the tumbler.

"Go."

Mia took off with the cup, and Clare returned to the bed, Sam close beside her. Mia was just now growing out of a habit of talking overly loud. It didn't bother Clare when they were at home, but on the bus or in the supermarket she felt embarrassed. People might think there was something wrong with her child. Or with her.

She turned her attention to the television. The news program was over, and *Jeopardy!* was on, the three contestants bug-eyed from nerves, smiling promiscuously, standing braced before the glittering, fateful controls. Clare heard the water running again and then the small, shuffling footsteps back. Mia's cup was not as full as Sam's, but she spilled more.

"Thank you, honey."

Mia handed off the cup, beaming, then climbed back on the bed, staking out new turf at her mother's knees. Clare took a sip purely for show and set the cup on the table. Then she picked up the thick magazine and started flipping the pages, backward first, which was cheating, since the pictures she enjoyed most were in the rear. Once through, she started again at the front, turning the thick shiny pages more slowly.

The magazine was Clare's reward. None of the clothes were anywhere near her budget, but she loved the sleek, manufactured fantasy.

Sam by now was transfixed by the television. She found the remote device under the mass of Mia's cast-off blankets and turned on the volume. The subject was mammals: fox, camels, hamsters, and yaks.

"Hamsters aren't mammals!" Sam shouted. "Mom, are hamsters mammals?"

"If they suckle their young, they're mammals," said Clare, studying a Ralph Lauren ad. If her daughter didn't know hamsters were mammals, it was her fault. She had forbidden pets in the house, hamsters and guinea pigs especially. No doubt they would give them all some pernicious disease, she thought. She pictured the vile rodent creatures scampering around her bed, dropping their contagions on the comforter, on the pillows.

"Miss Lenardi's class has a hamster," said Mia. "It made babies."

"If it's on the show," reasoned Clare, "don't you think they're right?"

Sam shrugged. She leaned closer into her mother and studied the Vogue. A blond sylphlike model, bare arms and legs, stood on a black sand beach, hands on hips, turned at the waist. Looking over her shoulder at the camera, she wore a pink halter dress, though the month was December. The clothes featured were pegged for the resort season, for women who bypassed the most bruising months of winter—February or March—in Morocco or the Caribbean. Clare had never been to the Caribbean, though she made it once halfway. The model in the photograph had almost no hips, the skin across her face taut and flawless like a porcelain mask. No doubt she was a teenager, closer in years to Sam than to Clare, which made Clare think of her age. Forty-two. Never again would her body look like that. She could be the model's mother.

She turned the page. The model was the same, only here she was costumed like a flamenco dancer: a full-length triple-tiered skirt in deepening shades of pink and a scoop-neck off-shoulder blouse. Clare noticed the pose: sitting on a rug on the sand, legs apart, her knees drawn up as if in stirrups. And she noticed how high she'd hiked up her skirt, the camera's coy hint at what was underneath. Daniel would chuckle and call it a beaver shot. She never told him so, but she had never heard that term before she met him. She found it disgusting.

"I like *that*," said Sam, pointing to the opposite page. The model was the same, but here she wore a pair of cuffed short shorts and a bolero jacket, her matching hat like a bellhop's. Everything was pink—it was a theme. Pink shorts, pink jacket, pink hat. Clare felt inadequate. She could never conform to so feminine an ideal. She smirked.

"Pink is for punks," she said.

Sam looked crushed.

"I mean, pink is for little girls." Clare paused. "It's not a color for grown-ups."

Sam pursed her lips. "Pink is for punks," she repeated, nodding. She was a quick study. Clare turned the page: the same child-model, this time in a pink strapless minidress, the attenuated skirt merely layers of taffeta bouffant. It was like a tutu. She stood on a boardwalk playing limbo, her back completely arched, her brilliant bare neck not quite grazing the bar. Circled around her, a dozen or so men watched, grinning, their skin the color of coconut shells.

"You could do that," Clare said, turning to Sam.

"I can! Watch!"

She leapt to the floor, arms extended behind her, her limber back descending. Her fingertips grazed the floor, then she pulled herself up.

"We learned in gymnastics."

Mia stared. "Do it again," she said, Clare seconding her. She was trying to teach her daughters to regard their bodies as precious and special. How many times had Daniel said that she denied their sexuality, that it threatened her? So what that she had only one lover before him. So what that she had never dreamed of half the things they did together in bed—she had always been game to try. Who was he to judge?

When she last spoke to him on the phone, Daniel called Samantha their little "nymphet," which she hated. It was a joke, he said, but she didn't find it funny. Lately, though, she had to wonder. Maybe he was right. They *were* sexual, Sam and Mia, whether they knew it or not. Clare was beginning to notice. Certainly backbends were sexual. Who knows—maybe so was sucking one's fingers. Until recently, she had been blind to this budding physicality, just as years ago she had been blind to her own. Maybe when Daniel was living with them, they had directed that energy only to him. But she saw it now, and what surprised her was that she welcomed it. She thought if they felt comfortable with that part of themselves now maybe they wouldn't end up thirty years later like her, alone.

Sam reclaimed her spot on the bed next to Clare, protecting her territory.

Mia caught sight of the pink taffeta dress in the magazine.

"Ooohhh," she cooed. She reached to touch the picture, knocking the *Vogue* from Clare's lap.

"You lost our page!" Sam exclaimed, and retrieving the magazine, she started flipping through the book in search of the tutu dress.

The game show was over. Clare had no idea who won. She turned off the television. Mia was sulking.

"What's wrong?" asked Clare.

Mia folded her arms across her chest and looked away.

"What happened in school?"

"I *told* you," she answered, still looking elsewhere. "The *egg*."

"I know. What else?"

"I drew a picture."

"Oh?"

Mia turned slowly to face her, nodding.

"Let's see it," said Clare, and the child was off.

Sam found the page she wanted and handed the magazine back to her mother.

Mia returned, a hopeful smile gracing her face.

"Look," she said.

She held out her treasure. It was a crayon drawing, the three letters of her name spelled in the teacher's block print in the lower right-hand corner. The picture itself was indecipherable. Rising in the center was a kind of ziggurat, lopsided and flat-topped, its color like primrose. Or was it a face—Clare couldn't be sure. The only elements she could make out with certainty were the sun, its rays like spokes on a wheel, and the hyacinth sky. There was also the outline of a circle, shaded in brown and misshapen, suspended mysteriously left of center. Clare folded her hands across the magazine and made the requisite sounds of awe and wonder.

"What is it?" asked Sam. She was sitting on her heels, her back as straight as the bedpost. Mia remained silent, her lips pursed to a wrinkled, contracted O, her face a shaggy-haired, miniature sphinx.

Perhaps Sam thought she could pry it out of her. "I know what it is," she said. "It's a house."

"Wrong," said Mia. It was Clare's turn.

"It's beautiful, but tell us what it is."

Mia was suddenly bashful. This was what she had wanted all along, to be the center of everything, all eyes on her.

"Do you like it?" she asked Clare.

"Of course I like it. But what is it? It looks to me like a house."

Mia didn't answer, and in the expanding moment, Clare heard the silence of the apartment house she inhabited with one hundred other people, most of them anonymous, though in the last few months she had begun to notice the women who lived alone. She heard the distant unintelligible hum of a neighbor's television, the sound track laughter playing always the same note for always the same duration. She heard the bathroom faucet dripping, clocked as a metronome. She pictured each tear-shaped drop, its bulge amassing under the tip of the cold steel orifice, the smooth weight of those collected molecules falling inevitably into the basin, every droplet a single, irretrievable loss. She felt that way, too, one inexorable moment to the next, every gesture in her working day, every aching breath at night.

"Tell us, Mia, *what is it?*"

The child turned her gaze to the picture, as if she had to make sure herself, or perhaps she had forgotten. "It's a chicken coop."

"Of course! A chicken coop! And pink! Wonderful! Where are the chickens?"

"Inside," Mia said. "They're sleeping, because they laid too many eggs." Mia paused and pointed to the odd, free-floating circle on the left. "That's an egg."

Sam folded her arms across her chest. "I don't see any *chickens*." Clare rose to Mia's defense.

"You can't see them because they're *inside*."

But Sam was unstoppable. "If it's a chicken coop, it should have chickens."

Mia was silent, searching her mother for support, then turning to the drawing as if it might offer its own rebuttal. Clare protested.

"They're inside, Sam. That's why you don't see them." She turned to Mia, softening her voice. "I love it, honey. Can I have it?" Mia stepped forward with the prize.

Sam folded her arms across her chest.

"Pink," she muttered, half under her breath, "is for punks."

Clare looked at her, astonished. Sam grew bolder.

"Pink is for punks!" She spat out the words, looking directly at Mia, and then paused, as if loading her ammunition. *"Baby!"*

A sound emerged from Mia's lips, muted at first, then loud. Clare felt her pulse rise. Mia was wailing. Clare opened her arms, her heart slamming into her throat. Mia half crawled, half was lifted onto her mother's lap, her arms and legs stiffened in distress. She was like a mollusk, the hard shell casing concealing the most simple of organisms. The magazine crashed to the floor, its pages folded under and awry, and the drawing fell, too. Clutching her lanyard, Sam retreated to the other side of the bed, which had been her father's side. Clare stroked Mia's head to calm her. She could hold Sam accountable, but that wouldn't completely be fair. Sam was only parroting what she had heard. With Daniel gone, the children were learning in ways Clare had never expected: from observation, from falsehood, from sleight of hand. They seized on anything as their model, though anything was not always appropriate. It was all she could do to be their mother; she couldn't police their thoughts and impulses. Whatever her words, they could never be taken back, and whatever her actions, they became their lesson. Clare felt completely to blame.

"I love pink," she said feebly, holding Mia close to her chest. "Did you know they have pink sand in Bermuda?"

It had been their honeymoon spot. Closing her eyes, she saw once again the blue palmetto wallpaper of the hotel room where they had slept. It was hurricane season, and they spent three days without electricity—only candles for light.

The bed, she recalled, was smaller than this.

SOLOMON AND HIS WIVES

I

Johanna pushed open the steel cafeteria door and saw the long particle board tables like lifeboats floating at sea. Clinging around the edges were women and men, some as old as the century, birthday hats strapped under their chins, their faces like cuneiform histories. They were having a party for members born in January. Chicken soup was on the menu. The smell of schmaltz was sickening.

Johanna had never seen so many old people assembled in one place, as if the entire population of a Ukrainian shtetl had time-traveled to the Bronx. She felt their collective gaze as she lugged sketch pads and pencils across the soiled floor, breathing through her mouth to avoid the stench. The din was overwhelming—the clash of trays, the shouting. Still, they noticed her and stared.

Hadn't they ever seen someone young?

Since when was thirty-five young?

She crossed the room to the director's office, passing the director herself, an ample redhead standing in the center of the converted basement wearing a worn glen plaid jacket and matching skirt, a tam-o'-shanter slant across her brow. The lunches were kosher, but there were no restrictions on the dress.

"Table two! Table two!" she shouted. "Move already!" Wedged inside the bountiful folds of her neck like a splint was a portable phone. Her voice was grating and shrill. Slowly, the denizens of table two came forward like sleepwalkers for their reward: half-pint cartons of skim and a mackintosh apple for those with teeth. Clutching their prizes, they shuffled back to their seats and began the arduous business of putting on coats.

Johanna stood in the tiny office. Mice droppings dotted the floor. She thought she might vomit. For a moment she panicked that she might be pregnant, though she knew that was impossible. That morning, she had lied again when Paul had asked, "Are you off the Pill or not?"

Crouching beside the window for air, she thought, *I hate this already.*

It was Paul's idea she take this job, though she had no experience teaching. He thought it might relieve her block—she hadn't sketched since September. He said if she could get outside herself, maybe she could break through. She didn't know why she believed him—what would a research biologist know about drawing—but she was desperate. Already, she had missed two deadlines for her book. She had never been late before. If she didn't have some illustrations by March, she would lose the contract.

But the first class was easy, as if she had a knack for teaching. Afterward, Frieda called her to the office. She asked how it went, but her second question seemed a reflection of her truer intent.

"Are you—*Jewish*?"

Johanna had the urge to say yes.

"Sort of. I mean, not really."

Confusion spread across Frieda's face like fog. The phone rang. Frieda picked up the handset and planted it in her neck. The question was dropped.

Johanna was not lying. She was Jewish by some measures, not by others. Her father had been Jewish; her mother was not, and she was raised as nothing. When she was seven, she had a bout with mumps, and soon after her mother, a high church Episcopalian, snuck her off to St. Michael's on Ninety-ninth Street to be baptized. Thus her last name, Schuler, became a deception.

Her father meanwhile was wrought with his own ambivalence. For his eighth wedding anniversary, he had his mother's silver menorah melted down and recast as candlesticks as a gift to his wife. But two years later, when he came upon the baptism papers in the breakfront drawer, he threw the candlesticks in a rage at the dining room radiator. They were dented and disfigured. Seven years later he died of a stroke, though Johanna's mother insisted it was depression that killed him.

Paul's name was Greek—Kalomeris—which, had Johanna taken it, would have been more misleading still. She had kept her name as a kind of vestige of her father and of her relationship to him, the gulf of seperation between them, how tenuous the connection.

Their children, if they had any, would be called Kalomeris. Paul wanted three. He would make a good father, everyone said. He could talk about their children as if they were already talking and walking, while Johanna remained loath to imagine them. The best she could do was to picture triplets, faceless and unindividuated, crawling about her feet like a litter of cats, their surname proof of her estrangement.

By the third week of class, Johanna began noticing the seniors' faces. Many of them had been refugees, though she could never tell who among them had been in the camps and who had not. It amazed her. One woman had spent the war safely hidden in a convent in Berne, yet every day she refused to eat, impassive as a tank. She wrapped her head in a scarf and never wore teeth, her mouth collapsed in a scowl. Johanna assumed the woman was ninety, until Frieda said she was only sixty-eight. Meanwhile Ruth Margolis found joy in anything—in even her glaucoma, because the laser therapy had made her eyesight better than ever. Tattooed on her arm were the numbers from Auschwitz.

Solomon was not originally in the class. Frieda needed to boost enrollment to sustain her funding, and she knew if Solomon joined, the women would follow. At seventy-two, he was the lunch program's leading bachelor, the widows all wooing him to their apartments with promises of homemade kasha varnishes and brisket. Once, on the bus to Atlantic City, Belle Gross and Cecile Coen had a fight over who would sit next to him. They were docked from the trip, and the next day Belle came to lunch with a bruised lip. Women outnumbered men three to one, and Solomon played them one against the other, taking his meals now with one woman, now with another. Frieda called him the King, after Solomon in the Bible. For the wives, not the wisdom.

"Whaddaya think?" he said to Johanna, eschewing introductions. It was his first class and he'd brought a photograph: black-and-white, the scalloped white edges frayed and torn. Inside was a smiling young man beside a big, old car, one shoe on the fender in wingtips, his bottom lip vaguely lascivious, as if the camera flash were a kind of foreplay.

"Is that you?"

"Who else? You like it or you don't?" His speech was studded with traces of what could only be Yiddish.

"Dashing."

"I mean me, not the Chevy."

She laughed. "You look like Kevin Kline." Solomon showed no recognition. Then she realized she had no idea whether the actor was even Jewish.

"Like a movie star," she corrected herself. "Only Jewish."

She studied his face, the skin cracked and lined like a tobacco leaf and shrunken, as if the bones beneath had receded. Though his turquoise skullcap served as camouflage, he was nearly bald, the pale crown of his head a smooth semiorb poised in contrast above his sinking cheeks, the swell and curve of his nose almost burlesque. He wore a red cable cardigan over a pressed shirt, his trousers ending in pert cuffs. Aside from his attention to dress, he was nothing like the man in the photograph; time had uglied him.

Yet his eyes were flirting.

"The *bubbes* here tell me you're an artist," he said, "so draw me my picture."

They were doing still lifes, she said, pointing to the bowl of fruit.

"What do you think, I'm blind?" he said, waving his hand imperiously. "I'm *asking*."

Before taking this job, Johanna might have thought him rude, but in the three weeks she had worked here she had learned otherwise. Solomon was trying to charm. She could tell in the unflinching way he gazed at her, as if he sensed something hidden behind her smile and he had set his mind on capturing it. She blushed.

"Why don't you draw it yourself?" She handed him a pencil. "Or draw the bowl." The class was short of men—there was only one other specimen, Herb Fine, who, having never married, lived with his deaf ninety-two-year-old mother and lamented daily about the ride that took them to the center, how the driver of the van hit the gas before they were seated. One day they'll have an accident, he whined, and then what?

"Here—sit here." She pointed to the chair beside Tova Braverman, who was envied by some for having the most children who had made aliyah. Four.

Johanna saw a knobby hand shoot out from under the table, swipe at something, then disappear. There was a soft thud and Tova shrieked, her Channel Thirteen tote upended on the floor. Among the contents was her milk carton, a white glossy pool forming on the linoleum.

Johanna felt relieved for the interruption.

Solomon was making her nervous.

After class, she gathered the sketch pads to put them away. Usually the seniors took home their work, but one sketch was left behind. The lines were faint and blurred from erasing, but the shape was undeniable. Someone had drawn the naked backside of a woman. The torso was turned slightly, the hair was pulled back in a loose ponytail not unlike Johanna's. On closer examination, it *was* Johanna. She looked for a signature. She turned it over. Scripted on the back in enormous baroque script was the name *Solomon A. Gershon.*

She had the feeling she was being watched, though the room was empty.

She felt violated.

That night as they prepared dinner, she told Paul about him, though she carefully omitted the portrait Solomon had left on the table. "He's seventy-two, and all the women are in love with him."

Paul kissed the rim of her ear.

"Don't you fall in love with him," he said. She laughed.

That night he made love to her twice, as if to remind her.

II

The next week Johanna presented Frieda's spider plant as a subject, pruning the withered bottom leaves to accentuate the lines. It was reproducing copiously, with a dozen miniature spider plants rising from runners in every direction. Johanna had six new students plus Solomon, swelling the ranks to eleven, though there were still only two men.

Solomon sketched quietly, wedged between Cecile Coen and Tova Braverman, the women debating nitroglycerin, tablets or spray. Unlike the other students, whose work Johanna had described to Paul as doodling, Solomon had talent. A sign painter by trade, before the war he had taken classes at the Art Students League. His drawings had texture and emotion, his spider plant an earnest replica, though he exaggerated the size and number of runners as if the plant were rioting with growth.

"It reminds me of fireworks," said Johanna. But when he stood up to leave, he tore up the drawing and scattered the pieces in the trash.

"Why'd you do that?" she asked.

Solomon pushed out his bottom lip. "I don't want it."

Cecile Coen cleared her throat, her pewter hair set upon her head like a Victorian bird cage and as nearly transparent. "But Solly," she said, "it was gorgeous."

"It's a plant. What do I want with a plant?"

"And what's wrong with taking it home?" pressed Tova, puckering her chin. Her own masterpiece was folded in quarters, though Johanna had suggested rolling them. Cecile pressed her hand on Solomon's shoulder, the turquoise ring on her pointer finger the size of a golf ball.

"*I* liked it," she said.

He shook her off. "I'm not interested in drawing any plant."

Johanna broke in. "What do you want to draw instead, Mr. Gershon?"

"Call me Solomon," he said and his hand landed on hers.

She pulled away, smiling politely, and repeated the question.

"What do I want to draw? What did Michelangelo draw? What greater work of art than the human form? How about that?"

"If you can wait until the end of the month," she said, "I'm bringing some clay models."

"At my age, I should wait?" He inched closer, smiling, and for a moment Johanna saw before her the arresting young face of the man beside the car. Outwardly she laughed, but in her mind she imagined drawing him herself. She saw him posing in his finest three-button suit, his profile in three-quarter turn, the background in shadow. Where would she begin: the rise of his forehead, the weighted lids on his eyes, curved like bowstrings, the line of his cheek, his lips.

Frieda's voice shot across the cafeteria.

"Mista Gershon, leave Mizz Schuler alone! She's a married lady."

"Married!" exclaimed Tova. "You got any children?"

Johanna froze.

She was used to the question, but fielding it here under the buzzing lights summoned all her feelings of shame and failure. Here she was, standing before a tribunal of elders, guardians of the race, intoning, *What have you done to secure the generations?* Married five years, three books in print, Johanna by now had no excuse. She felt a prickling heat rise up her neck.

Tova persisted.

"I'm asking, you got any children?"

"I'm sorry. I mean, no. I thought I said no."

"No children?"

"No—not yet." She forced a smile.

Tova nodded watchfully.

"And you write children's books?" asked Cecile.

She knew it was strange, that someone so fearful of having children would make her living illustrating books for them. She had never expected the dread that had overcome her on the subject, but now that the time had come, she found herself paralyzed. Privately, Johanna had come to suspect that work was a way of bridling her fear. But just when she needed it most, turning her attention to FSH levels and ovulation, she became blocked. Work, which she had thought would counsel her into motherhood, had abandoned her. How could she explain? She bit her bottom lip. She wanted to hide.

"Leave the girl alone," said Solomon, waving his newspaper vaguely like a flyswatter in the direction of the women. He was the only member who read the *Times* and not the *News*. He was also one of the few without grandchildren. "She doesn't need all you *bubbes* howling at her." He turned to Johanna and winked. She felt herself dissolve. Solomon had defended her, staking his claim on an otherwise undiscovered piece of her heart. It was another violation, vaguely pleasurable. She felt the blood rush at her temples. She saw herself crawling into his lap.

This was not what she came for.

This was ridiculous.

III

Paul came home with a stack of travel brochures about Greece. It was probably their last summer before children, he said, and he wanted to plan a trip that was spectacular. He had heard of a house for rent on Naxos near his grandparents' village. He still had relatives there. Just the thought made Johanna feel suffocated: a multigenerational convocation of people who had popped out of other people, all of them sharing genetic material. She couldn't possibly belong.

"Isn't it early to be thinking about this?" she said, staring down the cache of booklets on the coffee table.

"It's only four months from now, if we go in June."

But to Johanna four months was an unfathomable expanse. She pictured it like a mountain range, impassable and vast, breaking apart the land. It was all she could do to plan her weekly lesson—each one at the last minute. That was all the future she could take, one Tuesday to the next, and still she was unable to draw. He brushed her cheek with the back of his hand, leaned over, and kissed her.

"Who knows? Maybe we can start a family there." He put his arm around her, pulled her face to his, and kissed her again. He was looking to make love. She turned her head to the side.

"We were talking about the trip," she said.

"Yes. So?" He picked up her hand and kissed the knuckles.

"So let's talk about the trip."

"We were talking about having kids. I thought we could get a heads up right now. You know I think you'll be a wonderful mother."

"But about the trip—I can't go if I don't get those illustrations done. What if I forfeit on my contract? We can't possibly afford it."

"We can. And you won't."

"I won't what?"

"You won't forfeit. You'll figure it out."

He pulled her close. She shifted her weight away from him slightly and picked up a brochure on Santorini: rows of olive trees, unerringly straight, the history of the volcanic landmass in pictures, how most of the island was concealed under water. She felt she was half under water herself. Paul had presumed that he knew her better than she knew herself, and she resented that. Her mind raced with the fantasy of committing some transgression, something to prove him wrong. Then what would he say?

She looked at Paul and saw the concern on his face and the need.

"Do we have to decide now?" she asked.

She heard a trembling in her voice and wondered what was the source, annoyance or fear.

IV

Solomon became a regular student, bringing his own objects to sketch: his father's pocket watch from Lublin and a brooch belonging to his wife. She had died eight years before. Before class, he helped Johanna sponge down the tables and arrange the chairs. He called Johanna his "tall glass of water." Johanna found she liked the moniker.

By mid-February the group had distilled to a core of nine—Cecile was in the hospital for a hip replacement, and Herb had quit because he said the sketch pads made him feel confined. Johanna brought a stack of pocket mirrors and had them draw self-portraits. She showed them how to find a pose, but none of the women drew from life. They ignored the lines in their skin, slimming their cheeks and expanding the volume of their hair. Only Solomon was honest. Yet when Johanna saw his finished work, she was startled. She had come to forget his signs of age— the patchy discoloration across his cheek, the sacs beneath his eyes, the waffled folds of his neck. Gazing at him, she saw instead the eyes, nose, and mouth of a younger man, robust and virile.

"You can't blame them, making themselves young," he said later, collecting the pencils. He put them in her hand, closing her fingers over the lot, squeezing her hand with both of his.

"The body changes," he said. "But that's all."

V

The next week, Frieda told Johanna to cancel the anatomy lessons. Certain members had voiced objections.

"The ladies are saying it's indecent," she said, rolling her eyes like a teenager. *"Don't ask."*

The only alternative, she said, was closing the class to men.

"What about Solomon?" asked Johanna.

"The King? He would have to go."

Johanna protested.

"He can't go! He's my best student!"

"It's your choice," concluded Frieda.

That day, Solomon brought another photograph to class. In it rose a nineteenth-century brick tenement with two fire escapes that zigzagged down the front and a shallow rounded portico. It was on Rivington Street, he said. He had lived there as a child, and he wanted to draw it. He pointed to a second-floor window.

"See that? That's my bedroom I shared with my brothers, three of us. We used to hang out the window and place bets how many girls we could make turn their heads."

While the women copied landscapes from travel magazines, Solomon sketched his ancient home and the jagged grocer's awning next door. Every discernible detail was brought to the page: the Moorish cornices above the windows, the bas-relief scroll pedestals, the individual panes of glass. He claimed the likeness was remote, but Johanna saw an exact replica down to the latticed wood flower boxes. What he really wanted to draw, he said, was the view looking out—the synagogue across the street—but he couldn't. He hadn't a picture.

"I made my bar mitzvah there."

She asked if it was still standing.

"So I'm told."

"Why don't you go back and draw it from life?"

He shrugged with a certain detachment. "I like living life in the present."

By next week the drawing was finished. He lingered after class and offered it, rolled like a tube, to Johanna.

"It's beautiful," she said.

"For you."

"No, I couldn't possibly. Let's hang it on the wall."

"Please." He pleaded.

She relented.

The next morning, she had an overwhelming urge to see the building herself. She waited until Paul had left for work, then took the D train to Grand Street. She made her way to Rivington and then walked east.

Johanna recognized it immediately.

She stood before the building for nearly an hour, staring into the second-floor window, her breath shallow from nerves. Except for the graffiti and the metal intercom outside the door, the facade was unchanged. The storefront next door was now an herbalist, with hanks of hemp and lavender in the window. Sitting on the portico steps was a girl no older than sixteen wearing a green bomber jacket. The smell of Szechuan stung the air, pungent and sweet.

"Are you lost or something?" asked the girl.

Johanna shook her head, startled. She stepped back off the curb and into the street. An oncoming cab honked to make way, grazing her coat. She turned and dashed across the street, hoping to evade further questions. Looking up, she saw the synagogue. The tile above the door was smashed and gutted in places and the upstairs windows boarded up, but the ground floor was still in use, its latest incarnation a coffeehouse.

When she went home some time later, she felt invigorated. She was on a mission. She returned that afternoon with sketch pad and pencils. Taking her seat on the steps where the girl had sat, she faced the synagogue. Three hours later, she had drawn, with meticulous delineation, a perfect facsimile.

Her first sketch in six months.

VI

The following week she arrived early at the center, eager to give Solomon the picture. She rolled it in a mailer tube and carried it on the subway like a scepter. But Solomon wasn't there. He hadn't shown up for lunch, though he had signed up for it. Before class, Johanna asked Frieda if something might be wrong.

"They sign up, they don't show. They don't sign up, they show. *Whatever.*"

"So then what?"

"Someone calls, and usually they're home, like they forgot. Or they had to go to the doctor. These people have a million doctor appointments. You wouldn't believe." She pushed forward the Rolodex.

The line was busy.

Johanna called again after class.

Busy.

"Shouldn't someone check on him?"

Frieda was filing papers. She waved a handful at Johanna. "If I checked on every member who doesn't show, who would eat?" She shook her head. "Go ahead."

He lived on the opposite side of the parkway. Johanna loitered on the street until a postman came and unlocked the doors. She slipped in behind his cart and entered the elevator. It lifted. She drummed her fingers on the carrier tube, staring out the round window as each successive floor emerged from above and vanished beneath. She felt she was gazing out the porthole of a space capsule, traveling across time. Why was she nervous, her hands damp with fear?

The door opened after the first buzz and Solomon appeared, grinning broadly. He wore a dark suit and tie, the coat cut long, tailored from another age. He gestured her into the living room toward an oversized club chair and matching sofa, the murrey-red chenille worn and spotted. It was like the tired refreshments lounge of a revival movie theater. Johanna sat at the end of the sofa, winded, unsure why she'd come. The apartment was frowsty and overheated—the clank and hiss of the radiator like some off-key music. On the coffee table was a back-issue copy of *Natural History* and a chipped candy dish with *Masada* spelled in the center. Johanna took a mental picture of every ornament and fixture; here was his life laid bare—what he ate, what he read, how he filled his hours. She sensed a void. Despite the massive furniture, the apartment felt vacant, the loneliness as tangible as the coffee table or the coat stand.

He offered her coffee. She refused. He had been to synagogue, he said, to light the candles for his wife. It was the anniversary of her death.

"I'm sorry," Johanna blurted out. She felt tactless and intrusive. He refused the apology, waving it away with his hand.

"The last nine years we did nothing but fight." He sat in the chair beside Johanna, their bodies at right angles, the tips of their shoes nearly touching on the carpet.

"Three miscarriages. She blamed me, every one."

Johanna searched for something to say. Only once before had he mentioned his wife. Johanna wondered, *Was she beautiful?* She had wondered why he had no children. She saw the sadness flicker across his face. She felt unqualified to console him. The scent of his body was conspicuous, a smell of mortality and must.

What am I doing in this man's apartment?

"Eight years already she's gone," he said. "But what kind of a mensch am I? Let's talk about *you*." His hand touched her knee and lingered.

"Look," she said. "I brought you something." She tapped the drawing out of the tube and unrolled it, a great, unwieldy scroll. Her hands were shaking.

He studied the drawing for what seemed like forever. Johanna panicked. The room was sweltering. Was it the wrong synagogue? Was the whole idea a mistake? She so much wanted his approval.

"So?"

He nodded gently, forward and back, rocking his frayed angular body in private deliberation, a kind of davening. He turned to her.

"You did this?"

She nodded.

"You went to Rivington Street?"

She swallowed. "What do you think?"

"It's good."

"What do you mean *good?*"

He studied the picture.

"It's exactly right." The two ends of his mouth lifted in a smile.

She felt buoyant, like a child's toy launch cutting across a pond. He leaned inward, making the space between them vanish.

"May I?"

A quick intake of breath and she said yes, her pulse tripping with speed. He kissed the soft of her cheek. He kissed it again and then he shifted to her lips, kissing her there, and she kissed him back. He pulled away for a moment and looked at her, each of them silent until he kissed her again. She felt his fragile weight against her and she fell back into the sofa, his body alongside hers, his face rustling in her hair. He unhooked his suspenders and pushed up her dress. They made love in silence as if even the most fractured speech would force them to acknowledge the strangeness of their coupling and the unnaturalness, and they would have to stop.

VII

They met in the afternoons. At the end of each class, Solomon left with the rest of the students and Johanna put away the supplies. After, she went to his apartment. Always, they kept on most of their clothes; she was afraid of what she might see. He didn't challenge that. They kept to the sofa. She never saw the bedroom, and as the bath was off the hall she didn't need to. She was a reluctant lover, telling herself each time she crossed the parkway she would this day break it off. But then she stepped through his door and she could not turn back. She came to relish the lightness of his bones, the looseness of his skin. Intricately lined, it stretched across his frame in places as thin as paper and sallow. Straddled above her, his body seemed vulnerable and delicate, which she liked. It made her feel strong. She felt herself becoming a person more capable of love, more freely bestowing it.

She felt defiant.

She had no doubt that she loved her husband, that her life remained with him, but she could not explain her actions. Never before had she deceived him. Occasionally, it shocked her that she had taken a lover whose hands were rough as hide and liver-spotted, his flesh slack. Half the time he didn't enter her. He was not always able. She didn't mind. Her pleasure was ample, even without penetration, as she was aroused in a way she had never been before. She would come with little impact or friction.

As for Solomon, she was not sure exactly what he felt, but he seemed satisfied. She liked to think she offered him more than merely the thrill of being with a woman half his age. He had a way of putting his focus completely, exclusively on her. And if not explicitly on her, then on her life, her life beyond their weekly assignations, though his curiosity was not always without discomfort.

"So tell me about your husband," he started one day when a steady rain outside made her particularly reluctant to leave.

"Paul?"

"Is there any other? What's he like? What does he do?"

"He's a biologist."

"A biologist! So he is, shall we say, an expert about life?"

"He's a *plant* biologist. That's something different. He does research for pharmaceuticals."

"Is he like me?"

"What do you mean, *is he like you?*"

"Well, is he charming?"

She nodded hesitantly.

"And funny?"

She nodded again, this time wondering if that in fact were true.

"Is he Jewish?"

Johanna's heart sank. That question—again. If only she could answer it without giving anything away. If only she had an answer that was opaque, a substitute answer, to keep away questions like a scarecrow chases away birds, but she found she lacked the language. Glancing out the window she saw the rain had tapered off. Solomon continued.

"Why do I even ask? I already know." He stood up and offered to make a fresh pot of coffee.

Usually, however, their conversation was less provocative, and Johanna left Solomon's apartment feeling strangely restored.

She told herself that her relationship with Solomon was charitable and unselfish, that it was more therapy than adultery—therapy for him—and she could end it, she was certain, at any time.

Meanwhile on the days she didn't teach, she sat at her drafting table, drawing.

One afternoon after their lovemaking, they lolled side by side on the floor against the sofa, the coffee table pushed aside. Solomon said he was going for a week to Maryland. It was the week before Passover, and the lunch center would be closed.

"My niece, she sent me a ticket."

"Oh?"

"Fran. She wants me to move in."

"In Maryland?" Johanna played absently with his arm, tracing the length from his elbow to the tips of his fingers, his nails yellow and ridged.

"Silver Spring. She's got three screaming kids and a schmuck of a husband. I think what she really wants is a baby-sitter."

Johanna looked up.

"That doesn't sound like the job for you," she said.

"For that, my dear, you get a kiss." He leaned over and pressed his mouth against hers.

Johanna sunk into the floor.

Solomon broke away and whispered in her ear.

"The tongue is a muscle that knows no age."

VIII

Late one morning in March, Johanna noticed her birth control pills missing.

That night after dinner Paul stood up and went to the bedroom, returning with the foil of tablets.

"I found these in the hamper."

She searched for a denial. Her breath was short, her pulse driving and quick.

"They were extras."

"But they're half gone," he said, glaring.

She searched for an explanation.

"Okay. I said I would quit. I didn't say when."

"I can't believe it. You lied to me. I can't believe you lied."

She had wanted this not to happen. Always growing up and even when she married, she assumed she would have a family. Looking back, though, she was no longer sure how deeply she had considered it. Perhaps it was just the idea she fancied, as what she knew from her family of origin was not something she cared to re-create. Still, now was the time to conceive, now if ever, before she pushed the odds too far, but she was terrified. Not so much of pregnancy, the bodily mutation, but of motherhood, its permanence. Everything in her life, including her marriage, was reversible. But motherhood—the finality, the entrapment—that was devastating.

Paul threw the foil on the dining table. It knocked over the Little Mermaid salt shaker they had bought at Disneyland two years before on a lark, visiting his sister in Pasadena. She had three children then; now there were four. The night they arrived, after she opened her blouse to breast-feed, she touched Johanna's sleeveless shoulder asking, *Will you be next?*

Johanna looked up at the toppled cartoon figurine, its puddle of salt. It struck her as suddenly preposterous, that a woman unable to walk could become a children's heroine. What is a culture saying to girls when it offers as a role model a ravishing cripple?

Johanna felt steeped in guilt. She felt she had failed. She had deceived him on this matter and worse. Would that come next?

Should she tell him?

Did he suspect?

"I'm sorry," she whispered. She couldn't look him in the eye.

"It doesn't matter if you're sorry. I'm not putting up with this forever. You said you wanted a family. You said you wanted kids."

"I do."

He looked at her as if she were crazy.

"Then what the hell is your problem?"

This was the question she couldn't answer, even as she thought she knew why. What could she say? That she wasn't ready? That she felt herself a child? That she was afraid she might never do better than her parents before her, imparting to her children the same encasing loneliness her parents had imparted to her? That family was inevitably the site of all original sin, and she wasn't convinced that she might not wake up one day and have to break out? The grief was too great, and the shame. She pictured herself in a giant glass bubble, isolated and alone, feeling excruciating pain, unable to speak.

There was no way that she knew to let him in.

"I told you, I'm sorry."

"You have some serious thinking to do. I'm not staying married to a liar."

He snatched up the newspaper and stormed out of the room.

IX

Two more weeks passed before the center reopened. During that time Johanna's sleep disintegrated. She would doze off exhausted, propped up in bed at ten at night and awaken at three, her mind charged and alert. It was three hours at least before she could sleep again and sometimes she couldn't. After a few doses of coffee she worked through the morning. By mid-April she'd sent her editor most of the drawings that were due. After lunch, she'd take a walk down Broadway to tire herself for sleep, loitering in shops. She bought a pair of leather pants, though it was already spring and the days were warm. Handing her credit card to the woman at the register, she told herself, *I can't be getting pregnant, if I'm buying black leather pants.*

At the same time, she could not buy even the smallest household necessities. For more than a week, they'd been out of toothpaste. Each morning, Paul paraded around the apartment with only a towel around his waist exclaiming that he couldn't live like this, that he couldn't brush his teeth. But each time she entered a drugstore or supermarket, she swore the prices were fixed or the line to pay was too long and she would drift out the door, promising herself to try elsewhere.

Next went the dishwashing detergent and shampoo. She washed her hair with soap.

X

The following Tuesday, Johanna returned to the center. When she arrived, an ambulance was parked outside, doors shut, and a crowd had formed on the street, watching. The patient was inside. An old man, cardiac arrest.

Solomon.

She panicked.

She tried looking into the ambulance windows but they were curtained. A policeman pulled her away. The ambulance took off. Johanna rushed into the cafeteria, searching. Most of the members had left. Frieda leaned somberly against the dairy sink, in a red velvet beret.

Johanna asked, "Who was it?"

Frieda sighed. "*Was* is the operative word."

"FRIEDA, WHO WAS IT?"

"Herb Fine," Frieda said mournfully. She looked Johanna up and down. "Aren't you curious! You didn't see his mother?" She gestured toward the far wall. Mrs. Fine sat against the corner, winding a cord from the venetian blind around and around her wrist, her expression as lifeless as sand.

"Is he dead?"

"We'll see. They wheel them out. They work on them. Sometimes they come back. You never know."

"Where's Solomon?"

"The King? Haven't seen him." Frieda narrowed her eyes. "You can cancel. They all went home."

Johanna was glad to leave. She grabbed her bag and headed for the door. It was a brisk two-minute walk to Solomon's apartment. The elevator wasn't there, so she climbed the stairs. Five flights.

He opened the door on the second buzz.

"I'm so glad you're here," she said. She was out of breath.

"Where would I be instead?"

She entered the apartment as if it were hers, sure of her welcome, but there were changes. Windows were open, boxes stacked against the wall. On the table, a woman's purse.

"What's going on?"

He paused a moment before answering, as if her question hadn't registered. Johanna thought of repeating it but then he replied, half under his breath.

"Fran."

"The niece?"

He nodded. "She thinks she's moving me to Maryland."

Johanna sat down at the end of the sofa. This was not the whole story, she could tell. Something about him was different. Slower. Clipped, somehow. He didn't give his usual embrace when he shut the door. He seemed cut off from his usual self and more fragile. He was withholding something—Johanna wasn't sure what. Meanwhile her thoughts were racing.

"What do you mean, *moving?*"

He threw out a hand carelessly. "I'll go for a visit."

"Didn't you just come back from there?"

"I'll be back before summer." He reached toward her, set his hand high on her left thigh, and squeezed. Fran or no Fran, he still saw Johanna as one of his triumphs.

There was another pause, and Johanna noted that he hadn't answered the questions. He moved away from her now as if almost in a daze, as if every new moment were slightly disconnected from the one preceding.

"Coffee?" he offered.

She didn't answer, speechless.

"It's decaf. She threw out all my regular." He strolled into the kitchen.

Johanna glanced around the room. The stack of boxes reached halfway to the ceiling, all of them sealed and labeled. Leaning flat against the wall were a dozen or so more waiting to be assembled and filled. She walked over and touched the rough corrugated edges. Only then did they seem real.

She turned and walked toward the kitchen.

"They took Herb away in an ambulance."

Solomon turned to face her. Grief washed over his face.

"What happened?"

"His heart. I was scared it was *you*."

"Me? You should know I don't go that easy."

She laughed nervously. He kissed her cheek. She put her arms around him. He pulled away. Something was wrong.

There was a noise at the door, footsteps. A woman entered, groceries on each arm.

"Solly, you left the door open." She set the bags on the table. She was not much older than Johanna, early forties maybe, a little fuller in the waist.

"Are you the lady at the center?" The woman extended her hand.

Johanna took it limply. The woman's grip was firm.

Johanna wondered, *What lady?*

The woman continued.

"I hear he's very popular, though he says the food there is nothing to write home about." She dropped her voice. "Lucky for him, I can cook gourmet."

Fran.

"Don't listen to her *mishegas*!" said Solomon from the kitchen. "What does she know? She's my niece!" The kettle started to boil and he poured the water into the filtered contraption. Johanna turned to look. On the soft underside of his arm was an enormous purple bruise. The Band-Aid covering it looked woefully small.

"Thursday, he blacked out at my daughter Rachel's soccer match," started Fran with great composure. "They ran tests. They said he had an aortic aneurysm, a small one, but he has to be watched."

Johanna sunk into the gaudy chair. *Aneurysm.* What did it mean? She pictured some internal explosion, the veins and byways of the body spontaneously erupting.

She watched him from the chair as he poured the coffee into three diminutive cups, his hand gently trembling. Johanna shuddered. Even in his most familiar surroundings, he moved with frailty. He seemed suddenly old. Johanna had been having sexual relations with a seventy-two-year-old man. A man older than her father, were he alive. A man who at any moment could be dead.

Fran leaned in, whispering.

"He said Maryland doctors weren't good enough, so we had to come here." They had an appointment at Einstein that day at three. Solomon called out from the kitchen.

"Everyone ready for coffee?" From his voice Johanna could tell he was pleased to be playing host. She heard the rattle of the tray as he lifted to carry it.

Fran kept talking. "I wanted to see how much stuff he had before I ordered the boxes. Besides, I couldn't let him travel alone." She started emptying the bags: Ajax, paper towels, Mr. Clean.

Johanna felt like an interloper.

She cleared her throat and stood up.

"I hope you're not leaving," said Fran.

Solomon crossed into the living room with his tray of saucers and cups, his brow buckled in the effort. He joined them in a triangle on the carpet. Setting the tray on the table, he looked at Fran, his face lit with pride.

"Now, what kind of lies have you been telling my young lady friend here?"

"Nothing much, Uncle Solly."

"Whatever she said," Solomon spoke directly to Johanna, "I tell you it's not true." He smiled generously, but the gaze in his eyes hinted at distress, as if somewhere he knew he was standing at the brink of unavoidable loss.

"I should go," said Johanna. Her voice was nearly inaudible. She touched at the sleeves of her coat. Had she taken it off or was she wearing it all along? She made for the door.

"Stay for coffee," said Fran. "It's not every day we get to meet Solly's friends."

Johanna refused.

"Please!" Solomon cried out. "Stay!"

"I'm sorry."

"What about tomorrow?" he asked. His next words were addressed to Fran. "Did she tell you she's an artist?" Perhaps he thought that if she were roped into conversation Johanna might stay.

"Really? An artist?"

Johanna seized the opportunity and left. She raced down the stairs and into the street. She heard Solomon call out from the window three stories up. There was something desperate in his voice, but she did not go back. She couldn't, though she turned for a look. He was peering from the window just as she imagined he had on Rivington Street, just as he had said. Their eyes met and, for a moment, before he knew enough to conceal it, she saw on his face the fear. She was surprised. She hadn't thought that Solomon could be afraid of anything. But then, she hadn't thought of him as someone with *family*. He was cast in her mind as a single human entity, unhampered by kin, related to no one, the last doomed carrier of an inalterable parcel of genes that would never again come into flesh.

Yet there was Fran. Tall and ample, she looked nothing like Solomon. Her face bore no resemblance to his, and her mannerisms were different, too. She had a native confidence in everything she did: in her speech, in her walk, in the way she tallied in her head all his meager possessions. Yet she was family to him, and whatever their history, whatever their past together, here she was, ready to care for him.

Fran spoke of illness and catastrophe as if they happened every day. She could hedge disaster, watching it alight, on several fronts at once.

Is that what women learn from having children?

Johanna wondered.

She climbed the stairs to the elevated train. It eluded her still, how she had entered into that coupling, how it had gone so far. She would not go to his apartment again; it was over between them. Still, he was part of her, grafted onto her limbs. He was part of her history, embedded like some childhood memory.

She fingered her pocket for change. Paul, whenever they took the subway, always stood ready with two tokens in hand, one for her, one for him. He'd drop one into the slot, step aside, and then—this part she liked best—gesture her through the turnstile first, like some well-schooled old-fashioned gentleman.

ABOUT THE AUTHOR

Merin Wexler graduated from Harvard University, where she won a Knox Fellowship to Oxford University, and she earned her MFA from the Warren Wilson Program for Writers. She has been awarded the Heekin Foundation's Tara Prize for Short Fiction, among other prizes, and has won both an NEA/WritersCorps Fellowship and an NEH Fellowship. She lives in New York City, where she is currently writing a novel, forthcoming from St. Martin's Press.